EXPERIENCING

AMERICA'S STORY

THROUGH FICTION

ALA Editions purchases fund advocacy, awareness, and accreditation programs for library professionals worldwide.

EXPERIENCING

AMERICA'S STORY

THROUGH FICTION

Historical Novels for Grades 7–12

HILARY SUSAN CREW

AN IMPRINT OF THE AMERICAN LIBRARY ASSOCIATION
CHICAGO 2014

Hilary S. Crew is a former associate professor at Kean University, where she taught children's and young adult literature and was coordinator of the Educational Media Specialist Program. She has written numerous articles and three books in the field of children's and young adult literature, including *Is It Really Mother Dearest? Daughter-Mother Narratives in Young Adult Fiction* (2000); *Women Engaged in War: A Guide to Resources for Children and Young Adults* (2007); and *Donna Jo Napoli: Writing with Passion* (2010). She also reviews books for *VOYA* magazine. She earned both an MLS and a doctorate in communication, information, and library studies from Rutgers University.

© 2014 by the American Library Association

Printed in the United States of America
18 17 16 15 14   5 4 3 2 1

Extensive effort has gone into ensuring the reliability of the information in this book; however, the publisher makes no warranty, express or implied, with respect to the material contained herein.

ISBNs: 978-0-8389-1225-6 (paper); 978-0-8389-1991-0 (PDF); 978-0-8389-1992-7 (ePub); 978-0-8389-1993-4 (Kindle). For more information on digital formats, visit the ALA Store at alastore.ala.org and select eEditions.

Library of Congress Cataloging-in-Publication Data
Crew, Hilary S., 1942–
   Experiencing America's story through fiction : historical novels for grades 7–12 / Hilary Crew.
    pages   cm
   Includes bibliographical references and index.
   ISBN 978-0-8389-1225-6
  1. Historical fiction, American—Bibliography. 2. Young adult fiction, American—Bibliography.
3. Children's stories, American—Bibliography. 4. Historical fiction, American—Stories, plots, etc.
5. Young adult fiction, American—Stories, plots, etc. 6. Children's stories, American—Stories, plots, etc.
7. United States—History—Fiction—Bibliography. 8. United States—In literature—Bibliography.
9. Teenagers—Books and reading—United States. I. Title.
   Z1231.H57C74 2014
   [PS374.H5]
   813'.081099283—dc23
                  2014008471

Cover design by Kimberly Thornton. Cover illustration: village on the bank of North Yuba river, California, created by Blanchard and Cosson-Smeeton, first published in *L'Illustration, Journal Universel,* Paris, 1868. © Antonio Abrignani / Shutterstock, Inc.

Text design by Mayfly Design in the Minion and Cabrito Inverto typefaces.

♾ This paper meets the requirements of ANSI/NISO Z39.48–1992 (Permanence of Paper).

Contents

Introduction

The objective of this annotated bibliography is to provide a guide for school librarians, history teachers, and public librarians working with youth to historical novels about the United States from the colonial period to the era of the Iraq War, published between 2000 and 2013, that are appropriate for seventh to twelfth graders. The book also includes adult fiction titles for senior high school students. A concern about the lack of historical knowledge of American students is reflected in the 2010 Nation's Report Card on US History.[1] A study by the Southern Poverty Law Center found major failings across the states in teaching about the civil rights movement.[2] There is much debate over the use of historical novels to supplement the history curriculum over and above reading historical novels for pleasure, with discussions focusing on issues of accuracy, authentication, and the definition of historical fiction.[3] The novels included in this guide do, however, address important issues and topics addressed by the National Standards for History and in national testing. Examples include federal and state policies toward Native Americans, civil rights, child labor, immigration, and the internment of Japanese Americans during World War II.

Many states' recent adoption of the Common Core State Standards has further spurred the use of texts other than standard history textbooks for the teaching of history and social studies.[4] Well-researched and well-written historical novels can arguably contribute to the evaluation and comparison of different points of view on historical events and issues. M. T. Anderson's *The Pox Party* (volume 1 of *The Astonishing Life of Octavian Nothing, Traitor to the Nation*; Candlewick, 2006) and Edward P. Jones's *The Known World* (Amistad, 2003), for example, contribute to new ways of understanding the landscape of slavery. Historical novels offer readers opportunities to ask and debate questions regarding authors' interpretations and ideological standpoints in choosing how to tell their stories. The inclusion of historical novels that offer an alternative history of events, such as Philip Roth's *The Plot Against America* (Houghton Mifflin, 2004), can also raise important issues about fiction, imagination, and authenticity. Amy Huftalin and Louis Ferroli point out that historical novels "help teachers make history interesting and meaningful to students, while increasing students' pleasure in the reading of this genre," and provide charts aligning historical novels with other texts for the American Revolution, the Civil War, and the civil rights movement.[5] As one teacher who uses historical fiction stated, the "connection between informational texts with similar topics can be powerful as one genre can elegantly support and enhance learning from the other."[6]

There has been a move toward a more inclusive understanding of American history as more historical novels are published from the perspectives of voices representing different cultures, races, and ethnicities. Noticeable, too, is the wide range of topics covered by historical novels, ranging from discoveries in astronomy and medicine to the history of baseball. Recent novels contribute to different perspectives on the past, such as the effect of the Cold War on an Iñupiaq family in Debby Edwardson's *Blessing's Bead* and the Vietnam War seen through the lens of a female photographer in Tatjana Soli's *The Lotus Eaters*. An increasing number of novels are written in diverse narrative forms. Myra Zarnowski points out, for example, that Jen Bryant's multiple-voiced verse novel on the Scopes trial, raises "social issues from different perspectives."[7] The 1920s come to life in memorabilia, vintage postcards, and advertisements in Caroline Preston's *The Scrapbook of Frankie Pratt* (Ecco, 2011), and the Great Depression is experienced in arresting graphics in James Vance and Dan Burr's *Kings in Disguise* (W. W. Norton, 2006).

Writers explore the relationship between history as story and historical fiction. Allan Wolf writes that he has "allowed fantasy to play within the confines of fact. When it comes to historical fiction, history is the birdcage; fiction is the bird."[8] Wolf and many other writers of historical fiction are providing endnotes to their stories to strengthen their birdcages, including historical facts; distinctions between fact and fiction; and information about context, sources, and suggested readings. Authors often insert documentary material into the text of their novels. Jeff Shaara, for example, notes in *No Less Than Victory* (Ballantine Books, 2009) that the voices of his participants are based on primary sources such as memoirs, collections of letters, and interviews but that the book is a novel because there are always "everyday conversations that are not recorded for posterity." He emphasizes the importance of authenticity when he dares to "put words in the mouths of any of the historical figures" in his books.[9] Diane Glancy chooses to define her novel *Pushing the Bear: After the Trail of Tears* (University of Oklahoma Press, 2009) as "fictional, historical nonfiction."[10] But in writing about known facts, she also "wanted to know—the spirit, the emotional journey, the heartbeat during the march."[11] By reimagining the past through the lives and relationships of their protagonists, historical novels offer readers the opportunity to think about how events and issues affect individuals and their families. Several writers draw on their own experiences or the history of their family members to bring the past to life. As Ellen Klages reminds us, "History isn't just dates and facts and places. It's people and their lives and stories."[12]

Selection of Novels

The books annotated here are for seventh grade and up. To include a wide range of reading levels, books are featured that are suggested for grades 5 through 7 and for grades 5 through 8. Adult fiction titles for senior high school students are also included. Most books included here have publication dates between the years 2000 and 2013. Exceptions include four award-winning books published in the 1990s that were not included in *America as Story: Historical Fiction for Middle and Secondary Schools* (American Library Association, 1997).[13] Novels were selected for their literary merit and for their strength as historical novels. Many of the novels selected for this book are recipients of one or more awards or have been listed on various notable lists. Others were selected from among starred reviews in various journals.

Awards for books for seventh to twelfth grade include major American Library Association awards for youth literature: Newbery Medal, Coretta Scott King, Pura Belpré, and Printz awards. Other awards include the American Indian Youth Literature Award, the National Book Award for Young People's Literature, the Américas Book Award for Children's and Young Adult Literature, the Sydney Taylor Book Award, and the Western Writers of America's Spur Award. Awards recognizing a book's value as a historical novel include the Scott O'Dell Award for Historical Fiction, Notable Social Studies Trade Books for Young People, the Jane Addams Children's Book Award, and *Booklist*'s Top 10 Historical Fiction for Youth. Lists include ALA Notable Children's Books and YALSA's Best Books and Best Fiction lists (or Young Adult Lists).

Awards for adult novels include the National Book Award, the Pulitzer Prize for Fiction, and the Western Writers of America's Spur Award. Major awards for excellence in American historical fiction include the American Book Awards, the David J. Langum Sr. Prize, the Michael Shaara Prize for Excellence in Civil War Fiction, and the James Fenimore Cooper Prize. Also noted is a novel's inclusion on *Booklist*'s Top 10 Historical Novels. Awards for adult novels for teens include the Alex Award, Outstanding Books for the College Bound, and *School Library Journal*'s Best Adult Books for High School Students (which in 2010 was replaced by the web-based *SLJ* Best Adult Books 4 Teens).

Reviewing journals included *Booklist, Bulletin of the Center for Children's Books, Horn Book Magazine, Library Journal, Multicultural Review, School Library Journal, VOYA, History Teacher, Journal of American History, Social Studies,* and *Social Education.*

Abbreviations Used in Annotations for Prizes and Lists

American Library Association Notable Children's Book = ALA Notable

Américas Book Award for Children's and Young Adult Literature = Américas

Booklist Top 10 Historical Fiction for Youth = *Booklist* Top 10 HF

Booklist Top 10 Historical Novels = *Booklist* Top 10 HN

Coretta Scott King Book Award = King

David J. Langum Sr. Prize = Langum

James Fenimore Cooper Prize = Cooper

Jane Addams Children's Book Award = Addams

Michael L. Printz Awards = Printz

Michael Shaara Prize for Excellence in Civil War Fiction = Shaara

National Book Award = NBA

National Book Award for Young People's Literature = NBA (Y)

Newbery Medal = Newbery

Notable Social Studies Trade Books for Young People = NSSTB

Pulitzer Prize for Fiction = Pulitzer

Pura Belpré Award = Belpré

School Library Journal Best Adult Book 4 Teens = *SLJ* BAB4T

School Library Journal Best Adult Book for High School Students = *SLJ* BABHS

Scott O'Dell Award for Historical Fiction = O'Dell

Sydney Taylor Book Award = Taylor

Western Writers of America Spur Award = Spur

YALSA Alex Award = Alex

YALSA Best Books for Young Adults = YALSA BB

YALSA Best Fiction for Young Adults = YALSA BF

YALSA Outstanding Books for the College Bound = YALSA OB

Arrangement of Chapters

The arrangement of chapters is based with modifications on eras 2–10 of the US History Content Standards for Grades 5–12. I have omitted era 1, as the content is not addressed by historical novels chosen for this book. Historical novels do not always fit neatly into designated eras; I therefore have adjusted era headings and dates to better accommodate the historical time frame covered by the novels. Subheadings are used for specific topics where appropriate. Within headings, books appropriate for seventh grade and up are arranged alphabetically by the author's last name, and are then followed by a separate listing of adult novels appropriate for young people. For novels I provide brief bibliographic details, suggested grade levels, and relevant awards. Annotations provide a guide to historical context and themes. Each novel has one or more suggestions for discussion, with links to relevant resources when appropriate. Furthermore, a select bibliography with resources on historical fiction as well as the teaching and use of historical fiction in the classroom is included.

Notes

1. National Assessment of Educational Progress, The Nation's Report Card, "Summary of Findings," http://nationsreportcard.gov/ushistory_2010/summary.asp.
2. Southern Poverty Law Center, *Teaching the Movement*, September 2011, www.spl center.org/get-informed/publications/teaching-the-movement.
3. Eric Groce and Robin Groce, "Authenticating Historical Fiction: Rationale and Process," *Education Research and Perspectives* 32, no. 1 (2005): 99–120.
4. Common Core State Standards Initiative, www.corestandards.org.
5. Amy Huftalin and Louis Ferroli, "Literature That Increases Social Studies Knowledge and Skill in Text Reading," *Illinois Reading Council Journal* 41, no. 1 (2012–13): 11.
6. Allison L. Baer, "Pairing Books for Learning: The Union of Informational and Fiction," *History Teacher* 45, no. 2 (2012): 283.
7. Myra Zarnowski, "Historical Novels in Verse: A Fusion Genre," *Journal of Children's Literature* 36, no. 1 (2010): 37.
8. Allan Wolf, *The Watch That Ends the Night: Voices from the Titanic* (New York: Candlewick, 2011), 435.
9. Jeff Shaara, *No Less Than Victory: A Novel of World War II* (New York: Ballantine, 2009), ix–x.
10. Diane Glancy, *Pushing the Bear: After the Trail of Tears* (Norman: University of Oklahoma Press, 2009), 188.
11. Ibid., 189.
12. Hazel Rochman, "Talking with Ellen Klages," *Book Links* 17, no. 2 (2007): 26.
13. Rosemary K. Coffey and Elizabeth F. Howard, *America as Story: Historical Fiction for Middle and Secondary Schools* (Chicago: American Library Association, 1997).

Colonization and Settlement

(1585–1759)

Early Colonization

Carbone, Elisa Lynn. *Blood on the River: James Town 1607*. Viking, 2006. 237 pp. Grades 5–8. NSSTB, 2007.

Carbone integrates the writings of early settlers into her novel about the settlement of James Town, Virginia. Her main characters are based on real people, including the young narrator, Sam Collier, who describes in detail the voyage from London, his arrival in Virginia in 1607, and his experiences among the settlers until 1610. Sam, a page to Captain John Smith, tells readers how the site of James Town was chosen, the disagreements among the knowledgeable Smith and inexperienced "gentlemen," the difficulties settlers encountered in regard to governance and supporting themselves, and how the settlers' numbers diminished as they were killed and beset by disease and famine. The novel makes clear the relationship between the settlers and the different native tribes, including relations with Chief Powhatan. Sam's narrative incorporates a consciousness that it is they, the colonists, who are the encroachers on land that is already owned and has been named. Sent by Smith to live with the Warroskoyack tribe, Sam acquires hunting skills and knowledge of their culture, and he learns Algonquian. Quotations at the beginning of each chapter are taken from primary sources. In an afterword, Carbone extends Sam's narrative by summarizing the history of the settlement to 1644, including James Town's

"Starving Time," during the winter of 1609–10. She also explains how she uses her resources and provides suggestions for further reading.

1. Discuss the reasons the Virginia Company sent settlers to Virginia. How are the English "gentlemen" settlers represented?
2. Describe and evaluate the relationships among the various Native American tribes and the colonists from 1607 until 1610.
3. Compare Sam's description of the difficulties encountered by the settlers with accounts in primary sources. See "First-Hand Accounts" at the website Virtual Jamestown (www.virtualjames town.org/fhaccounts_desc.html#history).

Chibbaro, Julie. *Redemption.* Atheneum, 2004. Electronic text. Grades 9–12. American Book Award, 2005.

Chibbaro bases her novel on stories of early expeditions made a hundred years before the settlement of Jamestown by some who left Europe for religious reasons. Twelve-year-old Lily Applegate's father was persuaded to leave their village, Myrthyr, in England in the 1500s for the New World by Frere Lanther from the Rhineland, who is loosely modeled on Martin Luther, a leading figure of the Protestant Reformation. Similar to Luther, Lanther prints pamphlets and criticizes the Roman Catholic Church, but he betrays the Applegates by aligning himself with the local baron for the gain of his growing church. Lily describes the daily life, community, and work of a feudal village in England, but when her mother is forced to give up their croft, Lily and her mother sail to the New World with the baron, who hopes to find gold.

Lily is represented as a young Christian girl struggling with her religious beliefs as she endures the privations of the voyage, during which her mother is abused by the baron, and as she experiences the events that befall her when their ship is wrecked on the shores of the New World. Lily has to remind herself that the New World, with its unfamiliar birds, fish, and shells, and bounded by an impenetrable forest, has God's hand in its making. Through Lily's eyes readers see vivid scenes of the ship's wreckage strewn among the rocks, the divisions between the rich and poor survivors as they huddle over their separate fires, and the discovery of mutilated bodies thought to be those who had sailed before them. When the captain and his sailors take Lily's mother into the forest, Lily goes to search for her—alone with her fears of the devil and the "dogs-head" people, until the baron's son, Ethan, joins her.

Chibbaro's novel is also about Lily's assimilation into the New World, after her father finds her in the forest. At first, she did not recognize the man dressed in furs with strange markings on his face—he had been rescued and adopted by the Nooh people. Her father had learned their language and traditions, and taken a new wife. Lily describes the homes and lifestyle of the Nooh (Chibbaro notes that the tribes in her book are a composite of the "different tribes of Indians which proliferated in America both pre- and, for a short time, post-Columbus" [loc. 3074]). The plot does not gloss over Lily's encounters with violence in the New World, including capture by the Awthas, the cruel wolf clan that has been at war with the Nooh when Lily and her father set out to find her mother. But the Nooh and Awthas join forces in a murderous encounter with the privateers who kill Lily's mother and attack Lily and her father. Later, Lily tells readers about how her faith and perspective change as she is inducted into the Nooh tribe. In her notes, Chibbaro explains that the relationship between the Nooh and Awthas is "loosely based on the relationships between the clans of the Iroquois and Algonquin" (loc. 3074) and that she also based her story on documented cases of white settlers being adopted by Native Americans. Chibbaro briefly sums up the religious and political context of early explorations to the New World and provides information about her sources, including a bibliography.

1. Discuss how Protestantism affects the practice of religion in Myrthyr.
2. Discuss Lily's induction into the Nooh tribe.

Howard, Ellen. *The Crimson Cap.* Holiday House, 2009. 177 pp. Grades 5–7. NSSTB, 2010.

In 1687, ten-year-old Pierre Talon, living in a French settlement on the Gulf Coast, leaves his mother and siblings when he is chosen to accompany René-Robert Cavalier, Sieur de La Salle, on his latest expedition to search for the Mississippi River. Wearing the knitted crimson hat that belonged to his missing father, Pierre, struggling through swamps and rivers, is accompanying the fated expedition when La Salle and his personal staff are murdered. Pierre is stricken with fever and is cared for in a Hasinai village by the village leader's wife, who names Pierre "Tay'sha" (friend). He stays with the Hasinai for three years, learning their skills and culture, and the bond between them strengthens when he is tattooed as an adopted son. Later, when searching for his family, Pierre finds that the settlement where they were living had been burned and his siblings taken by the Clamcoëhs (Karankawa). Returning to the Hasinai, Pierre is taken prisoner by General de León, who, charged with setting up missions in the villages and locating members of La Salle's expedition, helps Pierre find his siblings.

Howard based her story on the actual person Pierre Talon and provides references to the primary sources that contain information on his life. In her notes, she describes what is known of Talon and his siblings from when they left Texas with the Spaniards to when they arrived in Mexico City in 1690, and through to their later lives. She also explains how her novel fits into the wider context of competition between France and Spain as they explored and made their claims to the New World.

1. Discuss what Pierre learns about the Hasinai culture that challenges the explorers' use of the terms *savages* and *civilization*.
2. Related website: For primary documents with eyewitness accounts by Pierre and his brother, Jean-Baptiste, see American Journeys (www.americanjourneys.org/aj-114/summary/index.asp).

Adult Fiction

Brooks, Geraldine. *Caleb's Crossing.* Viking, 2011. 306 pp. Langum honorable mention, 2011.

Caleb Cheeshahteaumauck, whose father was a leader of a band of the Wôpanâak (Wampanoag), Noepe (today Martha's Vineyard), was the first Native American to graduate from Harvard College in 1665. His story, imaginatively fleshed out from a few facts, is told by the fictional character, Bethia, daughter of Thomas Mayfield, a minister on the island who is engaged in converting the Wampanoag to Christianity. Twelve-year-old Bethia's first-person narrative weaves back and forth from the time she first meets Caleb in 1660 until the close of her life in 1715. Caleb studies with her father, then attends Master Corlett's school in Cambridge, before being admitted to Harvard College, which is bound by its 1650 charter to educate both "English and Indian youth of the country" (302). A brilliant student, he is represented as transcending the prejudice of other students while retaining a loyalty to his beliefs.

Bethia's character illustrates the limited choices available to women. More able than her brother, she is, nonetheless, advised by her father that she must accept her "destiny as a woman" (16). The rich social, cultural, and religious context of the novel is supported by descriptions of Noepe, Cambridge, and Harvard College, with details of the student body, the courses of study, and the fees (often paid in food and other goods). In her afterword to the novel, Brooks provides details of her research; known facts about Caleb; and information about the Mayhew family, whose history provides some of the biographical facts for the fictional Mayfields. The endpapers reproduce the only known document by Caleb, written in Latin.

1. Discuss Caleb's choice to leave his home.
2. Discuss the representations of Anne Bradstreet and Anne Hutchinson and how they add to Bethia's story about the status of women in seventeenth-century Massachusetts. See the related web page "Anne Hutchinson Banished, March 22, 1638," at Mass Moments (www.massmoments.org/moment.cfm?mid=88), and the website Anne Bradstreet (access via www.vcu.edu/search/index.php?).

Kent, Kathleen. *The Wolves of Andover.* Little, Brown, 2010. 300 pp.

In this prequel to *The Heretic's Daughter*, Kent imagines the life of Martha Allen. In 1673, Martha goes to Billerica, Massachusetts, to help her cousin Patience Taylor, who is expecting her third child. There she meets and falls in love with Thomas Carrier, an indentured servant, suspected of being the executioner of Charles I. The narrative shifts back and forth from Martha's growing fascination with Carrier to plotters who, hired on behalf of Charles II, make arrangements to sail to Boston to capture the regicide. Descriptions of Martha's household duties and seasonal farmwork are contrasted with scenes depicting London's underworld of baiting pits and taverns. While Martha and the Taylor household deal with wolves, grief over Patience's stillborn baby and the death of her young son, and fear of raids by Abenaki Indians, the men hired to find King Charles I's executioner finalize their plans and board the *Swallow*. But those who have no sympathy for Royalists thwart their plans. Through Thomas, who tells how he came to fight for Oliver Cromwell, Kent brings together key events of the English Civil War, the Protectorate of Oliver Cromwell, and the Restoration with the history of Massachusetts—home to John Dixwell, a judge who signed the warrant of execution for Charles I. Living under the name of James Davis, Dixwell organizes a ring of spies (including Patience's husband, Daniel Taylor) to protect regicides living in the colonies from Royalists and from informants keen to earn bounty money. Kent distinguishes fact from fiction, explaining that although the factual Thomas Carrier (also known as Thomas Morgan) is documented as having married Martha Allen Carrier, who was later hanged during the Salem witch trials, there is no evidence that he was Charles II's executioner; rather, this was a family myth.

1. Discuss the reasons Daniel Taylor and others were willing to protect regicides.
2. Related website: "John Dixwell, Regicide, c. 1607–89," BCW Project (www.british-civil-wars.co.uk/biog/dixwell.htm).

French and Indian War

Bruchac, Joseph. *The Winter People*. 2002; Penguin, 2004. 176 pp. Grades 7–9. *Booklist* Top 10 HF, 2003; NSSTB, 2003.

In 1759, fourteen-year-old Saxso and others are celebrating the good harvest in the Abenaki "mission village" of St. Francis (Odanak) on the Alsigontikuk River (the St. Francis River in Quebec) when a Scaticook Indian warns Saxso that the village is being surrounded by Robert Rogers (the "White Devil"), his Rangers, and Stockbridge Indians. When his mother and sisters are taken captive, the wounded Saxso follows them and devises a plan for their rescue.

Bruchac presents a different side to the attack on the village from that recorded in one of Rogers's dispatches to General Jeffrey Amherst (which is included in Bruchac's notes) that claimed that more than two hundred Indians were killed in St. Francis. In presenting the Abenaki side of story, Bruchac corrects the historical record, which indicates that Rogers's attack "wiped out" the Abenaki. He describes the relationship between the Abenaki and the French, deconstructs stereotypical representations of the Abenaki, differentiates Native American peoples and their different loyalties, and provides information on the life of captives. He explains in his notes that most of the characters are "real," for example, the white chief of St. Francis, Joseph-Louis Gill, son of a captive white man. Through Saxso's narrative, Bruchac provides readers with an understanding of Abenaki culture and their deep knowledge of and respect for their environment.

1. Discuss Rogers's raid from the perspectives of Saxso and the Abenaki. Contrast Saxso's description of the raid and burned village with Rogers's dispatch in Bruchac's notes.
2. Discuss the role of religion in the relationship between the Abenaki and the French.
3. Related website: Abenaki Culture and History (www.native-languages.org/abenaki.htm#tribe).

Salem Witch Trials

Duble, Kathleen Benner. *The Sacrifice.* 2005; Margaret K. McElderry Books, 2007. 224 pp. Grades 5–8. *Booklist* Top 10 HF, 2006.

Set in Andover, Massachusetts, in 1692, the story is told of how ten-year-old Abby Faulkner and her family are caught up in the Salem witch trials. When the news spreads that witches had been discovered in Salem Village, Abby's grandfather, Reverend Dane, warns the family that their father's "fits" could cause him to be considered an "oddity," which could bring danger to the family. When the "afflicted" girls are brought to Andover to identify witches in the community, Abby's family is among those chosen to parade before the girls. On this occasion, they pass the test, but as Reverend Dane continues to speak out against the trials, first Abby's Aunt Elizabeth and then Abby and her older sister, Dorothy, are accused of being witches and taken to Salem Township's jail.

Duble vividly describes the jail conditions: the stench, minimal food, and rats swimming in flooded cells. The choices set out before suspected witches at their trial are clear, as are the terms under which Abby's mother persuades her daughters to testify against her to gain their freedom. Duble bases her novel on her own family history, explains which of her characters are based on actual personages, and notes any changes of names and facts. The book includes a bibliography.

1. Compare Duble's fictionalized account with transcripts relating to the Faulkner family (click on "Search All Names in the Salem Witchcraft Papers") at the website Salem Witch Trials: Documentary Archive and Transcription Project (http://salem.lib.virginia .edu/texts/transcripts.html).
2. Discuss the ethical implications of the choices given to the accused at their trials.

Hemphill, Stephanie. *Wicked Girls: A Novel of the Salem Witch Trials.* Balzer + Bray, 2010. 408 pp. Grades 8–12.

In this verse novel, three girls—seventeen-year-old Mercy Lewis, servant to the Putnam family; seventeen-year-old Margaret Walcott; and twelve-year-old Ann Putnam—testify that they are "afflicted" by witches. Their narratives include familiar elements found in accounts about the Salem witch hunts, but the emphasis here is on the fictional background and lives of the girls, and their interrelationship with one another and with the "afflicted girls" Abigail Williams, Elizabeth Hubbard, and Susannah Sheldon. Hemphill shows how the girls' accusations bring them power and attention in a culture in which girls endured rigid familial discipline and were subject to sexual abuse. But revealed in the girls' dialogues are the slippages between their accusations and the truth, as well as the cracks that appear in their unified front.

Hemphill provides information about what is known about each of the real-life girls who testified and each of the accused. In an author's note, she includes information about various theories explaining the cause of the girls' affliction, but her main premise is that the "accusers 'faked' their affliction and knew what they were doing" (405). Her interpretation invites readers to think about the role of religion and witchcraft in colonial New England; the social and political structures of Salem; and the vulnerability of young women, no matter their different backgrounds and social class. A list of sources and websites is also provided.

1. Are there examples in the text pointing to the girls' faking their afflictions? Discuss key events that contribute to the ending of the accusations and trials.
2. Compare Hemphill's text with primary documents at the website Salem Witch Trials: Documentary Archive and Transcription Project (http://salem.lib.virginia.edu/texts/transcripts.html).
3. Related reading: Marc Aronson's *Witch-Hunt: Mysteries of the Salem Witch Trials* (Atheneum Books for Young Readers, 2003).

Adult Fiction

Kent, Kathleen. *The Heretic's Daughter.* Little, Brown, 2008. 331 pp. Langum, 2008; *SLJ* BABHS, 2008.

In December 1690, nine-year-old Sarah Carrier and her family moved to Andover, Massachusetts, to live with her grandmother. When smallpox breaks out, Sarah leaves to stay with her aunt and uncle, but once home in April 1691, there are accusations of "witchery" against the Carriers. During a time when people feared disease and Indian attacks, they blamed the Carriers for spreading smallpox. Other factors included the hatred of Mercy Williams (fired for lying and stealing), the sharpness of Martha Carrier (Sarah's mother) in disputes, and the fortuitous change in the wind that saved their fields but burned those of a neighbor. Martha is arrested on May 31, 1692, and two of her brothers the following July—then Sarah and her brother Tom in August. Kent delineates the lack of reason governing their trials and vividly describes the dreadful prison conditions for incarcerated women and children. Also mentioned are those who begin to question the proceedings, including Increase Mather. Martha, proclaiming her innocence and refusing to save herself by confessing to a lie, is hung on August 18, 1692.

Herself a descendant of Martha Carrier, Kent weaves her own family history into a well-researched portrait of seventeenth-century Salem, a society in which belief in witchcraft existed alongside a religion that emphasized repentance from damnation. Martha Carrier's earlier life is imagined in the prequel novel *The Wolves of Andover* (Little, Brown, 2010).

1. Discuss the role of confession in the Salem witch trials.
2. Related website: The website Salem Witch Trials: Documentary Archive and Transcription Project (http://salem.lib.virginia.edu/texts/transcripts.html)—search under "Carrier" by clicking on "Search All Names in the Salem Witchcraft Papers."

Slavery in the New World

Draper, Sharon. *Copper Sun.* Atheneum, 2006. 302 pp. Grades 9–12. *Booklist* Top 10 HF, 2006; King, 2007; NSSTB, 2007.

The village of fifteen-year-old Amari welcome the pale-faced strangers with a feast, but celebration changes to scenes of bloodshed as Amari's family and the other villagers are killed. Amari is shackled and marched to the coast, where she is branded. During the sea voyage, she is raped, and in Charles Town, South Carolina, she is sold to a plantation owner as a gift for his sixteen-year-old son, Clay. Fifteen-year-old Polly, an indentured white girl, is instructed to "tame" the "savage" slave girl (90). The girls, assigned to the kitchen under the slave cook Teenie, form an uneasy alliance that strengthens into friendship.

Set in 1738, Draper's story exposes through the girls' alternating perspectives a patriarchal socioeconomic system in which there is disregard for human life and dignity, including sexual abuse, whippings, and life-threatening conditions in the rice fields. When Mr. Derby murders his wife's newborn mixed-race child, the doctor who has been entrusted with reselling Amari and Polly, gives them, along with Teenie's young son, a chance to escape. In contrast to the many slaves who were traveling north, Amari insists that they follow the advice of an old slave and travel south. They make their way to Fort Mose, Florida, a refuge for escaped slaves, indentured servants, and Native Americans. Draper provides information about Fort Mose; St. Augustine; and Francisco Menendez, a former slave who became captain of St. Augustine's black militia. She also provides a list of resources.

1. What does Draper's story convey about the economic benefits of slavery on a rice plantation?
2. Discuss Polly's position as an indentured servant and Amari's position as a slave.
3. Describe examples of passive and overt resistance to slavery.
4. Related reading: Glennette Tilley Turner's *Fort Mose and the Story of the Man Who Built the First Black Settlement in Colonial America* (Abrams, 2010).

Adult Fiction

Morrison, Toni. *A Mercy*. Alfred A. Knopf, 2008. 167 pp. ALA Notable, 2010; *Booklist* Top 10 HN, 2009.

In 1682, Jacob Vaark, an Anglo-Dutch farmer and trader from Milton, Massachusetts, rides to Maryland to collect his debt from a Portuguese plantation owner. He refuses the offer of slaves in recompense, although he covets D'Ortega's house. A slave mother begs Vaark to take her daughter, Florens. Florens joins Lina, a servant woman who Vaark took from her Native American village when it was ravaged by smallpox, and Sorrow, another ill-used orphan who survived a shipwreck and was handed over to Vaark by a man who had abused her. With help from two white indentured laborers, Scully and Willard,

Florens and Lina work on the farm with Jacob's wife, Rebekkah. In a multiple-voiced narrative, the characters tell their different stories and versions of the events that unfold after Jacob's death from smallpox, before he could move into the mansion he had built with profits from the Barbados molasses trade.

Morrison provides a kaleidoscopic view of the different groups that populated America in the 1680s, making visible the different ethnic, racial, and religious divisions in a milieu in which slavery is already extant. At the center of story is Florens—in love with the never-enslaved blacksmith who crafts the mansion's iron gates. But Florens has never come to terms with being separated from her mother, who believed it was "a mercy" to send her away. Her mother tells her about her own bondage with the warning, "To give dominion of yourself to another is a wicked thing" (167).

1. Discuss Morrison's characters and what they convey about the divisions among different groups of peoples in the 1680s.
2. Discuss Jacob Vaark's involvement with slavery despite his criticism of the slave trade.
3. Discuss the significance of the mansion at Milton for Jacob and others.
4. Florens's mother states that there is "no protection" against misuse by men (162). Discuss the ways this applies to all women characters in the book.

CHAPTER 2

Revolution and the New Nation
(1760–1820s)

Avi. *Sophia's War: A Tale of the Revolution.* Beach Lane Books and Simon & Schuster, 2012. 302 pp. Grades 5–7. *Booklist* Top 10 HF, 2013.

There are, writes Avi, three threads to this story: the treatment of American prisoners on British prison ships anchored off New York City, the secret dealings between Major John André and Benedict Arnold regarding plans for a British attack on American-held West Point, and the fictional story of Sophia. Twelve-year-old Sophia, despite her loyalty to the Patriots, is enamored of the charming young British officer who boards at her family's house in British-occupied New York in 1776. But John André refuses to help her brother, William, a follower of Thomas Paine, who is imprisoned on the *Good Intent* and subsequently dies. Three years later, Sophia, eager to avenge William's death, agrees to be a house servant at General Clinton's British headquarters so that she may spy on Major André and his secret correspondence as Anderson with a Mr. Moore (Arnold) concerning West Point. When André voyages up the Hudson to meet Arnold, Sophia sets out to warn West Point of the intended attack and Arnold's treachery. Her action results in the Patriots' arrest and the hanging of André as a spy. As Avi's story makes clear, André's decision to dispense with his British uniform and don civilian clothing for his journey back to New York was a major factor in his indictment.

Avi's story includes background material to the American Revolution and detailed descriptions of New York under British occupation, the conditions on prison ships, and the circumstances and reasons for André's arrest. Avi inserts quotes from the secret correspondence between Anderson (André) and Moore and provides maps, a glossary, and a bibliography.

1. Discuss the strategic importance of West Point in relation to the outcome of the War of Independence.
2. Sophie is conflicted over her role in André's hanging. Was his death justified? For a detailed assessment of his case, see the web page "John André: Case Officer," (https://www.cia.gov/library/center-for-the-study-of-intelligence/kent-csi/vol5no3/html/v05i3a07p_0001.htm).
3. Related website: "John André (1750–1780)," Spy Letters of the American Revolution (www.clements.umich.edu/exhibits/online/spies/index-people.html).

Blackwood, Gary. *The Year of the Hangman.* 2002; Penguin and Speak, 2004. 264 pp. Grades 7–10. YALSA BB, 2003.

"By the winter of 1776, the American Revolution seemed doomed," writes Blackwood in a preamble to his alternate history in which the Patriots are defeated. Blackwood's story begins in 1777 with fifteen-year-old Creighton Brown, who is forcibly shipped off to his uncle, Major Gower, in Charles Town in the Carolinas by his mother, who feels that she has no control over her wayward son after his father, a career soldier, was reportedly killed in Carolina. But when Creighton arrives, Gower has just been appointed lieutenant governor of Florida. On their voyage to Pensacola, Creighton and Gower are attacked by the Patriot Benedict Arnold and escorted to New Orleans, where Gower is confined. Creighton, posing as an indentured servant, is hired by Benjamin Franklin, the former ambassador to England and France, who has his printing shop in New Orleans. In his work for Franklin, Creighton begins to question assumptions about English superiority that had shaped his upbringing and comes to see another side to British rule. As he meets with members of the Patriots, he realizes that they have been misrepresented in England. Meanwhile, Creighton reluctantly agrees to spy for Gower and helps him escape, but his uncle betrays him by leaving him behind.

Embedded in the adventure-filled plot that includes the rescue of Creighton's imprisoned father are themes of colonialism, war, and loyalty. Blackwood assembles and rewords excerpts from Franklin's writings on peace and war. There are detailed descriptions of New Orleans in 1777 and of the printing process. In his notes, Blackwood distinguishes between fictional and actual characters and between historical facts and his alternate history in which the British capture Washington.

1. Discuss the changes Blackwood makes to the historical record. Discuss events when defeat may have been a possibility.
2. Discuss Creighton's changed attitudes toward British colonialism and the Patriots.

Elliott, L. M. *Give Me Liberty.* Katherine Tegan/Harper Collins, 2006. 376 pp. Grades 5–8.

Nathaniel Dunn's father abandons him when their ship docks at Leedsgate, Virginia, in 1772 after a voyage from England, during which his mother died. His father is indentured to a plantation owner near the Blue Ridge Mountains, and Nathaniel is sold to a Virginian plantation owner who goes bankrupt in 1774. Nathaniel is rescued from the bullying blacksmith who is ready to buy him by Basil Wilkinson, a musician and tutor, and taken to Williamsburg, where he is hired out as an apprentice to Edan Maguire, a carriage maker. They arrive to see the House of Burgesses displaying support for the Patriots. Nathaniel, however, also hears the arguments of Maguire against Williamsburg's enforcement of the Non-Importation Agreement, which is affecting his declining business. When the Patriots form the Virginian Regiments, Nathaniel enlists as a fifer and is present at the Battle of Great Bridge, near Norfolk, in 1775. Nathaniel's friendship with Moses, an escaped slave who joins Lord Dunmore's Royal Ethiopians, forces him to think about the contradictions between upholding slavery while fighting for liberty.

References are made to the philosophies undergirding the struggle for liberty and independence, to Patrick Henry's speeches, and to Thomas Jefferson's writings. Historical figures include Henry and Jefferson, as well as Peyton Randolph (first president of the Continental Congress). In a lengthy note, Elliott expands on the issues and characters of her story. She closes with quotes from Thomas Paine's *Common Sense.* An annotated time line and extensive bibliography are included.

1. Discuss the effects of the Non-Importation Agreement on Williamsburg's merchants.
2. Discuss ideas in Jefferson's *A Summary View of the Rights of British America* in relation to the Declaration of Independence, available at the World Digital Library (www.wdl.org/en/item/117/).

Hughes, Pat Raccio. *Five 4ths of July.* Viking, 2011. 304 pp. Grades 7–10. *Booklist* Top 10 HF, 2012.

On July 4, 1777, in East Haven, Connecticut, Jake Mallery, a spirited fourteen-year-old, spends time with his friends. When his father refuses to let him be a cabin boy on a privateer, Jake continues to help with his father's farm and ferry business and then joins the militia on July 4, 1778. He is taken prisoner with his best friend, Tim Morris, during the British attack on East Haven in July 1779 and endures unspeakable conditions on the prison ship *Bonhomme,* anchored in Wallabout Bay in Brooklyn. Especially vivid are descriptions of daily life on board, where skeletal prisoners, beset by bad food, filth, and illnesses, struggle to stay alive. Tim is killed when Jake and others engage in mutinous behavior. Jake finally escapes in 1781.

The progress of the Revolutionary War is woven into the story of Jake and his family, including the career of Benedict Arnold (Jake's hero). Arguments made by "Refugees," or Tory sympathizers, are heard from Mr. Pickett, who, with his wife, helps Jake regain his health after escaping from the *Bonhomme* by swimming to Long Island. Jake, in turn, hears how the Patriots imprisoned Pickett and his son "in the name of liberty, and without a trial" (248–49), for acting upon their beliefs. Themes of liberty are also woven into Jake's conflict with his father and his romance with an indentured servant, Hannah.

In her notes, Hughes provides information about prison ships, explains how Jake Mallery is based on a real boy, and tells about her research regarding young people during the Revolutionary period.

1. Discuss Jake's opinions on the Revolutionary War.
2. Discuss Mr. Pickett's arguments for being a Loyalist.

Klass, Sheila Solomon. *Soldier's Secret: The Story of Deborah Sampson.* Holt, 2009. 215 pp. Grades 6–9. *Booklist* Top 10 HF, 2009; NSSTB, 2010.

In 1983, Deborah Sampson was proclaimed "Official Heroine of the Commonwealth of Massachusetts" (212). Klass's story of Sampson's service during the American Revolution as the enlisted soldier Robert Shurtliff begins with the unmasking of her disguise by a Dr. Binney, who rescues a fevered Shurtliff from an army hospital. In her first-person narrative, Sampson documents her life from her birth in 1760 in Plympton, Massachusetts Bay Colony, including her difficult childhood as a "give-away child," her ten years as an indentured servant, the threat of an unwelcome suitor from whom she runs to enlist in the Fourth Massachusetts Regiment in May 1782, and details of her service until her honorable discharge in October 1783. She describes her first experience of serious combat, the missions that bring her to the attention of senior officers, and her work as an aide to General Paterson. She also explains how she lives as a woman among men.

Klass points out that Shurtliff's relationship with fellow soldier Roger Snow is invented. In her notes, Klass tells about Sampson's marriage to Benjamin Gannet and how she, later, spoke about her experiences before theater audiences. A chronology is provided.

1. Sampson states that she "never wanted to be a boy or a man" (25). Discuss her character and the reasons behind her choice to enlist.
2. Discuss how the relationship between Shurtliff and Roger Snow is used to speculate how it might have been for a woman to experience war disguised as a male.

3. Related website: *The Female Review* (Library of Congress), at the Internet Archive (http://archive.org/details/femalereviewlife00 mann).

Paulsen, Gary. *Woods Runner.* Wendy Lamb, 2010. 164 pp. Grades 6–9. NSSTB, 2011; YALSA BF, 2011.

Thirteen-year-old Sam lives with his parents in western Pennsylvania, and they have just learned about Lexington and Concord. Sam is hunting when he sees smoke and returns to find his settlement burned, corpses of his neighbors, and the tracks of his captured parents. Using his skills as a *courier de bois*, Sam catches up with the party of British soldiers and Iroquois who are holding his parents captive. But he is caught up and severely wounded in a surprise attack on the captors by Coop, the leader of a band of men who are looking to join the Patriots. Under Coop's care, Sam survives to continue his search. Throughout Sam's journey, Paulsen shows a dark and often hidden side of the fight for freedom, including an undercover informal spy network that enables Sam to rescue his parents.

Paulsen emphasizes the brutality that is part of a war for freedom. Sam witnesses, for example, the cold-blooded murder of a family by Hessians and then adopts the small girl they fail to kill. Sam's narrative is interspersed with segments that provide facts about weapons, British and American soldiers, fighting tactics, orphans, prisoners of war, and treatment of the wounded. Statistics on the dead and wounded during eight years of fighting are included in Paulsen's afterword.

1. Paulsen states that there is a tendency to focus on "rousing stories of heroism and stirring examples of patriotism, all clean, pristine, antiseptic" (162). To what extent does he provide perspectives on the Revolutionary War different from those given in other accounts?
2. Compare Paulsen's representation of the Hessians to other accounts of their role in the war.

Schweizer, Chris. *Crogan's Loyalty.* Oni Press, 2012. 176 pp. Grades 7–10. *Booklist* Top 10 Graphic Novels for Youth, 2013.

Framed within a contemporary story of a falling out between two brothers, this novel (one of a series of historical adventures about the Crogan family) goes back to 1778, when two brothers find themselves on opposing sides during the American Revolution. Will Crogan, the younger brother and a Patriot, accuses his older brother, Charlie—schooled on the East Coast and hanging around the "Macaroni Boys"—of being a turncoat. Charlie regards Will as belonging to a side that decides philosophical debates by acts of violence, such as tarring and feathering those who preach against rebellion. After initially attacking and then recognizing each other in a chance encounter in the woods, they are torn between loyalty to each other as brothers and their loyalty to their different causes. Charlie, in particular, risks losing his life and honor in endeavoring to be loyal both to his Hessian commander, Captain Unterbrüsch, and to Will as he helps Will escape from his troop and aids him in his search for Bess, the daughter of a nonpartisan family with whom Will has fallen in love.

Schweizer's fast-action plot and dramatic graphics convey the desperation of brothers who must make life-and-death choices. The text raises different views on what it means to be loyal to one's country, the different positions taken by Native Americans toward the war, the illegal settlement of Native American lands, and how war affects even those who do not actively wish to take sides.

1. Discuss Captain Unterbrüsch's view that Charlie is a "good man" but not a good soldier (170).
2. Discuss Will's decisions and actions as a Patriot and as a brother.
3. Discuss the representation of Captain Unterbrüsch in relation to what you have read about Hessians' role in the Revolutionary War in other fictional or informational texts.

Adult Fiction

Cornwell, Bernard. *The Fort: A Novel of the Revolutionary War.* Harper-Collins, 2010. 468 pp.

In 1779, the Massachusetts government launched the Penobscot Expedition to dislodge from Majabigwaduce (now Castine, Maine) the British, whose goal was establish a new province, New Ireland, which would provide shelter for Loyalists and deter rebel privateers. Cornwell's novel provides a well-researched, detailed, and entertaining account of the ill-fated expedition, the "worst naval disaster in United States history before Pearl Harbor" (451). The narrative switches from Brigadier General Francis McLean, his Eighty-Second Regiment, and Captain Mowat (commander of the three British sloops in Majabigwaduce Harbor) to the American brigadier generals Solomon Lovell and Peleg Wadsworth and Commander Dudley Saltonstall, whose fleet was the largest assembled by the Patriots during the War of Independence. Despite the Americans' initial success in gaining the high ground in front of McLean's unfinished fort, they lost momentum. For the following weeks, Lovell dug in while conducting a running dispute with Saltonstall, who, seeing the harbor as a trap, refused to enter and engage the British sloops. The fort, he insisted, was to be gained first. Cornwell describes the frustration of Wadsworth and sea captains under Saltonstall as the weeks pass with only a few assaults and counterassaults, which give McLean time to strengthen his fort and the British navy time to arrive.

Cornwell explains the reasons for the Americans' retreat, including Saltonstall's decision not to stand against the British fleet, which resulted in his court-martial. Special attention is given to two figures celebrated in poetry: the British lieutenant John Moore ("The Burial of Sir John Moore at Corunna," by Charles Wolfe), and Lieutenant Paul Revere, who is presented in a very different light than he is in Henry Wadsworth Longfellow's poem. Cornwell includes excerpts from letters, orders, journals, and depositions from the book *Documentary History of the State of Maine* and includes the titles of other works in his extensive research notes.

1. Compare the representation of Paul Revere with how he is represented in other works of fiction, poetry, and informational texts.
2. Discuss the arguments Lovell and Saltonstall make to not attack the British.
3. Related website: "A Naval Disaster: The Penobscot Expedition," Maine History Online (www.mainememory.net/sitebuilder/site/592/page/952/display).

Shaara, Jeff. *Rise to Rebellion.* Ballantine, 2001. 492 pp.

Drawing on letters, diaries, and historical accounts, Shaara tells the story of American Independence from 1770 to 1776 through the voices and different perspectives of various figures, focusing especially on Benjamin Franklin, John Adams, George Washington, and the British general Thomas Gage. Shaara provides detailed biographical material for all his protagonists. In his introduction, he provides background information on the Seven Years' War; the restrictions and taxes the British levied against the colonies, including the Stamp Act of 1765; and Samuel Adams and the Sons of Liberty. Beginning with the Boston Massacre of 1770 as experienced by a British sentry facing an unruly mob, Shaara provides a detailed, multiple-perspective account of the slow but inevitable move toward independence. The complexity of issues is made clear from the standpoint of "radicals" and those wishing to reconcile with the king, as well as those representing Parliament and the empire, such as Thomas Hutchinson and Gage. The evolving positions of Franklin and Adams are laid out with clarity, as are the tensions and fervor among delegates during meetings of the Continental Congress and the signing of the Declaration of Independence.

Shaara leavens the text with characterizations of his protagonists and their personal relationships. The novel concludes with Washington in New York, where his troops hear the words of the Declaration of Independence even as General Howe's fleet sails toward Long Island, thus setting the stage for the second volume: *The Glorious Cause: A Novel of the American Revolution* (Ballantine, 2002).

1. Compare Shaara's treatment of the Boston Massacre with accounts in textbooks.
2. Analyze the arguments for independence that John Adams presents in the novel.
3. Related reading: David McCullough, *1776* (Simon & Schuster Paperbacks, 2006).

Revolution and Slavery

Amateau, Gigi. *Come August, Come Freedom: The Bellows, The Gallows, and the Black General Gabriel*. Candlewick Press, 2012. 231 pp. Grades 7–10.

Beginning with Gabriel Prosser's childhood, Amateau traces his life as a slave and the path he follows to rebellion. As "milk brother" to Thomas Henry, son of Thomas Prosser, Gabriel is taught to read and write by Mrs. Prosser, but his relationship with young Thomas Henry changes when Gabriel is beaten for repeating Patrick Henry's speech that ended, "Give me liberty or give me death." He is sent to Richmond with his brother, Solomon, to be apprenticed to the blacksmith Jacob Kent, whose forge is a gathering place for those who discuss politics and liberty. After seven years, he returns to Brookfield Plantation and arranges to be hired out so that he can earn the money to manumit Nonny, the girl with whom he has fallen in love. His growing determination to fight for freedom is fueled by news of the Saint-Domingue slave rebellion led by Toussaint L'Ouverture and by a chain of events in which he has to relinquish his hard-earned money to Thomas Henry.

The novel provides details of Gabriel's rebellion in 1800, of the reasons for its failure, and of Gabriel's capture and imprisonment before he is hung. Amateau places the novel in the context of Richmond's development. On her website, Amateau distinguishes fictional and historical characters and events. She identifies each inserted document and explains, for example, that official documents and Gabriel's trial transcripts are authentic but that Thomas Prosser's journal is fabricated and modeled on an unpublished plantation journal of the same period.

1. Related website: For discussion questions, resources, and research notes, see the author's website (www.gigiamateau.com/contact.php).

Anderson, Laurie Halse. *Chains: Seeds of America.* Simon & Schuster, 2008. 316 pp. Grades 7–9. ALA Notable, 2009; NBA finalist, 2008; NSSTB, 2009; O'Dell, 2009; YALSA BB, 2009.

When their owner dies, Isabel and her little sister Ruth are taken away from Rhode Island to New York, where they are bought by the Locktons, Loyalists to the core. Isabel describes her never-ending work in an affluent household on Wall Street and records the abuse to which she and her sister are subjected. Anderson provides a rich, in-depth portrait of New York in 1776: the layered society, from mistress to servant to slave; the geographic layout of the island, with its streets and buildings; and its transformation into a barricaded city. Isabel is persuaded to spy for the Patriots by a young slave boy, Curzon, but she overhears the arguments of other slaves who believe the British will free them. Anderson's story illustrates how slaves were caught up in the fighting between the British and the Patriots. Isabel also observes the effects of the British invasion on New York.

The diary format of this book runs from the first chapter, "Monday, 27th, 1776," to the last, "18th–19th January, 1777," when Isabel escapes from New York with Curzon. Quotes from primary materials head each chapter. In the appendix, Anderson provides information about the historical personages included in her story, attitudes toward slavery during the American Revolution, and the 1776 Great Fire of New York.

1. Isabel states that she is "chained between two nations" (182). Discuss various characters across different social classes and loyalties and how they perceive freedom and slavery.
2. Discuss how the events of 1776 affected the citizens of New York City.

Anderson, Laurie Halse. *Forge.* Atheneum Books for Young Readers, 2010. 297 pp. Grades 5–8.

In this sequel to *Chains: Seeds of America*, Curzon, who has served as a substitute in the army for his master, James Bellingham, is rescued from a prisoner's brig in New York by Isabel. They find work in Morristown, New Jersey, but later part company. After reenlisting in the Continental Army, Curzon fights in the Battle of Saratoga and marches south with his company, arriving at Valley Forge, Pennsylvania, on December 21, 1777. He describes the conditions endured by the Continental Army through the winter of 1777–78, such as the lack of shelter, food, and clothing. He is one of the starving men in rags who marches barefoot in the snow and struggles to build log cabins with "little equipment and less training" (87) while eating "fire cake" day after day. Through the character of Curzon, who is recaptured by Bellingham, now an assistant to the committee from Congress, Anderson addresses issues of liberty and slavery. Curzon hears General Nathanael Greene's plans to provision the army; overhears current political events from committee members, including the news that the French will support General Washington; and observes Baron von Steuben's new drill techniques that bring military discipline to an untrained army. Anderson's resource material includes readings and information on the role of African Americans in fighting both for the Patriots and the British.

1. Discuss reasons Curzon and the majority of men did not desert or mutiny.
2. Discuss the measures that turned starving and ill-equipped men into "soldiers ready for war" (278).
3. Related reading: Russell Freedman's *Washington at Valley Forge* (Holiday House, 2008).

Anderson, M. T. *The Pox Party.* Vol. 1 of *The Astonishing Life of Octavian Nothing, Traitor to the Nation.* Candlewick, 2006. 351 pp. Grades 7–12. *Booklist* Top 10 HF, 2007; NBA (Y), 2006; YALSA OB, 2011; Printz honor, 2007.

Anderson, M. T. *The Kingdom on the Waves.* Vol. 2 of *The Astonishing Life of Octavian Nothing.* Candlewick, 2008. 561 pp. Grades 7–12. Printz honor, 2009; YALSA BB, 2009.

Anderson's award-winning novels present a well-researched new perspective on the relationship between slavery and America's struggle for liberty and independence through the character of Octavian, a young African American slave who has had an unusual upbringing. In volume 1, Octavian, whose mother claims to be an African princess, receives a classical education at the Novanglian College of Lucidity as part of an experiment by Mr. Gitney to "divine" whether he belongs to "a separate and distinct species" (49). Because of growing unrest in Boston, the college moves to Canaan, where in 1775 Gitney and Sharpe arrange a "pox party" at which guests and slaves are inoculated with infected strands of hair from smallpox victims. The horrific death and autopsy of his mother drive Octavian to escape. Avoiding capture, he is persuaded to join the Patriots, for there was "need to stand with his Brother Man & resist the Tyranny of Those Who Own Us" (246). After taking part in a raid on Hog Island, Octavian is captured and taken back to Canaan, where he is fitted with an iron mask. Dr. Trefusis, Octavian's former tutor, rescues him, and they flee to Boston to seek refuge with the British, who they believe are more sympathetic to the freeing of slaves.

In volume 2, Octavian is employed as a violinist with an orchestra at Faneuil Hall, but when rebels lay siege to Boston and Charles Town is burned, Trefusis organizes their escape by ship to Norfolk. Here, Octavian enlists in Lord Dunmore's Royal Ethiopian Regiment, composed of slaves who agree to fight for Dunmore in return for their freedom. After the burning of Norfolk, Dunmore's fleet retreats to Gwynn's Island in Chesapeake Bay, where smallpox breaks out. Octavian eventually escapes with the fleet to New York and from there makes his way to the college to confront Gitney and replace the records of the experiment with his own record.

Inserted in the text are transcriptions of eighteenth-century documents, including Dunmore's "A Proclamation," in which he declares "all indentured Servants, Negroes, or others . . . free that are able and willing to bear Arms" (118), and a letter from George Washington to Richard Henry Lee of Virginia, warning him that Dunmore must be "crushed" (264). Volume 2 shows how farmers and citizens in the Virginian countryside, Patriots and Loyalists alike, are caught up in the war. In both novels, the style and diction of Octavian's narrative reflect the time in which it would have been written. Philosophical and scientific theories extant at the time are interwoven throughout the texts.

1. Identify and compare perspectives on the American Revolution presented in these novels to those presented in textbooks.
2. Anderson explains how he constructs his fictional narrative from primary sources. Compare his example of the "composite" mob scenes in Boston with the report he uses as a source in his author's note in volume 1.
3. Discuss reasons that slaves are drawn to fight for the British, or alternatively decide to fight with the Patriots.

Adult Fiction

Hill, Lawrence. *Someone Knows My Name.* W. W. Norton, 2008. 486 pp. *SLJ* BABHS, 2008.

Eleven-year-old Aminata Diallo, born to a free Muslim family around 1745, is captured by slave traders and taken to Bance Island, where she is branded and shipped to Sullivan's Island, South Carolina, and sold to Robinson Appleby, an indigo plantation owner on St. Helen's Island. Aminata describes the horrors of the forced march and sea passage, as well as her life on the plantation, where she is raped by Robinson, but where the Muslim overseer also teaches her to read and write. After Aminata marries Chekura, a young man from her homeland who lives on another plantation, their baby is taken away, and Aminata is sold to Solomon Lindo, a Jewish indigo inspector who lives in Charles Town. In 1775, Aminata accompanies Lindo to New York, where Sam Fraunces, a tavern owner, helps her escape. After the Philipsburg Proclamation, she helps the British to document black Loyalists who wish to go to Nova Scotia by entering their names in the ledger titled "The Book of Negroes." In 1783, she sails to Shelburne, Nova Scotia, where black Loyalists are unable to procure land and are forced to live apart from white Loyalists. In 1792, Aminata leaves Nova Scotia for Sierra Leone, which the Sierra Leone Company promises will be a colony without slavery. Aminata's final destination in 1802 is London, where she testifies before a parliamentary committee on behalf of abolitionists in their efforts to end the slave trade.

Aminata's voice brings to life the history of the places where she has lived, been a slave, and worked. Characters based on actual people include Sam Fraunces; John Clarkson, who organized the exodus to Sierra Leone; and the English abolitionist William Wilberforce. Hill used as the basis for his novel "The Book of Negroes," which contains the names of those who had served or lived behind British lines and who sailed from New York for Nova Scotia and other colonies. He provides research notes and a bibliographic essay.

1. Analyze and discuss British polices toward slaves and slavery.

The New Nation

Anderson, Laurie Halse. *Fever 1793.* 2000; Aladdin Paperbacks, 2002. 251 pp. Grades 6–9. *Booklist* Top 10 HF, 2001; YALSA BB, 2001.

In August 1793, yellow fever is spreading quickly through Philadelphia. Fourteen-year-old Mattie's mother falls sick, and Mattie is sent with her grandfather to stay outside the city. On the way, Mattie succumbs to the fever and is taken by her grandfather to Bush Hill, which Stephen Girard has transformed into an efficient hospital. When Mattie recovers, she returns with her grandfather to a ransacked coffeehouse. Returning on the day that General Washington reenters the city (November 11), Mattie's mother finds out that her daughter has dealt with intruders and her grandfather's death, and has reopened the coffeehouse.

Anderson vividly describes the desolation of a city left with the dead and dying; those who cannot flee drench their clothes in vinegar and wear "tarred ropes around their necks" (73). Anderson includes medical responses to yellow fever, such as Dr. Benjamin Rush's bloodletting treatments, disparaged by French doctors. She also provides information on topics such as the Free African Society, the "moving" capital of the United States, and various real-life personages mentioned in the text.

1. Discuss the reasons given for the outbreak and spread of the fever, as well as the controversies between Dr. Rush and the French doctors at Bush Hill over the treatment of yellow fever victims.
2. Related website: The Great Fever (www.pbs.org/wgbh/amex/fever/peopleevents/e_science.html).
3. Related reading: Jim Murphy, *An American Plague: The True and Terrifying Story of the Yellow Fever Epidemic of 1793* (Clarion Books, 2003).

Bradley, Kimberly Brubaker. *Jefferson's Sons: A Founding Father's Secret Children.* Dial Books, 2011. 360 pp. Grades: 5–9. ALA Notable, 2012; NSSTB, 2012.

In 1805, Sally Hemings told her son, seven-year-old Beverly, that he must never call Thomas Jefferson "Papa." Through the different viewpoints of Beverly and his younger brother Maddy (Madison), and from the perspective of Peter Fossett, the young son of Jefferson's enslaved blacksmith, Bradley's story provides a comprehensive depiction of slavery and life at Monticello that includes what it meant to be a slave. Jefferson's three slave sons and their sister, Harriet, were promised their freedom at the age of twenty-one, but Bradley uses the difficulties Beverly experienced after leaving home to explain the contradictory slave laws pertaining to freed slaves and those of mixed heritage.

The lives of Sally Hemings's children are placed in the context of Jefferson's household, which also included his daughter Martha and her children, who come to live with Jefferson at Monticello. The relationships between Sally Hemings and Jefferson, between Jefferson and his slave children, and between Martha and Jefferson's "other" family are subtly drawn. The novel charts the decline of Jefferson's estates and his mounting debt, which led to the auction of 130 slaves after his death in 1826. Bradley includes information about what is known about the future of Beverly, Madison, their younger brother Eston, and the Fossett family and provides a list of resources.

1. Discuss the contradiction between slavery and the ideas in the Declaration of Independence. Related website: Thomas Jefferson's Monticello (www.monticello.org/site/jefferson).
2. Compare Bradley's representation of Jefferson as slave owner with the information and opinions in the essay "Thomas Jefferson and Slavery" (www.monticello.org/site/plantation-and-slavery).

Ketchum, Liza. *Where the Great Hawk Flies.* Clarion, 2005. 263 pp. Grades 5–8. NSSTB, 2006.

Ketchum bases her novel on the true story of her Pequot grandmother, a midwife, and her grandmother's white husband, who lived in Vermont during the eighteenth century. Set in Vermont in 1782, after the end of the War of Independence and two years after the Indian raid near Royalton, Ketchum's story centers on the family of thirteen-year-old Daniel Tucker, whose Pequot mother is respected as a "doctress," and eleven-year-old Hiram Coombe and his family, the Tuckers' new neighbors who have moved back to the area after the raid, which destroyed their home and farm. Both Hiram, still suffering from the trauma of the raid, and his mother show animosity toward the Tuckers, failing to understand that it was the Caughnawaga, not the Pequot, who aided the British in the raid. The unexpected arrival of Daniel's Pequot grandfather, a *powwaw* who builds a wigwam, is followed by the arrival of Hiram's Uncle Abner, who has escaped from a British prison after being captured in the raid and seeks revenge by burning the wigwam and attacking Daniel. But the emphasis in Ketchum's story is on the rejection of prejudice and revenge as Abner is ejected from the community with the support of friends and neighbors. Hiram's respect for Daniel's family grows when Daniel's mother helps with the birth of Hiram's mother's twins. The motif of the red hawk that follows Daniel's family is highlighted in poetry and in the text. Ketchum's extensive notes cover her family history and the history and language of the Pequot.

1. Discuss the reasons for Hiram and his family's attitudes toward the Tucker family.
2. Related website: Mashantucket Pequot Museum and Research Center (www.pequotmuseum.org).

Expansion and Reform

(1801-1870)

Gratz, Alan. *The Brooklyn Nine: A Novel in Nine Innings.* Dial, 2009. 299 pp. Grades 6–9. *Booklist* Top 10 HF, 2009.

In these short stories, Gratz combines nine generations of family history with the history of baseball. The novel begins with the first inning in 1845 in Manhattan, New York, in a story featuring Felix Schneider, an immigrant boy from Bremen, Germany, and ends with the ninth inning in Brooklyn, New York, in 2002 in a story about Snider Flint. The historical background is integral to each generational story. Felix's story is set in the context of Kleinedeutschland (Little Germany), the clothing industry, and the history of Alexander Cartwright and the Knickerbockers. When fire consumes East Manhattan, Felix, a fast runner who has dreamed of playing baseball, is injured. He has to sew suits all day but he also makes his own baseball. His son Louis's story is told within the context of the Civil War. Louis trades a blinded Confederate soldier his father's homemade ball for a bat—the kind he has seen used only by the "finest players on the Excelsiors"—before taking the soldier back to the rebel lines (57). In 1908, Walter Schneider learns about prejudice when his father changes their name to Snider, and about segregation when he learns that pitcher "Cyclone Joe" Williams can never play for a National League team.

Connections are also made between baseball and popular culture as baseball becomes a national pastime. Frankie, Walter's daughter, meets the famed sportswriter John Kieran, and Frankie's daughter Kat plays in the All-American Girls Professional Baseball League during World War II. In 1957, Kat's son watches the movie *Duck and Cover* and knows that the Dodgers are moving from Brooklyn to Los Angeles. In 1981, Kat's grandson achieves a "perfect game." The last story connects to the first as Snider Flint handles the baseball made by Louis Schneider in 1845 and searches for the stories behind baseball memorabilia, including a bat that belonged to Babe Herman of the Brooklyn Robins. Gratz seamlessly integrates baseball and history and provides extra information for each inning.

1. Identify examples of baseball's connections to American popular culture.
2. Related reading: Nelson Kadir, *We Are the Ship: The Story of Negro League Baseball* (Jump at the Sun and Hyperion, 2008).
3. Related website: A "virtual scrapbook" of women baseball players from 1945 to 1954, including interviews and newsreels, is at the website of the All-American Girls Professional Baseball League Players Association (www.aagpbl.org).

Adult Fiction

Carey, Peter. *Parrot and Olivier in America.* 2009; Vintage International, 2011. 381 pp. *Booklist* Top 10 HF, 2010; NBA finalist, 2010.

Carey's novel is based on Alexis de Tocqueville's visit to America in 1831, which resulted in his two-volume work *Democracy in America.* In this "improvisation," Carey's chief characters are the aristocrat Olivier de Garmont and Parrot (John Larrit), the son of an English journeyman printer. Their stories, covered from the childhood of each, take place after the French Revolution and provide a background to the rest of the novel. Olivier's life is in danger in the July Revolution of 1830, so he is dispatched to America to report on the prison system. Parrot is forced to accompany him as spy, protector, and *secrètaire.* Once in New York, Olivier makes plans to visit and write about prisons for his *Penitentiary System in the United States,* but he increasingly spends time on his work on democracy. His knowledge of America expands during a tour with Philip Godefroy, a wealthy farmer from Connecticut whose life is illustrative of the classic American rags-to-riches story. Olivier's ultimate rejection by the freethinking Amelia Godefroy is based on his inability to abandon his aristocratic upbringing. Parrot exemplifies the self-made man who successfully builds his life from scratch as he establishes an artists' colony with his wife on the banks of the Hudson.

Ideas from Olivier's writing that appear in *Democracy in America* are inserted into the novel's text—rich in descriptions of American democratic society, politics, and culture in the mid-nineteenth century.

1. Discuss Olivier's observations of American democracy.
2. Analyze the relationship between Olivier and Parrot and how it reflects the status of individuals in an aristocracy versus a democracy.
3. Related website: The Alexis de Tocqueville Tour: Exploring American Democracy in America, with links to the text of *Democracy in America* (www.tocqueville.org).

Harrigan, Stephen. *The Gates of the Alamo.* 2000; Penguin, 2001. 592 pp. Spur, 2001.

This novel begins with a ceremony honoring the Alamo and the recognition of ninety-one-year-old Terrell Mott, a former mayor of San Antonio and last surviving hero of San Jacinto. Back home, Mott reminisces about events leading up to the Alamo, back when he was sixteen years old. Harrigan covers events leading up to the siege of the Alamo, the siege itself, and the aftermath through the different perspectives of Mott; his widowed mother, Mary; the botanist Edmund Gowan, who stayed in the Mott's inn in Refugio in 1835; and others, including members of the Mexican Army. The lives of these fictional characters become embroiled in the growing hostilities between the Mexican Army and the "Texians." As a result of their circumstances, the Motts and Gowan are inside the fort when the siege of the Alamo begins in 1836.

There are vivid accounts of the battle inside the fort as Mrs. Mott helps the wounded, and as Edmund and Terrell fight alongside historical figures: Davy Crockett, Colonel William Travis, his slave Joe, and

Jim Bowie. The experiences of the Mexican Army's march toward Béxar (San Antonio), the character of Santa Anna, and accounts of his orders are narrated from the perspectives of Sargento Blas Ángel Montoyer and Lieutenant Telesforo Villaseñor. After the siege, Mrs. Mott, searching for her son, who had been sent out of the fort to seek help, sees the evidence of the slaughter of Texans at Goliad; there are also descriptions of the rout of the Mexican Army as a result of Sam Houston's attack at San Jacinto. The novel addresses the settlement of Texas; Mexican laws, including laws addressing immigration and slavery that affected the American colonists; and the arguments made for and against the independence of Texas. Harrigan dispels some of the myths and dubious accounts of the Alamo and relies on, for example, Colonel Travis's letters and Colonel Juan Almonte's field diary of the siege.

1. Analyze the different perspectives regarding Texas's independence from Mexico.
2. Discuss the representation of Santa Anna and his motives.
3. Compare the representation of the siege of the Alamo with accounts in textbooks or other informational texts.
4. Related reading: William C. Davis, *Three Roads to the Alamo: The Lives and Fortunes of David Crockett, James Bowie, and William Barret Travis* (HarperCollins, 1998).

Immigrants and Their Stories

Preus, Margi. *Heart of a Samurai: Based on the True Story of Nakahama Manjiro.* Amulet Books, 2010. 301 pp. Grades 5–9. ALA Notable, 2011; *Booklist* Top 10 HF, 2011; Newbery honor, 2010; NSSTB, 2011.

This novel is based on the life of Nakahama Manjiro, who in 1841, at the age of fourteen, was swept away in a storm from his Japanese village in a fishing boat and stranded on Bird Island with three companions. Near starvation, they are rescued by the whaling ship *John Howland.* Unlike his friends, Manjiro demonstrates a willingness and ability to learn English and whaling skills, and he is given the name "John Mung, whale hunter," by Captain Whitworth, who adopts Manjiro as his son. In New Bedford, Massachusetts, Manjiro, now aged sixteen, helps on the captain's farm, attends school, learns navigation skills, and is apprenticed to a cooper—all while dealing with prejudicial attitudes. After finding gold in California, he returns to Japan, where he is imprisoned before being allowed to return to his family. Soon afterward, he is called on to serve as a samurai teaching English.

In an epilogue, Preus outlines Manjiro's life as a samurai, in which, among many other achievements, he helped bring about an end to the Japanese policy of isolation. Preus includes information about Commodore Matthew Perry's visits to Japan and the treaty signed between Japan and the United States in 1854. Interspersed with the text are black-and-white illustrations, many of which are attributed to John Mung. Preus makes clear where she has fictionalized her story and provides a glossary and a bibliography.

1. How does Manjiro's perspective provide a different lens to look at American society and culture in the nineteenth century?
2. Discuss how Preus shows America's progression toward industrialization compared to that of Japan, which is described as "sealed and shuttered" (68).

Yep, Laurence. *The Journal of Wong Ming-Chung: A Chinese Miner.* Scholastic, 2000. 219 pp. Grades 5–7.

In 1852, "Year Two of the Era, Prosperity for All," Wong Ming-Chung's parents send him to join his uncle, Precious Stone, in California. Wong, known as "Runt" because of his small stature, explains that he records the events of each year in his diary "by both the American and Chinese calendars" (4). In his diary entries, Wong describes his family's poverty but tells how, once his uncle sends back money, his family is promoted to "guest" status in a social hierarchy in which wealth confers privileges. Wong's diary entries reproduce the experiences of thousands of Chinese who left China for California—the Gold Mountain. After a miserable sea voyage during which many die, Wong is taken to San Francisco's Chinatown, where he is provided with shelter before traveling to Sacramento. From there he travels to join his uncle at the Chinese mining camp at Big Bend. His diary entries include descriptions of San Francisco and Sacramento in the early 1850s.

The name "Golden Mountain" is "poetical," Wong soon realizes, when he sees the abandoned mines and cabins. He describes the methods used to extract the remaining fragments of gold from ice-cold water and the difficulties of working in wintry weather. He writes about the laws of discrimination against the Chinese miners: a tax of three dollars per month for a license to work in the mines, and laws that deny the Chinese any legal standing, such as testifying in court. Dishonest Americans are, therefore, able to force the Chinese to give up their claims, as happens at Big Bend, and the Chinese have no recourse. Wong also writes about the mechanization of gold mining, with the result that the Chinese begin to find new work and opportunities in California. By 1853, Wong, like many Chinese, finds that California has become home.

In the epilogue, Yep imagines Wong returning to San Francisco's Chinatown after a few years back in China and becoming a prominent figure fighting against anti-Chinese laws. In the "Historical Note," Yep provides the background to California's gold rush, the effects on the environment, and more about the Chinese who came to Gold Mountain.

1. Discuss how Yep uses Wong's diary to show the importance of education for Chinese immigrants like Wong.
2. Discuss the effects of discrimination against the Chinese miners and mechanization of the mines on Chinese immigrants.
3. Related website: "The Chinese in California, 1850–1925," Library of Congress (http://bancroft.berkeley.edu/collections/chineseinca.html).

Institution of Slavery

Lester, Julius. *Day of Tears: A Novel in Dialogue.* 2005; Hyperion, 2007. 192 pp. Grades 7–10. ALA Notable, 2006; *Booklist* Top 10 HF, 2005; King, 2006; NSSTB, 2006.

Lester's multiple-voiced drama is based on records of the largest slave auction in American history, in Savannah, Georgia, on March 2–3,

1859, when Pierce Butler sold more than four hundred slaves from his family's plantation to pay off his gambling debts. The fear and emotional pain of being sold as a slave is especially heard in the voice of thirteen-year-old Emma, who, despite the fact that she has cared for Butler's two young daughters, is sold away from the plantation and her family. Slaves, slave owners, slave auctioneers, and abolitionists voice their different views on slaves and slavery. Slavery is also a source of dissension in the Butler family, members of which are divided over the issue. An author's note provides background information about the family (including Pierce Butler's wife, Fanny Kemble, the well-known actress, writer, and abolitionist) and about the plantations and slaves. Online references to the auction known as "The Weeping Time" are also included.

1. "Rather than ending slavery, we need to expand slavery westward. . . . With slavery, America will become prosperous and strong" (47). Butler's argument can be used as a starting point for discussing the opinions of Southern slave owners on slavery and westward expansion.
2. Compare the different attitudes voiced about slaves and slavery from slave masters, slave sellers, and slaves themselves.

Adult Fiction

Chevalier, Tracy. *The Last Runaway.* Dutton, 2013. 305 pp.

When jilted by her fiancée, Honor Bright leaves Bridport, England, in 1850 and accompanies her sister, Grace, who is traveling to Ohio to marry Adam Cox, a Quaker living in Faithwell. But Grace dies from yellow fever, and Honor is left to journey alone until she is taken in by Belle Mills, a milliner. When Adam Cox collects her and takes her to his home, Honor realizes that she cannot stay with him and his widowed sister-in-law. Accepting Jack Haymaker's offer of marriage, she joins his mother and sister on the Haymaker farm. The story shows Honor adjusting to nineteenth-century Ohio, with its isolated towns and farms surrounded by forest. She is described as comparing the sense of permanence conveyed by Dorset's tamed meadows and stone and brick buildings with the sense of restlessness and temporality that characterizes Ohio. Her letters to England convey details of social and domestic life, including the importance of quilts and quilting.

The main focus of the novel is on Honor's first encounters with runaway slaves and her awakening to the reality of slavery. Honor, a devout Quaker, respects the equality of all people, but in Ohio she finds that, even in the Quaker community, an "abstract principle becomes entangled in daily life" and loses "its clarity," becoming "compromised and weakened" (227). Honor learns of the contradictions and compromises people make regarding slavery and the 1850 Fugitive Slave Law through her friendship with Belle, whose home is a stop on the Underground Railroad; her relationship with Belle's brother, Donavan, a slave catcher; and the experience of the Haymakers, who suffered the death of Jack's father and the loss of their farm in North Carolina for helping a runaway. When a runaway slave dies, Honor can deny her conscience no longer, and she takes actions that eventually lead her to leave the Haymakers and Jack to live with Belle, where she gives birth to her daughter. But both she and Jack recognize their need to make different choices, and they decide to move west. Honor's thoughts and actions provide insight into Quaker beliefs and practices. Chevalier includes a bibliographic essay.

1. Discuss the Haymaker family's attitudes about the abolition of slavery and the Fugitive Slave Law.
2. Related website: "Fugitive Slave Law of 1850," Ohio History Central (www.ohiohistorycentral.org/entry.php?rec=1483).

Jones, Edward P. *The Known World.* Amistad, 2003. 388 pp. ALA Notable, 2004; Pulitzer, 2004; YALSA OB, 2011.

In July 1855, thirty-five-year-old Henry Townsend, a freed slave and owner of a plantation and thirty-three slaves, lies dying. Set in the fictitious county of Manchester, Virginia, Jones's novel maps in detail the landscape of slavery. Through the story of Henry and his wife, Caldonia, Jones illumines the fact that there were also black slave owners. Henry's father, Augustus, had paid William Robbins, a white slave owner, for his son's freedom, only to see his son become a slave owner who sees slaves as a source of wealth. Jones's story tells of the complex relationships among slave owners, freed slaves, and plantation slaves—all of these exemplified in the close-knit group of Fern Elston, a free black woman, and her former pupils, who include Henry, Caldonia, and the children of Robbins and his black slave Philomena.

Stories woven around each character illustrate how the insidious practice of slavery affects all of them, including patrollers who capture and sell freed slaves; the conflicted sheriff, John Skiffington, and his rogue deputy and cousin, Counsel (a former plantation owner); and Moses, who has ambitions to marry Henry's widow. But there are also those who eschew slavery, and plantation slaves who triumph over adversity. The nonlinear narrative weaves back and forth in time as characters' lives unfold leading up to and beyond the Civil War. An interview with Jones is appended.

1. Henry's father tells Henry that he had never thought that the "first slaveowner" he ordered off his land would be his "own child," to which Henry replies that he has "done nothing that any white man wouldn't do" (138). Discuss Henry's justification for being a slave owner.
2. Discuss how the characters John Skiffington, Moses, Celeste, and Alice experience and respond to their known worlds of slavery.

Kidd, Sue Monk. *The Invention of Wings.* New York: Viking/Penguin, 2014. 369 pp.

Kidd's novel, written in six parts from 1803 to 1838, is based on the life and work of the sisters Sarah and Angelina Grimké, who grew up in Charleston, South Carolina. Sarah Grimké's first-person narrative alternates with that of the fictional character Hannah "Handful" Grimké, who at the age of ten is given as a maid to eleven-year-old Sarah as a birthday gift. Handful, a skilled seamstress like her mother, Charlotte, tells about their servitude under the Grimkés. She describes the punishment meted out to Charlotte for rebellious acts and how she missed Charlotte when a slave trader abducted her. After thirteen years, Charlotte escapes from the plantation where she was taken. Back at the Grimkés, she creates a record of her family history in a story quilt. Hannah also tells about her mother's and her own involvement with the (real-life) Denmark Vesey, who planned a slave uprising for which he and his coconspirators were hung.

The narrative of Sarah Grimké reveals that, even as a girl, she possessed the ideals that led her to become a well-known abolitionist and supporter of women's rights—she attempted to refuse Hannah's gift and was devastated when forbidden to use her father's library as soon as it was discovered that she had taught Hannah to read and write. Kidd traces the evolution of the close relationship between Sarah and her younger sister Angelina, who shared Sarah's values. They both rejected a life based on slavery, moved north, became Quakers, and spoke out publicly for abolition in their work for the American Anti-Slavery Society. The sisters' story clearly shows how radical they were in advocating for both abolition and women's rights. The sisters' personal lives are woven into the novel, including Angelina's marriage to the abolitionist Thomas Weld. At the close of the novel, Sarah helps Hannah escape Charleston.

In her author's note, Kidd explains how she has "blended fact and fiction" and distinguishes fictional and historical figures in the text, one of whom is women's rights activist Lucretia Mott. She includes an account of Angelina's and Sarah's work for abolition and women's rights issues beyond where the novel ends. She also provides additional information about Vesey and includes information about Harriet Powers and her slave quilts, as well as a list of books for further reading.

1. Discuss Handful's comment to Sarah: "My body might be a slave, but not my mind. For you, it's the other way round" (201).
2. Discuss the arguments in one of the following pamphlets: Sarah Grimké, "An Epistle to the Clergy of the Southern States" (http://antislavery.eserver.org/religious/grimkeepistle), and Sarah Grimké, "Letters on the Equality of the Sexes" (http://nationalhumanities center.org/ows/seminarsflvs/Grimke%20Letters.pdf).
3. Discuss the significance of slave quilts for African American history.

US Government Policy and Native Americans

Bruchac, Joseph. *The Journal of Jesse Smoke: A Cherokee Boy.* My Name Is America. Scholastic, 2001. 203 pp. Grades 5–7.

In his journal entries from October 1837 to May 25, 1838, sixteen-year-old Jesse, who has attended Mission School at Brainerd until its closure, records his life with his mother and younger sisters on his family's Tennessee farm, which he has managed since his father's murder. But Jesse, like other Cherokees, is living under threat of the government's plans to remove them to the west, despite Chief John Ross's efforts to avert or at least to delay their departure and his directives to the Cherokees to hold fast. In diary entries up to May 25, 1838, Jesse notes the departure of the first emigrants who leave for the west, the increase in soldiers, and the building of stockades. On May 26, 1838, Jesse records the "fist" pounding on the door, a signal of the beginning of his family's journey on the Trail of Tears. He describes the cruelty and unjust treatment of the Cherokees during the roundup, the terrible conditions during the weeks spent in the summer heat in the stockade, and the preparations Cherokee leaders made for the eight-hundred-mile journey. Included in the diary are Winfield Scott's orders to his soldiers for "the Removal." From October 2, 1838, Jesse's diary entries describe the physical and emotional toll of the journey, during which he works as a courier between detachments. Jesse uses his journal to record statistics, such as on lives lost and the cost of the forced emigration. His entries cover the historical background to the Cherokee Removal and refer to Cherokees' anger at their betrayal by those who signed the Treaty of New Echota, thereby agreeing to the terms of the Removal.

In an epilogue, Bruchac imagines Jesse and his family's future up to and beyond the Civil War as they settle near Tahlequah, the new Cherokee capital. Bruchac's historical note, supplemented by photographs, covers the history of the Cherokees before, during, and after the Removal. Information about Cherokee culture and the Cherokee language are integrated into Jesse's diary.

1. Discuss the emotional and physical effects of the Removal on the Cherokees.

2. Related website: "Trail of Tears and the Forced Relocation of the Cherokee Nation," National Park Service (www.nps.gov/nr/twhp/wwwlps/lessons/118trail/118trail.htm).

Erdrich, Louise. *The Game of Silence.* HarperCollins, 2005. 256 pp. Grades 5–8. ALA Notable, 2006; *Booklist* Top 10 HF, 2006; Newbery honor, 2010; O'Dell, 2006.

Erdrich, Louise. *The Porcupine Year.* HarperCollins, 2008. 193 pp. Grades 5–8. ALA Notable, 2009.

Erdrich, Louise. *Chickadee.* HarperCollins, 2012. 196 pp. Grades 5–8. O'Dell, 2013.

In these books, sequels to *The Birchbark House*, Erdrich continues the story of Omakayas and her family. Set in 1850, *The Game of Silence* covers the forced removal of the Ojibwe to land further west. Men, women, and children have already warned them that the Bwaanag (a native tribe of the Dakota and Latrobe people) resent the intrusion of the Ojibwe into their lands on the Great Plains. The Ojibwe are "caught between two packs of wolves," as they are also told that their land now belongs to the government, that they must leave their home to make room for more white settlers, and that land payments would be made to them to resettle farther west (21). After hearing the news that the government has cheated the Ojibwe, Omakayas's family has no choice but to leave. As the family travels through Bwaanag territory, the "game of silence" that the children play to win prizes becomes a game of life and death.

Set in 1852, *The Porcupine Year* follows the journey of Omakayas's family as they continue to Lac du Bois, in northern Minnesota, where they join Aunt Muskrat and her family. During their journey, the young men Animikiins and Quill are taken for a year by members of the Bwaanag tribe. However, Erdrich's story also incorporates the friendship that "presaged the good relationship" between the Ojibwe and Dakota today (192), as the young men form friendships with their captors. As in *The Game of Silence*, this book voices the distrust of the US government, which plans to create one large homeland for all the Anishinabe (the Ojibwe and Chippewa people) near the territory of the Bwaanag. In both novels, the language, culture, and spiritual life of the Ojibwe are woven into stories of the everyday life of Omakayas's family. *The Porcupine Year* closes with Omakayas's emergence into womanhood.

In *Chickadee*, set in 1866, Omakayas, now the mother of eight-year-old twins; her husband, Animikiins; and their family are forced to move from their remote home in the woods to follow the trail of their son Chickadee, who has been kidnapped from the sugar maple camp by Batiste and Babiche Zhigaag. Pulled out of his family wigwam in the night and bundled into a mail sack, Chickadee is taken to the Zhigaags' shack on the plains, where they treat Chickadee as their servant. Chickadee is kidnapped a second time by a priest and nuns, who find him alone at the shack and take him to their school back across the Red River, where they attempt to erase his Native American identity by baptizing him and giving him "a proper name" (89). Chickadee escapes and spends days making his way northward through the woods until he meets his Uncle Quill driving in an oxcart convoy to trade furs and other goods in St. Paul, Minnesota. The story shifts back and forth from Chickadee's journeys to those of Omakayas and of Two Strikes and Animikiins, who track Chickadee as far as the oxcart trail. The family is finally reunited in Pembina, Dakota Territory.

There are descriptions of the family's journey across new territory and their adaption to the treeless Great Plains, where oxcarts and horses take the place of canoes. Chickadee's lone journey through the woods illustrates his close relationship with the natural world and his ability to survive using the skills and knowledge of the Anishinabe people. Readers see a description of mid-nineteenth-century St. Paul, with its large, wealthy homes on the bluff, through Chickadee's eyes. He envisages a future in which those in power will swallow the forests and natural life on which the Anishinabe people depend.

1. Discuss the ethics of the US government's plans for the removal and relocation of the Ojibwe and the effects of that plan on the Ojibwe.
2. Identify, analyze, and discuss some of the important values of Ojibwe culture and way of life.
3. Discuss how living on the Great Plains changes Omakayas's family.

4. Discuss what can be ascertained about the economy and culture of the Great Plains from Chickadee's descriptions of trading in St. Paul?

5. Related website: NativeTech: Native American Technology and Art (www.nativetech.org/shinob/#history).

Adult Fiction

Conley, Robert. *Mountain Windsong: A Novel of the Trail of Tears.* 1992; University of Oklahoma Press, 1995. 240 pp.

The forced removal and relocation of the Cherokee from east of the Mississippi to Arkansas Territory from 1835 to 1838 is told as a story, shared by grandfather with his grandson, about the love between Oconeechee and Waguli. Oconeechee had fallen in love with Waguli (which means "whip-poor-will"), a young Native American who is captured when General Winfield Scott's soldiers drive Cherokees from their homes at gunpoint. After two failed escapes and a brutal whipping, Waguli gives in and walks like a "ghost" along the trail (110). Vividly described are the horrific conditions of the grueling six-week trek, the many deaths along the route, and the sense of hopelessness among the survivors. Oconeechee, convinced that Waguli is alive, spends the following four years searching for him.

Conley places his story into context by providing, in a separate narrative, a full account of the history of negotiations and treaties between the State of Georgia and the US government over the cessation of Cherokee lands, including the articles of the 1835 treaty, the amendments that sealed the fate of the Cherokee, and divisions among the Cherokee in regard to the signed treaty. Extracts from James Mooney's *Historical Sketch of the Cherokee, 1900* provide details of the different waves of Cherokee relocation to Arkansas, which resulted in more than four thousand deaths. The "crime" of the government against the Cherokees is laid out in a letter to President Martin Van Buren from Ralph Waldo Emerson (74–78).

1. Compare Conley's novel to textbook accounts of the Trail of Tears.
2. Discuss the approach taken by President Andrew Jackson in regard to the Cherokee and how it was different from that of previous presidents.

Glancy, Diane. *Pushing the Bear: After the Trail of Tears.* University of Oklahoma Press, 2009. 197 pp.

In the sequel to *Pushing the Bear: The Trail of Tears* (Harcourt Brace, 1996), Glancy writes about what happens to her fictional characters Maritole, a young Cherokee woman; her husband, Knobowtee; his brother, O-ga-na-ya; and others after their arrival at Fort Gibson, Indian Territory, 1839. Maritole's family continues to suffer the emotional, physical, and socioeconomic costs of their removal from their lands and their nine-hundred-mile walk, and Knobowtee wrestles with plowing the stony, inhospitable land, while Maritole mourns the death of their baby and her mother on the trail.

In her afterword, Glancy writes that her main themes are politics, religion, and gender. The political background to the Cherokee removal is particularly conveyed through the attitudes of O-ga-na-ya, whose bitterness over the signing of the Treaty of New Echota results in his participation in the murders of signers John Ridge and his son, and Elias Boudinot. His desire for revenge and his increasing dependence on alcohol cause dissension with his brother, who focuses on rebuilding what has been lost. There are divisions between Christians and traditional "conjurers" as they both work to uplift a dispirited people. *Baptist Missionary Magazine* issues are inserted into the text and report on the spiritual health of the Cherokee while ignoring their hunger, poverty, and despair. Reverend Busheyhead, a historical person, perseveres with his translation of the Bible, "stretching and bending the old language" into the "new message of Christianity" (128). The failure of the government to grant the Cherokee compensation owed for their property is highlighted by the insertion of primary documents from the Cherokee National Papers listing reclamation and spoilage claims.

By 1847, schools were being established and a new generation born. Glancy explains that the one narrator in the novel is "speaking in a *daguerreotype* style of writing," so that, like a pinhole camera, the narrator throws a "brief spot of light" on lives that had "blurred or obliterated parts" (191). She provides a list of characters and a short list of works she consulted in her research.

1. Discuss divisions within the Cherokee, including the divisions between the "old settlers" and the new arrivals.
2. Related website: For primary documents relating to the Cherokee, see the University of Oklahoma Libraries' website Western History, Native American Manuscripts, Finding Aids (http://digital .libraries.ou.edu/cdm/search/collection/NAMfinding/searchterm/ Cherokee/field/collec/mode/all/conn/and/order/nosort).

Westward Expansion

Blos, Joan W. *Letters from the Corrugated Castle: A Novel of Gold Rush California, 1850–1852.* Atheneum, 2007. 310 pp. Grades 5–7.

The "corrugated castle" is the prefabricated iron home ordered by Eldora's uncle and aunt, the Holts, when they move to San Francisco from New Bedford, Massachusetts, in 1850. In letters to her cousin Sallie, Eldora provides details of their new home and of the growing city where accommodation is scarce and prices are high because of the influx of people arriving with gold fever. Her correspondence tells readers about her growing friendship with Mexicans—Miguel and his younger sister, Luciana—and about the arrival of John Hall, a newspaperman from Michigan, with his fourteen-year-old son, Luke. Hall's news dispatches about San Francisco, the gold mines, and Monterey, and letters from Luke, who goes out to the "diggins" but soon returns to work in a mining store, are interspersed among Eldora's letters. When she has news of the mother whom she has not seen or heard from since she was a small child, Eldora decides to go and live with her in Salinas Valley, where her mother owns mines and ranches. Eldora's letters describe the different lifestyle and culture of her mother's home, and she eventually decides to return to San Francisco. The novel reproduces the atmosphere of San Francisco, with fascinating details of everyday life as California becomes the thirty-first state during the time of gold fever.

1. Discuss the decisions made by Eldora and Luke and the reasons for them.

2. What do the letters tell us about the access to education for young people in the West?

Holt, Kimberly Willis. *The Water Seeker.* Holt, 2010. 309 pp. Grades 6–9. YALSA BF, 2011; NSSTB, 2011.

In 1833, Amos Kinkaid's mother, Delilah, died in childbirth in Bittersweet Creek, Missouri. Amos's father, Jake, a water dowser turned trapper, takes Amos to his brother, Gil, a preacher who runs a mission for the Otoe with his wife, Rebecca, in Pretty Water, Nebraska. When Rebecca succumbs to smallpox, Amos and Gil live with the neighboring Block family until Jake and his Shoshone wife, Blue Owl, take Amos back to Bittersweet Creek, where they live with Delilah's sister; her husband, Homer; and their son, Finn. When trapping is no longer viable as a way to make a living, Jake is hired as a scout for Isaac Bolton's wagon train, and in April 1848, the family travels the two thousand miles from Independence, Missouri, to Oregon, arriving November 1848. The journey to Oregon's Willamette Valley is described in detail and without romanticism from the perspectives of Amos and other characters: Homer is drowned and Jake loses a leg. Amos, an artist, sketches portraits of those who die for their relatives. Central to story are the connections forged among Amos's family and others. At the close of the novel in 1859, Amos is married with a son and is a successful water dowser. Amos's coming of age blends seamlessly with the historical setting, and elements of magic realism present Delilah as a constant presence in her son's life.

1. Discuss reasons people set out for the West and their preparedness for the challenges ahead.
2. How does Holt's novel represent the effects of pioneering life on the composition and social life of families? Discuss how Blue Owl is perceived and her role in Amos's family.

McKernan, Victoria. *The Devil's Paintbox.* Knopf, 2009. 357 pp. Grades 6–9. NSSTB, 2010; YALSA BB, 2010.

Fifteen-year-old Aiden and his younger sister Maddy are orphans, starving on their drought-stricken farm in Kansas in 1865 when Jefferson Jackson agrees to let them join his wagon train to Oregon, provided that Aiden will work to pay for their passage at a timber company near Seattle. There are descriptions of the emigrants and everyday routine of life on the trail, but three main events shape Aiden's journey: his rescue from drowning by Nez Percé Indians; the arrival of a company of the US Army, some of whom have smallpox (the "devil's paintbox"); and the drowning of Maddy. Aiden is delivered to Napolean Gilivrey and indentured until his debts are paid. He has become a successful logger and a popular contender in arranged fights when Tupic, his Nez Percé friend, arrives to ask for his help in procuring smallpox vaccine for his tribe. McKernan covers the history of smallpox vaccination, its production, and its distribution in the time the novel is set. A central theme is the prejudicial treatment of Native Americans by the US Army and others, particularly in the "understanding" that they not be vaccinated against smallpox. In her notes, McKernan discusses whether Native Americans were deliberately infected with the virus.

The novel provides a window into a changing and volatile frontier, with descriptions of Seattle on the edge of industrial development. Aiden is represented as a tough young man who has to fight, and even kill, to survive in a harsh environment.

1. How do the careers of Jackson and Gilivrey illustrate a changing frontier?
2. Discuss the policies of the US Army and what they reveal about attitudes toward Native Americans.

Wilson, Diane Lee. *Black Storm Comin'.* 2005; Margaret K. McElderry, 2006. 291 pp. Grades 7–10. *Booklist* Top 10 HF, 2006; Spur, 2005.

In 1860, the Wescott family is traveling to California in a wagon train when twelve-year-old Colton is accidentally shot by his father. Colton is left to take charge of his sick mother, newborn Willy, and his two younger sisters as his father gallops away on their saddle horse, leaving them somewhere in Utah Territory. Colton, whose mother is black, receives no help from the racially prejudiced boss of the wagon train. The death of his brother Willy, the deliberate slaughter of two of his four oxen, and his mother's growing weakness force Colton to seek help in Dayton, Nevada's Chinatown, where a Chinese woman doctor takes in the family. When Colton sees the advertisement for "expert" riders, "preferably orphans," younger than age eighteen (91), he walks through the night to the Pony Express office in Carson City. After demonstrating that he can sit on a bucking horse that he acquires from a local livery stable, he finally persuades the superintendent that he is capable of negotiating the trail over the Sierras in high winds and blizzard conditions.

Wilson's historical adventure story incorporates details of the delivery of US mail by the Pony Express: fast horses capable of negotiating mountain trials, frequent exchanges of horses at stations during the route, and rules for riders (who had to be white). A major theme is racial discrimination, in a political context in which there was fierce debate regarding free and slave states and tension because of the pending presidential election and the threat of civil war. Colton, whose father is white, finds himself in difficult situations—suspected of being "colored" while passing for white, he identifies with people of color, including his mother's half sister in Sacramento, to whom he delivers the freedom papers sent by his mother. The novel contains vivid descriptions of Colton's journeys and the scenery and towns of the American West.

1. The Pony Express operated only from April 1860 to October 1861. Discuss the reasons it was unsustainable.
2. Discuss the racial discrimination that Colton and his mother encounter on their journey.
3. Related reading: Christopher Corbett, *Orphans Preferred: The Twisted Truth and Lasting Legend of the Pony Express* (2003; Broadway, 2004).

Wolf, Allan. *New Found Land.* 2004; Candlewick Press, 2007. 521 pp. Grades 7–12. YALSA OB, 2009; YALSA BB, 2005.

President Jefferson charged the Lewis and Clark Expedition with finding the most "direct and practical all water route" to the Pacific Ocean for "purposes of commerce" (11). The voices of thirteen members of the Corps of Discovery share the difficulties and wonders of their journey from their different perspectives. Oolum, a fictional character based on Lewis's Newfoundland dog, narrates the overall progress of the expedition. Embedded in these narratives are the prejudices and ignorance that the travelers carry into what they believe are undiscovered and unnamed lands. The novel is divided into seven parts, each covering a specific stretch of the journey from 1803 up to and including the return journey in 1819. A two-page map that lays out the explorers' route prefaces each part.

In poetry and prose, Wolf builds his fictional account on diaries and letters of the expedition. Wolf includes Jefferson's letter of instruction, excerpts of passages from *The Journal of the Lewis and Clark Expedition* (edited by Gary Moulton), and selected letters from *Letters of the Lewis and Clark Expedition, with Related Documents: 1793–1854* (edited by Donald Jackson). Also provided are lists of further reading and Internet resources, summaries of what happens to chief characters after their return from the Pacific, and a "miscellany" of facts and figures relating to the expedition.

1. How does the Louisiana Purchase of 1803 influence the objectives of the Lewis and Clark Expedition?
2. Analyze the different attitudes of Native American nations toward the expedition and its members.
3. Compare Wolf's novel to the resources at Gary E. Moulton's website Journals of the Lewis and Clark Expedition (http://lewisand clarkjournals.unl.edu).
4. Related website: "*New Found Land* Study Guide" (www.allanwolf .com/books/lewis_clark/nflstudyguide/).

Adult Fiction

Glancy, Diane. *Stone Heart: A Novel of Sacajawea.* 2003; Overlook Press, 2004. 156 pp. YALSA OB, 2004.

"Once you were Shoshoni, then Hidatsu, then Charbonneau. Now you'll speak *horse* in Shoshoni for the White man" (13). In this novel, written in the form of a journal, Sacajawea identifies herself and the reason she has been chosen to accompany Lewis and Clark. Glancy presents a fictional record of the Lewis and Clark Expedition from 1804 to 1806. Glancy dispels the legends of Sacajawea's leadership during the expedition, noting that it was only on the return journey that Sacajawea led William Clark and a group of men over a mountain pass. Rather, Sacajawea's voice, richly imagined by Glancy, records how she collects roots and berries and translates Shoshoni for Lewis and Clark when they reach the Shoshoni tribe from which she was kidnapped and of which her brother is now chief. Through her journal, written in the second person, Sacajawea presents a different perspective of the expedition: an awareness of the "presence" of the land and "the voices of the plants" (30), an awareness of how the land is being taken away. Her observations and comments, including those on her treatment by Toussaint Charbonneau, are juxtaposed to dated excerpts from the diaries of Lewis and Clark. Central to her narrative is the child Jean Baptiste, whom she carries like a "bird's nest" on her back (10). Her death is recorded after the birth of her second child, Lizette, in 1812.

Glancy includes President Jefferson's 1803 letter of instructions to Captain Lewis, a bibliography, and observations on her research into Sacajawea's journey.

1. Compare Glancy's representation of Sacajawea with other accounts of Sacajawea's life.
2. Identify and analyze an instance when Sacajawea's perception differs from accounts in the diaries of Lewis and Clark.
3. Discuss the significance of Glancy's objective of writing a novel in which Sacajawea tells her own story. Related website: "Author Interview: Diane Glancy," C-SPAN (www.c-span.org/video/?282348-1/author-interview-diane-glancy).

Wheeler, Richard. *Snowbound.* 2010; Forge Books/Tom Doherty, 2011. 304 pp. Spur, 2011.

John Charles Frémont was known as "the Pathfinder," for his expeditions in the West, including his surveys of the Oregon Trail in 1842 and in 1843–44. Beginning with Frémont's court-martial in 1847, Wheeler focuses on Frémont's privately funded and disastrous fourth expedition in 1848–49. The expedition's stated purpose was to survey a railroad route across the continent to San Francisco along the thirty-eighth parallel. Against advice, Frémont is determined to cross the Wet and Sangre de Cristo Mountains with thirty-three men (including Charles Preuss, his cartographer) and 130 mules in one of the worst winters people could remember. The voices of Frémont; his guide, Bill Williams; and seven of his company vividly describe the increasing severity of the weather and terrain as they cross mountains, desert, and canyons in deep snow until they are lost in the San Juan Mountains.

In separate chapters, men voice their private thoughts about Frémont's leadership while mules and men's lives are lost; in other chapters, Frémont presents his justifications for his decisions. Wheeler's novel deconstructs the romance associated with expeditions when the lure of the West was further fueled by news of gold. Additional voices are Frémont's wife, Jessie, who describes her journey across the Isthmus of Panama, and Frémont's father-in-law, Senator Thomas Hart Benton. In his notes, Wheeler addresses the perception of Frémont by his biographers, gives his own analysis of Frémont's character, and refers to the "contradictory" sources documenting Frémont's fourth expedition.

1. Discuss Frémont's character and leadership and their effect on the expedition.
2. Discuss Frémont's expeditions as part of the exploration of western America.
3. Related website: "Rivers, Edens, Empires: Lewis & Clark and the Revealing of America," Library of Congress (www.loc.gov/exhibits/lewisandclark/lewis-after.html).

CHAPTER 4

The Civil War and Reconstruction
(1850–1877)

Civil War

Bruchac, Joseph. *March toward the Thunder.* Dial, 2008. 298 pp. Grades 7–10.

Fifteen-year-old Louis Nolette, an Abenaki Indian, enlists in the Union Army in 1864 and is assigned to the Irish Brigade. In the trenches outside Petersburgh, New York, he reflects on the reasons he signed up: the money that would enable him and his mother to buy some land; the status conferred by a uniform so that he is no longer insulted for being an Indian; and his support for the abolition of slavery. Bruchac draws on his own family history, modeling the fictional character of Nolette on his great-grandfather, who, like Louis, served in the Irish Brigade in 1864 and whose pension record from the National Archives is reproduced in Bruchac's notes. In short chapters, Louis's experiences in war are narrated from April 15 to August 24, 1864, when he is wounded during an attack at Reams Station and taken to the Depot Field Hospital, where his mother, a "doctress," collects him and takes him home.

The novel includes details of the strategies and logistics of battles and engagements, descriptions of the fighting and wounded, and the day-to-day routines of life in camp. Especially emphasized are the relationships that Louis forms with his fellow soldiers, as well as how enlistment was extended to Indians and African Americans once casualties mount. Louis becomes close friends with a Mohawk Indian and with members of the US Colored Troops, a new regiment. Louis's Irish sergeant draws attention to the common bond between the Irish and the Abnenaki, who were both subjected to being crushed by the English. An extensive history of the Irish Brigade is provided with information on actual historical figures included in the novel.

1. Discuss the ways Bruchac represents the Civil War from the perspective of an Abenaki Indian.
2. Discuss the representation of Union Army generals and the conduct of the war.

Durrant, Lydia. *My Last Skirt: The Story of Jennie Hodgers, Union Soldier.* Clarion, 2006. 199 pp. Grades 5–8. NSSTB, 2007.

Durrant fictionalizes the life of Jennie Margaret Hodgers, who served as the soldier Albert Cashier with the Ninety-Fifth Illinois Infantry, Company G, during the Civil War. In her first-person narrative, Jennie describes her early life in Ireland and the first time she decided to pass herself off as a young man, to earn money she could not earn as a young woman. Jennie continues to find it advantageous to look for work as a man after she and her brother emigrate to America, first in New York and later on the Cleary farm in Illinois under the name Albert Cashier. She then is persuaded by a friend to enlist. Jennie's description of her training and active service includes details of the siege of Vicksburg and other military activities. Her female identity is suspected only by her friend Frank Moore, for whom she has romantic feelings. Jennie's narration continues beyond the Civil War. In 1911, she lived as Albert Cashier until she was injured and her real identity discovered. In 1913, she is living as Jennie Hodgers at the Illinois Soldiers' and Sailors' Home in Quincy, Illinois.

Durrant explains in her notes that Moore is based on "the 95th Illinois's historian Wales Wood who, unlike the fictional Moore, survived the Civil War and made frequent mention of Cashier in his history of the regiment." She notes that Hodges retained her war pension and was given a full military funeral. Information about Camp Douglas and a bibliography are included.

1. Discuss strategies Jennie uses to disguise her gender and the problems she faces in assuming a male identity.
2. Identify other women who assumed a male identity so as to serve as soldiers in the Civil War.
3. Related reading: Anita Silvey, *I'll Pass for Your Comrade: Women Soldiers in the Civil War* (Clarion, 2008).

Elliott, L. M. *Annie, Between the States.* Katherine Tegan Books/HarperCollins, 2004. 488 pp. Grades 7–9.

On July 21, 1861, Annie Sullivan and her mother are staying on her aunt's farm, which has been taken over by the Union Army. They tend wounded Union soldiers, including a grateful Thomas Walker, and hide in the cellar as Union soldiers retreat from the first battle of Manassas. Back home in Fauquier County, Union and Confederate soldiers cross, camp, and skirmish in Annie's fields as she and her brothers, Laurence and Jamie, become engaged in the war. Her older brother Laurence enlists in the cavalry with Jeb Stuart, and in 1863, her younger brother Jamie joins the controversial John Mosby's Rangers, who raid Union supply wagons. Annie not only tends to the wounded but also warns Stuart and Jamie about Union troop movements and, at great risk, hides Confederates. She wounds a Union picket when saving one of the family's freed slaves who had been kidnapped—for which she is incarcerated in a Union prison for six months.

Elliott's novel sets Annie's story within a meticulous account of the background and progress of the Civil War, including dates, battles, and casualties, as well as how the war affects Annie's family: raids that deplete their livestock and resources; inflated food prices; and how civilians are caught up in the war, such as with the 1862 Conscription Bill. Conflict in Annie's family centers on the fight between Laurence and Jamie when Jamie joins John Mosby's Rangers, and Annie's marriage to Captain Walker in 1864. The issue of slavery is central to the story and a topic of discussion between Annie and Walker. In her notes, Elliott expands on issues central to story and provides information about characters and events. She explains, for example, that Annie was "inspired by several northern Virginian women" (459). Headings with date and location preface each chapter. A bibliography and time line are provided.

1. In what ways do Annie and her brothers represent conflicted attitudes toward the war?
2. Discuss the attitudes toward John Mosby's Rangers by the Confederate and Union armies. Related website: Col. John Singleton Mosby, 1833–1916 (www.womacknet.net/features/jsmosby/mosby.htm).

Klein, Lisa. *Two Girls of Gettysburg.* Bloomsbury, 2008. 393 pp. NSSTB, 2009.

In 1961, Rosanna McGreevey arrives in Gettysburg, Pennsylvania, from Virginia to stay with her widowed sister and her young children and becomes best friends with her cousin Lizzy Allbauer. In alternating chapters, Lizzie and Rosanna tell about their experiences in the Civil War from different perspectives and how war changes their lives. Lizzie, whose father and brother enlist in the Union Army, is forced to put aside her wish to attend the Ladies' Seminary in order to run her father's butcher's shop; Rosanna goes back to Virginia; marries her former beau, John Wilcox; and becomes a camp follower and nurse with the Confederate Army. Rosanna describes the modern facilities of Chimborazo Hospital, which stand in stark contrast to nursing conditions in the field, where she becomes skilled in dealing with wounds and disease. Lizzie, meanwhile, describes the work involved in running her father's business and the changes she makes in butchering and preserving when it is no longer feasible to keep livestock in Gettysburg.

Although the novel charts major campaigns and battles, the emphasis is on the changes war brings to civilians' lives and the way civilians contribute to the war. Lizzie, for example, provides geographical information that helps General George Meade plan his strategy for the Battle of Gettysburg. The issue of slavery is addressed throughout the plot and in the differing views of Lizzie and Rosanna, but the book does not include direct references to Abraham Lincoln's Gettysburg Address.

In her author's note, Klein distinguishes fictional characters who are based on actual people—for example, Lizzie Allbauer—from those who are invented characters. She identifies resources she used for her research and provides a list of books for further reading.

1. In what ways is the topology of Gettysburg shown to be important to the outcome of the battle? Related website: Historical Society of Pennsylvania's "A Map Study of the Battle of Gettysburg," with primary sources (http://hsp.org/education/unit-plans/a-map-study-of-the-battle-of-gettysburg).
2. Identify and analyze how citizens of Gettysburg in the novel were affected by war before, during, and after the battle.

Myers, Walter Dean. *Riot.* 2009; Egmont, 2011. 176 pp. Grades 7–12. *Booklist* Top 10 Black History Books for Youth, 2014.

In this novel, written as a screenplay, Myers presents a dramatic recreation of the four-day New York City Draft Riots in 1863, which he describes in his notes as the "bloodiest civil disturbance in American history" (160). When President Lincoln institutes a draft lottery after the Battle of Gettysburg, Irish immigrants are enraged. Their protests include expressing fears that they would be fighting to free enslaved African Americans, who would then compete for their jobs. They are angry because the wealthy can buy their way out of the lottery for three hundred dollars. Many take to the streets to attack black people, and some set fire to the Colored Orphan Asylum. Myers's main character is fifteen-year-old Claire Johnson, whose Irish mother and African American father work at the Peacock Inn. Other characters include Claire's best friend, an African American; young Irish people caught up in the fervor of the events; gang members who use the opportunity to threaten and loot; war-weary soldiers who fire their weapons at protestors; and police and others who attempt to protect the victims of violence. Walt Whitman and the instigator John Andrews also make appearances.

Myers's novel reveals different viewpoints and attitudes about the war and slavery. He explains how social and economic divisions led to the riots. The book includes a time line, a history of slavery, and information on the plight of Irish immigrants in New York, together with visuals from leading newspapers of the time.

1. Discuss how various characters' views reveal racial, social, and economic divisions in New York City.
2. Related website: A comprehensive account of the New York 1983 Riot is available at "NY Draft Riots" (www.vny.cuny.edu/draftriots/Intro/draft_riot_intro_set.html).

Paulsen, Gary. *Soldier's Heart: Being the Story of the Enlistment and Due Service of the Boy, Charley Goddard in the First Minnesota Volunteers: A Novel of the Civil War.* 1998; Turtleback, 2000. 106 pp. Grades 7–9. YALSA BB, 1999.

Paulsen's story is based on the life of Charley Goddard from Winona, Minnesota, who lied about his age and enlisted with the First Minnesota Volunteers when only fifteen years old. In this book, Charley signs up at Fort Snelling, where he receives training before traveling to Maryland and battle. Readers see the grim reality of combat from Charley's perspective: the fear and tension, the horror of walking through the mounting bodies of the dead, and the times when he is filled with the urge to kill as he charges the enemy with his bayonet. After his first experience in the field, he is given raw pork and drinks water tinged red with blood. Details are provided about Charley's uniform, his training and weapons, and the unsanitary conditions of army camps.

The phrase "soldier's heart," Paulsen explains in his foreword, is what is now known as post-traumatic stress disorder, unrecognized and therefore untreated in the Civil War. In the book, Charley, like his actual counterpart, is wounded at the Battle of Gettysburg and left with mental and physical wounds that do not heal. The real Charles Goddard died in December 1868, at twenty-three years old. Paulsen provides a map of Charley's journey from Minnesota with the locations of his battles and a reading list about the Civil War.

1. Discuss the phrase "soldier's heart" and its application to Charley.
2. Related reading: Jim Murphy, *The Boys' War: Confederate and Union Soldiers Talk about the Civil War* (Clarion/Houghton Mifflin, 1990); Michael Shaara, *The Killer Angels: A Novel of the Civil War* (1974; Random House, 2004).

3. Related website: First Minnesota Volunteer Infantry Regiment (www.1stminnesota.net); for a photograph and biography of Charley Goddard, see the page "Charles E. Goddard" at the First Minnesota site (www.1stminnesota.net/1st.php?ID=1161).

Peck, Richard. *The River Between Us.* 2003; Puffin, 2005. 176 pp. Grades 7–12. *Booklist* Top 10 HF, 2004; O'Dell, 2004; YALSA BB, 2004.

In 1916, fifteen-year-old Howard and his young twin brothers visit their grandparents in Grand Tower, Illinois. Grandmother Tilly's story takes Howard back to 1861, when Grand Tower begins to experience the first stirrings of the Civil War. When the last steamboat arrives from New Orleans (before the blockade by the North), two young women disembark—the fashionable young Delphine, and her companion, Calinda—representatives of the "free people of color." Tilly's mother, Mrs. Pruitt, offers to takes them in, and Tilly; her twin brother, Noah; and her younger sister, Cass, are soon disarmed by their boarders despite the town's suspicions that they are spies. When Noah leaves to join the Thirty-First Illinois Infantry regiment organized by "Black Jack" Logan, Tilly and Delphine are sent to Cairo, Illinois, to bring him back. But sixteen-year-old Noah is in a hospital tent suffering from dysentery. Amid terrible conditions, he is nursed back to health by his sister, found fit for service, and takes part in the Battle of Belmont in Missouri, returning without an arm.

Peck's novel illustrates the impact of the war on a small Illinois town with divided loyalties. But Peck's story is also a family history, as Howard learns about his relationship to Noah and Delphine. In his notes, Peck writes about the history of the *gens de couleur* and the strategic position of Cairo and the Battle of Belmont.

1. Discuss how Peck uses his story to show divisions between supporters of the South and North.
2. Discuss the effects of the Civil War on Delphine and Calinda.
3. Related website: "The Battle of Belmont" (www.nytimes.com/1865/07/01/news/battle-belmont-general-grant-s-first-official-report-very-brief-but-satisfactory.html).

Philbrick, Rodman. *The Mostly True Adventures of Homer P. Figg.* Blue Sky Press and Scholastic, 2009. 224 pp. Grades 5–8. ALA Notable, 2010; Newbery honor, 2010; NSSTB, 2010.

When the uncle of seventeen-year-old Harold enlists him illegally in the Union Army as a substitute for the local magistrate's son, his brother, twelve-year-old Homer, is determined to find Harold before he is killed in war. He escapes from his uncle's farm in Maine but does not get far before being captured by the villains Stink and Smelt. The first-person narrative of Homer, a gifted truth stretcher who is equally perceptive at detecting others' duplicity, describes with flair the series of adventures that eventually lead him to his brother at the Battle of Gettysburg. These include his arrival at Jeremy Brewster's home, where Homer learns about the beliefs of Quakers and the Underground Railroad and escapes his captors when he outwits them on behalf of Brewster, who is sheltering slaves. Later on in his journey, he participates in a traveling medicine show run by Professor Fleabottom—a Confederate spy. Before he joins his brother in holding the regimental flag on the Gettysburg battlefield, Homer has landed in a balloon among Confederate troops, met Jeb Stuart and Colonel Chamberlain, and has ridden a horse across five miles of battleground to reach Union lines. His experiences at Gettysburg opens his eyes to the awfulness of war. Embedded in Homer's odyssey are themes and facts about the era of the Civil War, and Philbrick expands on key figures and topics with short but informative notes, such as "Conscription Law," "New Ways of Waging War," and "Emancipation Proclamation." The glossary "Civil War Slang" is also appended.

1. Discuss Harold's decision to enlist in relation to conscription law and his subsequent imprisonment for mutiny.
2. What are the different attitudes toward war expressed in Homer's narrative?

Wells, Rosemary. *Red Moon at Sharpsburg.* 2007; Penguin, 2008. 240 pp. Grades 7–10. ALA Notable, 2008; *Booklist* Top 10 HF, 2008.

In 1861, twelve-year-old India Moody narrates how the Civil War changes lives across all levels of society in Berryville, in the Shenandoah Valley, as friends move away or die. The latter include her schoolteacher; the younger sons of the Trimbles; her large landowning neighbors; and her father, a harness maker, who enlists as an ambulance driver and dies from camp fever after the Battle of Sharpsburg (Battle of Antietam) in 1862. The horror of war is made clear as India searches for her father among the thousands of dead. Paralleling the progress of the war are stories of betrayal. The Trimbles' possessions are burned by a former friend, now a Yankee captain, when they refuse to hand over a fugitive who has killed Union soldiers. Slavery is addressed in the differing opinions as to the cause of war; and through the story of the Trimbles' slaves, Micah and Ester, who in the fire lose the proof that the Trimbles had granted them their freedom and ten acres. They and India are betrayed when they shelter Henry Bedell, a wounded Yankee soldier. The story of the real Henry Bedell is provided in Wells's notes.

The effect of war on Southern women is illustrated by India and her mother leaving their home to work in the home sewing business of India's aunt Divine. India, however, had been introduced to botany and chemistry when helping Emory Trimble collect specimens. She plans to attend Oberlin College and be a scientist. The advances and limitations of Civil War medicine are integrated into Wells's novel through Emory, who goes to Chimborazo Hospital. Imagined to be ahead of his time, he has already realized the importance of hygiene and sterilizing surgical instruments. Wells includes a reading list.

1. Wells hopes that her story reveals the "profound immorality of war." Discuss examples in her story that illustrate that objective.
2. Discuss the representation of Southern women and their attitudes toward the war. What is expected from them in regard to war?
3. To what extent are Micah and Ester "free" in 1864 compared to how the Trimbles had envisaged their freedom in 1848?

4. Related website: "Emancipation Proclamation," National Archives (www.archives.gov/exhibits/featured_documents/emancipation_proclamation/).

Adult Fiction

Brooks, Geraldine. *March.* 2005; Penguin, 2006. 280 pp. Pulitzer, 2006.

In Louisa May Alcott's novel *Little Women* (first published in 1868), Mr. March, father of Meg, Jo, Beth, and Amy, goes to fight in the Civil War. In *March*, Brooks imagines how the idealistic philosopher-educator is tested by the exigencies of war while serving as a chaplain in the Union Army. March, in telling his own story, reveals that there are sides to the war he cannot write about in his letters to his wife, including the brutal reality of combat and his own failings.

One of the hardest realities that March, an abolitionist, confronts is the racist attitude toward slaves and slavery held by Union soldiers. Brooks's story also covers a lesser-known aspect of the Civil War: liberated plantations in the South. March is assigned to be superintendent of contraband on a plantation run by the inexperienced Ethan Canning, an attorney from Illinois, who demands "the maximum amount of labor" from his workers to produce the cotton needed for the "Union cause" (109).

March's narrative shifts back and forth from when he was an itinerant peddler to his present experiences in the Civil War. The narrative switches to Mrs. March when she visits the gravely ill Mr. March in the hospital and is made aware of all that he has hidden from her. In her afterword, Brooks explains that her sources for March's character were Bronson Alcott's letters and autobiographical writings and the letters and journals of Ralph Waldo Emerson and Henry David Thoreau. She notes where her fictional Mr. March differs from Bronson Alcott.

1. The Penguin edition includes a "reader's guide" with an interview with Brooks and discussion questions.
2. Related reading: Louisa M. Alcott's *Hospital Sketches* (1863; Bedford/St. Martins, 2003).

Doctorow, E. L. *The March.* 2005; Random House, 2006. 384 pp. *Booklist* Top 10 HN, 2006; Shaara, 2006.

Set in Georgia and both North and South Carolina, Doctorow charts General Sherman's march through the South in 1864. Doctorow introduces a cast of fictional and historical personages whose different perspectives provide a wide-angled lens as the army loot and burn their way across the South. These include Sherman and members of his Union Army; the freed slave girl Pearl; Mattie Jamieson, wife of the plantation owner who fathered Pearl; Emily Thompson, daughter of a Southern judge who attaches herself to army surgeon Wrede Sartorius; Union soldier Stephen Walsh, who received three hundred dollars for enlisting; and Arly and Willie, who, freed from jail to fight the Confederates, subsequently adopt whichever uniform or disguise is expeditious for their survival. Doctorow conveys the social and cultural upheaval in the South through the voices and experiences of these and other representative characters.

The pain and devastation of war is seen from fire-consumed Columbia, South Carolina, to scenes of rape and looting. Distant assessments of the war are heard from historical figures such as War Secretary Edward Stanton and Ulysses Grant. Doctorow acknowledges that the Civil War was the first war in which photography was used to document events by addressing the issue of photography and the veracity of historical record. Toward the close of the novel, he paints a detailed portrait of President Lincoln before his assassination.

1. Discuss Sherman's attitudes toward the objectives of the war and the effects of his strategies on the South.
2. Discuss how selected characters are transformed by the war.

Frazier, Charles. *Cold Mountain: A Novel.* Atlantic Monthly Press, 1997. 356 pp. ALA Notable, 1998; NBA, 1997; *SLJ* BABHS; YALSA OB, 1999.

Toward the end of the war, Inman, sickened by his experiences on the battlefields, walks away from the field hospital where he is recuperating from a neck wound and embarks on the difficult journey to Cold Mountain and to Ada Monroe, daughter of the former minister of

Black Cove. The narrative alternates between the account of Inman's odyssey and the story of Ada, who, more at home with books and a sketchbook, is left alone after the death of her father, knowing little about farming. She is saved by the arrival of Ruby, who agrees to help. The novel provides richly detailed descriptions of the land through which Inman travels—a landscape that shapes the lives of people who live in its coves and traverse its ridges and woods. But the darkness of war follows Inman, and the false perception of war as heroic is set against its brutal reality. Killings are extant in the mountains as the Home Guard hunt and massacre deserters and as outliers join the lawless. The detrimental effects of war are shown on those whom Inman meets, including a young widow, left with a young baby, who has Federal troops raid her home. Ruby and Ada use a bartering system in an economy in which "scrip" is worthless and inflation is rampant. The novel closes in 1874 as Ada and Ruby find peace on the farm that has prospered under their labor.

1. Discuss Inman's reasons for desertion.
2. Discuss how the war has affected the people who live in the shadow of Cold Mountain.

McBride, James. *The Good Lord Bird*. New York: Riverhead Books/Penguin, 2013. 417 pp. NBA, 2013.

In 1856 in Kansas Territory, John Brown takes the young slave boy Henry Shackleforth away from his home after a confrontation among Brown, Henry, and Henry's father's owner during which Henry's father is shot. Brown's character and his single-minded mission to end the institution of slavery are seen through the unique, often humorous perspective of Henry, who, wearing a flour sack, is mistaken for a girl by Brown and retains his new gendered identity throughout the novel. He is also given the name "Onion" by Brown and holds on to the good-luck feather from the "Good Lord Bird." In Part 1, Henry accompanies Brown and his sons as they weave back and forth through Kansas (a battleground of abolitionists and pro-slavers); and Henry is present at Brown's infamous massacre of white homesteaders. After the battle at

Osawatomie during which Brown fights Missouri rebels, Henry separates from Brown. In Part 2, Henry documents his two years in the slave state of Missouri, where he works as a maid in a hotel and brothel where slaves plan an unsuccessful uprising. In Part 3, Henry is reunited with Brown and accompanies him on a fund-raising tour that includes Boston, New York City, Philadelphia, and Canada, before they take part in the preparations for the attack at Harper's Ferry. Brown gives Henry and others instructions to gather together, or "hive," free and enslaved African Americans who Brown assumed would be ready to fight for their freedom. Henry describes the scenes outside the armory during the long hours that Brown and his men are trapped inside until the arrival of Lieutenant Jeb Stuart.

Filtered through Henry's perceptive eyes are a detailed portrait of Brown and descriptions of Brown's small but changing army of followers, including his sons. The text includes the various attitudes toward Brown held by slaves, abolitionists, and well-known figures such as Frederick Douglass and Harriet Tubman, whom Henry meets while traveling with Brown.

1. Compare Henry's perception of John Brown with representations in other texts. In what ways does McBride's choice of narrator affect how Brown and his mission are presented?
2. Compare McBride's description of the attack on Harper's Ferry with other accounts. Give examples of how McBride blends fact and fiction.
3. Discuss Henry's views of Brown's planned attack on the armory.
4. Related reading: Russell Baker, *Cloudsplitter* (HarperFlamingo, 1998); Tony Horwitz, *Midnight Rising: John Brown and the Raid that Sparked the Civil War* (New York: Holt, 2011).

Oliveira, Robin. *My Name Is Mary Sutter.* 2010; Penguin, 2011. 364 pp. Shaara, 2011.

By the outbreak of the Civil War, Mary Sutter is a seasoned midwife, but her wish is to be a surgeon. When she is turned down by Albany Medical College and by Dr. James Blevens, who refuses to teach her, she answers Dorothea Dix's 1861 circular calling for women to serve as nurses "in the tradition of Florence Nightingale" in Washington, DC (83). Refused by Dix because she lacks letters of recommendation and because she is too young, Mary is taken on at the Union Hotel Hospital by Dr. William Stipp. Mary and Stipp work together for much of the war. Mary joins Stipp on the battlefields, where she is eventually entrusted to perform amputations on her own.

Mary's ambition to be a surgeon is placed in the context of gender inequality, the pull between her duty to family and work, and the state of medical knowledge and practice of the time. Her story is also placed in the context of the conduct of the war, as the narrative switches from Mary's story to the perspectives of those directing events, such as President Lincoln and his advisers, to the perspectives of her enlisted brother and brother-in-law. Sutter is portrayed as a determined and dedicated woman who, after the war, is the first graduate of Elizabeth Blackwell's School of Medicine.

1. What do Mary Sutter's experiences have to say about women and the medical profession prior to and during the Civil War?
2. How did Dorothea Dix change the role and perception of women who volunteered as nurses?
3. Describe medical practices that contributed to the death toll in the Civil War. How did the war contribute to medical knowledge?
4. Related website: "Exhibits," National Museum of Civil War Medicine (www.civilwarmed.org/museum/exhibits/).

The Era of Reconstruction

McMullan, Margaret. *When I Crossed No-Bob.* Houghton Mifflin, 2007. 209 pp. Grades 5–8. YALSA BB, 2009.

Set in Smith County, Mississippi, in 1875, during Reconstruction, twelve-year-old Addy is a member of the outcast O'Donnell clan. The clan owns the land known as No-Bob and has a reputation for meanness. Deserted by her mother, Addy is taken in by the schoolmaster Frank Russell and his wife, Irene. Addy is shattered when she and

Frank's sister, Little Bit, witness the burning of the black schoolhouse and church by the Ku Klux Klan, which resulted in the death of their young friend Jess Still. But the worst is not over for Addy: her father, thought to have long gone to Texas, arrives to collect his daughter, and she is soon back with the O'Donnells—now members of the Ku Klux Klan. Addy listens to the invective of Klan members, ex-Confederates, who resent the enfranchisement of freed slaves when their own voting rights have been curtailed. Threatened by plans for her marriage to a Klan member, Addy runs from No-Bob and, in hiding, is able to foil a Klan lynching. Her loyalty to her father is set against what she knows is right.

The effects of the Civil War on the South are described including the destroyed towns and railroads, the scarcity of food, and slaves freed without having any resources. But in 1877, as Rutherford Hayes is elected nineteenth president, there are signs of prosperity: new sawmills, a railroad, and the success of Frank Russell's new store. McMullen's novel also addresses the unjust treatment of the Choctaws, forced to leave their settlement in Smith County.

1. Discuss why some people regarded the Fifteenth Amendment in 1870 as a threat. Related website: "Reconstruction," Voting Rights and Citizenship (www1.cuny.edu/portal_ur/content/voting_cal/reconstruction.html).

Taylor, Mildred D. *The Land.* 2001; Penguin, 2003. 400 pp. Grades: 7–10. ALA Notable, 2002; King, 2002; O'Dell, 2002; *Booklist* Top 10 HF, 2002; YALSA BB, 2002.

In this prequel to her Newbery Medal winner *Roll of Thunder, Hear My Cry* and other books about the Logan family, Taylor sets her story about Paul-Edward Logan in the 1870s and 1880s, during Reconstruction. Paul, the son of a white plantation owner whose mother was his father's slave and then his housekeeper, first describes his early years in Georgia, where he and his sister, Cassie, were educated and brought up alongside their white half brothers—with differences. Taylor shows what it is like for Paul to be a man of color who looks white when he is whipped and told by his father that for his own safety, he must never again "hit" or "sass" a white man, including his brother (83). When his friend Mitchell attacks a white man, Paul and Mitchell escape by train to Mississippi, aided by a white woman who hires them. After two years, they leave and work in the brutal Mississippi lumber camps.

In the second half of the novel, "Manhood," Paul describes two backbreaking years clearing forty-nine acres for a dishonest white landowner who breaks his contract. Refusing the offer of sharecropping, Paul finds the means to secure the land he desires. Taylor's story about discrimination and violence against African Americans during Reconstruction also includes those from a cross section of society, black and white, who offer Paul friendship and help. In an epilogue, Taylor writes about her great-grandfather, whose history forms the basis for her novel.

1. What do the attitudes of white landowners and bankers toward Paul's desire to own land imply about the social and economic effects of the abolition of slavery?
2. What does the ownership of land signify for Paul, his mother, and Mitchell?

Development of the Industrial United States

(1870-1899)

Bartoletti, Susan Campbell. *A Coal Miner's Bride: The Diary of Anetka Kaminska.* Scholastic, 2000. 219 pp. Grades 5–8. NSSTB, 2001.

"By 1900, nearly thirty-eight thousand Poles had settled in the anthracite coal region of Pennsylvania" (197). In her diary beginning April 16, 1896, thirteen-year-old Anetka records how she and her brother, Josef, leave their *babcia* (grandmother) in Sadowka, Poland, to join their father in Lattimer, Pennsylvania. He has arranged for Anetka to marry the miner Stanley Gawrych, who has paid their steamship passage. When they arrive, Anetka finds that she is to be a mother to Stanley's three young daughters. Josef, meanwhile, becomes a breaker boy, and his hands are swollen and cracked, with red tips, after the first day. Anetka's diary entries describe life in the patch villages; the endless drudgery of housework, including picking coal on the culm banks; and her efforts to be a good mother. Included are figures on mine accidents, the numbers of men killed, and the numbers of widows and fatherless children. On January 29, 1897, Stanley dies in a roof fall. Anetka is, as she writes, a widow who now looks after boarders, her father, and a brother before she is even fourteen years of age.

Anetka charts growing unrest among miners as the company makes discriminatory laws against immigrant workers, such as a 3 percent tax for alien workers. Leading the debate about whether the miners should join the United Mine Workers and advocating strike action is the young Leon Nasevich, who accompanied Anetka and Josef on their voyage. Anetka describes the growing strike movement that culminates with the Lattimer Massacre, of September 10, 1897, in which strikers were shot. In her "Historical Note" to this title in the *Dear America* series, Bartoletti expands on the czar's ethnic cleansing in Poland, the working and living conditions of the miners and their families, and the Lattimer Massacre. Photographs depicting mine scenes are included.

1. Identify reasons Polish workers were ready to leave Poland to work in the Pennsylvania coal mines.
2. Analyze the attitudes of the mine bosses toward immigrant workers that led to the miners' strike action.
3. Related reading: Susan Campbell Bartoletti, *Growing Up in Coal Country* (Houghton Mifflin, 1996). *See also* Pat Hughes, *The Breaker Boys* annotation, later in this section.

Hobbs, Will. *Jason's Gold.* Morrow Junior Books, 1999. 221 pp. Grades 5–9. YALSA BB, 2000; NSSTB, 2000.

After making his way from Seattle to New York, fifteen-year-old Jason Hawthorne is working as a newsboy when he sees the headline "GOLD IN ALASKA" on the first page of the *New York Herald*, on July 17, 1897. He returns to Seattle and joins the stampede to the Klondike goldfields, stowing away on one of the overcrowded steamships. There are scenes of chaos in Scagway and Dyea as "stampeders" unload their packs and livestock before climbing trails over mountain passes that will take them to the rivers and lakes that lead to Dawson City. Turning back from the White Pass trail, which is choked with people toiling in thick mud and hundreds of dead horses, Jason tackles the "Golden Stairs" of the Chilkoot Pass. Vivid descriptions of the terrain and maps enable readers to follow Jason's journey by foot and canoe. He is badly injured by a moose and is forced to winter in a cabin before completing the remaining 250 miles down the Yukon River to Dawson City. In June 1898, Jason joins his brothers, partners in a thriving sawmill.

Integrated into Hobbs's well-researched story are facts and figures, including the price of "packing" and food. Hobbs conveys the frenzy of gold fever that persuaded men to leave their families and forfeit their savings. When those men went "bust," they were forced to return home; others lost their lives. Jason meets actual historical figures in his story, including Jack London. Hobbs explains that some incidents are based on real events.

1. Discuss Jason's observations on how the Klondike gold rush affects the Canadian Northwest.
2. Discuss Hobbs's use of one of his real personages to substantiate and add to the historical information presented.

Hughes, Pat. *The Breaker Boys.* Farrar, Straus & Giroux, 2004. 247 pp. Grades 6–9, NSSTB, 2005.

Set in 1897 in Hazelton, Pennsylvania, Hughes's story centers on the Lattimer Massacre. Events are told from the perspective of twelve-year-old Nate Tanner, whose family operates the Lattimer colliery. Nate, expelled from boarding school, bikes to where the miners live at Harland patch, where he makes friends with Johnny, a breaker boy, but hides his true identity. He plays baseball with Johnny and the other boys even as he hears about proposed union action and his grandfather's declaration that he will never deal with union leaders. The coal operators argue that they are threatened by the railroad owners, who already control the shipping and distribution of coal, resulting in shrinking profits. But Nate has seen how the miners live and the company store's high prices. Demonstrating his loyalty, Nate takes another boy's place in the Harland breaker and experiences the "choking dust" and excruciating pain of "redtop" fingers as he picks out slate from coal (166).

Nate watches as the union march on the Lattimer colliery, on September 10, 1897, becomes a massacre when the sheriff and his deputies shoot nineteen men—some in the back—and wound thirty-nine others. Nate reads the conflicting newspaper reports about the shooting but knows what he saw. In her notes, Hughes distinguishes where she parts from using factual names. She quotes from the *Philadelphia*

Record of March 10, 1898, on the trial and acquittal of the sheriff and his deputies, which took place on February 1, 1898.

1. Compare Hughes's novel with the account of the Lattimer Massacre on the Pennsylvania Historical and Museum Commission's website (http://explorepahistory.com/hmarker.php?markerId=1-A-3BA).
2. Related reading: Michael Burger, *Breaker Boys* (Compass Point Books, 2012).

Murphy, Jim. *The Journal of Brian Doyle: A Greenhorn on an Alaskan Whaling Ship.* Scholastic, 2004. 188 pp. Grades 5–8.

It has been estimated from detailed records kept that one-third of the seamen on whaling ships in the nineteenth century were teenagers, and some like Brian, running from an abusive parent (176). In his fictional diary, dated from April to September 9, 1874, Brian records his tasks on the *Florence,* such as climbing the rigging, watching and hunting for whales, and learning navigation skills. He provides information on the harpooning and dismembering of whales for their oil, baleen, and ambergris; on the use to which these products were put; and on how profits were shared. But the whales they see and succeed in killing are far and few between, and after a voyage to Hawaii, the captain decides to sail to Alaska. Brian charts their progress, describing the increasingly dangerous conditions until the ship becomes trapped and crushed by ice. He writes about the grueling journey of his boat crew over the ice to an inhospitable coast and his solitary and dangerous trek to the Cape Lisburne whaling station for help.

In his notes to this book in the *My Name Is America* series, Murphy outlines the growth of the whaling industry in the nineteenth century, pointing out that overfishing of right whales resulted in their disappearance from the Atlantic coast, thus causing whaling fleets to travel further afield. He provides facts about the increasing numbers of whales killed as newer methods of killing and processing were developed and new industrial products obviated the need for whale oil and baleen in the United States. Photographs of Arctic whaling ships are included.

1. What information does Brian's diary give about the composition of a whaling crew, the relationships among the crew, and the expected conditions and dangers they face during a voyage.

2. Discuss how Brian's diary represents the advantages and disadvantages of traditional sailing ships in comparison to the newer steamships.

Napoli, Donna Jo. *Alligator Bayou.* Wendy Lamb Books, 2009. 280 pp. Grades 7–10. YALSA BF, 2010.

Napoli's story about a little-known aspect of immigration and prejudice toward Italian immigrants in the South focuses on the lynching of five Sicilian immigrants in Tallulah, Louisiana, in 1899. When fourteen-year-old Calegero's mother dies, he leaves Louisiana to live with his father's friend Francesco in Tallulah. Francesco and his brothers and cousins live together as one family. They grow fruit and vegetables and have their own grocery, but they are subject to the bigotry and threats of the dominant white patriarchy of Tallulah. Perceived as neither black nor white, discriminatory laws prevent Sicilian young people from attending the white school in Tallulah. Sicilians are also denied jobs and prevented from living in town. Calegero describes the conflict in his family as he and his young cousin determine to speak English and become American. Francesco resists segregation laws in their grocery by serving African Americans before white customers if they are first in line. Francesco's dispute with Dr. Hodges over a trespassing goat results in the killing of the goat and the shooting of Dr. Hodges. Although Dr. Hodges is not killed, members of the white community administer their own justice. Calegero escapes and travels by skiff down the Mississippi River to Baton Rouge. Napoli's afterword provides a detailed description of the community of Tallulah, based on her research.

1. Compare Napoli's story with the article by Edward F. Haas that she recommends in her afterword: "Guns, Goats, and Italians: The Tallulah Lynching of 1899" (*North Louisiana Historical Journal* [1982]:

43–58, also available via Google search at www.rootsweb.ancestry
.com/~lamadiso/articles/lynchings.htm).

2. Discuss the newspaper responses to the lynching reported in the
Haas's article. What attitudes are revealed in regard to immigrants'
standing in relation to laws and justice?

Napoli, Donna Jo. *The King of Mulberry Street.* 2005; Yearling, 2007. 245
pp. Grades 5–8. ALA Notable, 2006; NSSTB, 1996.

In Naples in 1892, nine-year-old Beniamino's mother puts him on a
ship bound for America wearing his first pair of shoes, in which she
hides the holy tassels from his grandfather's prayer shawl. It is not until
they are ready to sail that Beniamino realizes that his mother is not
coming with him. Once at Ellis Island, he avoids being swept up into
the illegal *padroni* system in which boys earn their ship's passage by
working as slave labor, and he escapes before he is placed in an orphanage. Soon he is fending for himself on the streets of New York without
food, shelter, or knowing English. Now known as Dom, he integrates
himself into the street culture of Five Points, where he meets Gaetano.
Smart and resourceful, Dom refuses to beg or steal, and together, he and
Gaetano build a successful sandwich business. Key to Dom's survival is
his willingness to work and his commitment to honesty, friendship, and
cooperation, which earns him the title "King of Mulberry Street."

Napoli does not sugarcoat Dom's life as an immigrant; for example, he is whipped and held prisoner by a *padrone* while looking for
his friend who has been murdered. The novel provides a vivid sense
of nineteenth-century New York and its various ethnic communities.
Napoli explains that her inspiration for her novel came from a story
about her paternal grandfather, who came alone to New York at the age
of five and later became a successful sandwich vendor.

1. Discuss Beniamino's mother's decision to send her son alone to
America.

2. Discuss what Dom learns about surviving on the streets of New
York.

Peck, Richard. *Fair Weather.* Dial Books, 2001. 139 pp. Grades 5–7. *Booklist* Top 10 HF, 2002; NSSTB, 2002; YALSA BB, 2002.

In 1893, Rosie Beckett's mother receives a letter and railroad tickets from her sister, Euterpe, inviting thirteen-year-old Rosie, seventeen-year-old Lottie, and seven-year-old Buster to stay with her for a week so that they can visit the World's Columbian Exposition and expand their education beyond a one-room schoolhouse. In her first-person narrative, Rosie gives her impressions of Chicago, with its mansions and new Art Institute, and she acts as guide to the exposition. Her ecstatic descriptions of the "White City" and its architecture are accompanied by a photo of the Court of Honor; postcards featuring views of the fair; and portraits of singer Mary Russell and Buffalo Bill, whom they meet when attending the latter's Wild West Show, which is described in detail. Euterpe takes Rosie and Lottie around the Women's Building, where they view the art of Mary Cassatt and hear Susan B. Anthony speak about women's suffrage. Their irascible grandfather takes Buster to the Transportation and Fisheries Buildings. The family rides the new elevated train and enjoys the entertainment at the Midway Plaisance, where they listen to Scott Joplin and ride on the giant Ferris wheel. Peck discusses the far-reaching effects of the fair in his author's notes. Additional side notes to this warm, humorous family story are Euterpe's problems, Rosie's introduction to Chicago society, and Lottie's romance—all of which illustrate the era's system of social class.

1. Discuss examples of advances in science and technology that are demonstrated at the fair. For more information, see the Chicago History Museum's website on the World's Columbian Exposition (www.chicagohs.org/history/expo.html).
2. Provide examples of how the fair influenced American culture.

Wright, Barbara. *Crow.* Random House, 2012. 297 pp. Grades 6–9. NSSTB, 2012.

Eleven-year-old Moses Jackson's grandmother had given birth to his mother in slavery. In 1898, in Wilmington, North Carolina, his father, a city alderman and reporter for the *Record*, the only "Negro daily in the

South," gives a speech on National Memorial Day about the progress black people had made in establishing a solid middle class in Wilmington (61–62). Moses describes how this optimism changed beginning with a white supremacist rally at Fayetteville protesting an editorial written by the *Record*'s editor, Alex Manly, criticizing a Mrs. Felton, who had suggested that white women were in danger from black men and advocated lynching. Later, Moses witnesses armed militia groups and "Red Shirts" from South Carolina who intimidate black people from voting in state elections, and he helps Manly escape a lynch mob.

Wright's story documents the hate and violence against the black community, culminating in a riot as the Democrats, under Alfred Waddle, seize control of the city government and issue the "White Declaration of Independence" that denies black people work and governance in Wilmington. The exodus of the black middle class from Wilmington in 1898 is represented by Moses's father, who is informed that a one-way ticket to Richmond has been purchased for him. Despite the tragic ending, Moses's friendship with his white friend is a sign of hope for the future. In a detailed historical note, Wright provides more information about the aftermath of the riot, in which black men were shot. She quotes from Manly's editorial, Waddle's speech at Fayetteville, and the "White Declaration of Independence."

1. Discuss the political context that led up to the riot, the socioeconomic context that contributed to the establishment of a middle-class black population in Wilmington, and the effects of the riot on Wilmington's black population. Related website: "Wilmington Race Riot Report," North Carolina Office of Archives and History website (www.history.ncdcr.gov/1898-wrrc/report/report.htm).

Yep, Laurence. *The Traitor: Golden Mountain Chronicles, 1885.* HarperCollins, 2003. 310 pp. Grades 6–8. NSSTB, 2008.

In this novel set in 1885 in Wyoming Territory, Otter Young and his son, Joseph, are caught up in the massacre of Chinese mine workers working for the Union Pacific Railroad Company at Rock Springs. In alternating chapters that begin on June 14, the voices of Joseph and Michael

Purdy, an illegitimate white boy, tell about their friendship, which grows amid mounting tension in the mines. Joseph works alongside his father in Mine Number Six and describes the growing escalation between Chinese and Westerners in the mines. Joseph explains that *Westerners* is his "father's polite word for *Americans*" (4). Both Chinese and Westerners, both paid by the ton, argue over the company's assignment of coal "rooms" in the mine. American miners are fired, and Michael hears the angry voices of Westerners who claim that the Chinese are stealing their jobs and should be driven out. On September 2, the armed "Patriots" and their followers attack the miners, set fire to Chinatown, and chase survivors into the wastelands, thus beginning a territory-wide expulsion of the Chinese. In the final chapter, dated December 8, Joseph tells of their resettlement in San Francisco, where his father continues to work for better conditions in Chinatown, just as he had fought against the passing of the Chinese Exclusion Law in 1882. Yep also writes about the prejudice leveled against Michael in Rock Springs because his father did not marry his mother.

In his notes, Yep places the novel in the context of his Chronicle series, which covers the history of seven generations of the Young family from the time they leave China in 1849 to the 1990s. He explains how he uses the historical record for his fictional narrative and provides a bibliography of articles and books.

1. Related website: "'To This We Dissented': The Rock Springs Riot," History Matters: The US Survey on the Web (http://historymatters .gmu.edu/d/5043/).
2. Assess and discuss how the Chinese Exclusion Act of 1882 restricted Chinese immigration and Chinese workers already in the United States. Related website: Chinese Exclusion Act of 1882 (www.our documents.gov/doc.php?doc=47).

Native American History

Bruchac, Joseph. *Geronimo.* Scholastic, 2006. 360 pp. NSSTB, 2007; Spur, 2007.

In 1886, thirteen-year-old Willie is traveling on a train with Geronimo and other Chiricahua Apaches who are being taken from Fort Bowie to Florida as prisoners of war. As he details the steps of the journey, Willie, who (besides his parents) is Bruchac's only fictional character, revisits the past as he remembers the massacre of his parents and how he became known as Geronimo's grandson. Bruchac provides much historical information about Geronimo, including the murder of his first wife and children by Mexicans in 1851, his life on Warm Springs Reservation from 1858 to 1877, and the series of events leading up to Geronimo's final surrender to General Miles at Fort Bowie in 1886. Bruchac corrects some of the so-called well-known facts about Geronimo, and Willie's knowledge of Geronimo goes well beyond the warrior that people flock to see.

Primary sources integrated into the text include directives from President Grover Cleveland that document the policies and broken promises of the US government and US Army concerning the Chiricahua. But Bruchac also includes statements of support for the Apaches by individual army officers who have come to know their captives. Willie's narrative goes on to cover the Chiricahaus' eight years of captivity, including the separation of Geronimo and other Apache leaders from their wives and children from November 1886 to April 1887; the forced removal of Apache children to the Indian Industrial School at Carlisle; the deaths of Apaches from malaria and tuberculosis; and the series of moves they are forced to make from Pensacola to Fort Pickens to Mount Auburn, Alabama. Reference is made to Lozen and other well-known leaders and to the role of Apache army scouts. Willie, like other Apaches, later enlists in the US Army while still a prisoner of war. In 1884, Geronimo and the remaining Apaches are given the choice to transfer to Fort Sill in Oklahoma, which becomes Geronimo's home until his death in 1909. In his afterword, Bruchac explains that it was 1912 before the Apaches were formally released as prisoners of war, after which some of "Geronimo's Band" chose to move to Mescalero, New Mexico. Bruchac provides a detailed annotated chronology of events and a bibliography.

1. Compare the facts in Bruchac's novel with other accounts in textbooks or other informational texts.
2. Discuss the motivations of Apache scouts in the novel.

Carvell, Marlene. *Sweetgrass Basket.* Dutton Children's Books, 2005. 243 pp. Grades 7–10. ALA Notable, 2006; *Booklist* Top 10 HF, 2006; Addams honor, 2006; NSSTB, 2006.

In this free-verse novel, the alternating voices of twelve-year-old Sarah and her older sister, Mattie, members of the Mohawk tribe, tell how they leave home to attend the Carlisle Industrial School, which, in 1879, was the "nation's first off-reservation school for Native Americans" (n.p.). The girls describe the harsh, cruel regime of the school under the thumb of Mrs. Dwyer, including, along with the curriculum, hours of physical labor and the requirement that they march to meals, lessons, and work. The book makes clear how the school strips away the identities of Native American children: their names are changed to "good" names, they are denied the use of their own languages, and they are forbidden to keep "any Indian things from home" (198).

Carvell drew on the "experiences of her husband's great-aunt Margaret who attended the Carlisle Industrial School in the early 1900s" to write her novel (back flap). She explains that although Native children came from western states, the Mohawk tribe had "350 children at the Carlisle school during the time of its existence," from 1879 to 1918. Phonetic pronunciations are also provided for Mohawk words used in the text.

1. In what ways and to what extent do Sarah, Mattie, and others resist the school's regime?
2. What assumptions does Mrs. Dwyer hold about Native Americans?
3. Discuss the belief of Mattie and Sarah's father that it is best for them to attend the Carlisle Industrial School.

4. Related website: Carlisle Indian Industrial School (http://home
   .epix.net/~landis/histry.html).

Adult Fiction

Maltman, Thomas. *The Night Birds.* 2007; Soho Press, 2008. 370 pp. Alex, 2008; YALSA OB, 2009; Spur, 2008.

In 1876, fourteen-year-old Asa, who "grew up in the shadow of the Great Sioux War" (3), meets Aunt Hazel, a woman with epilepsy released from an asylum and sent to live with the Sengers in Kingdom Township, Minnesota. From Hazel, Asa learns the history of his family. She tells how her father, Jakob, moved his family from Missouri to Milford Prairie, Minnesota, in 1859, when his printing press was destroyed by his father-in-law because Jakob had printed an antislavery pamphlet. On the prairie in Minnesota, Jakob's family members forge relationships with the Dakota who live across the Waraju River. However, the expansion of German immigrants into the prairies, with their insatiable demand for land, is destroying the Native Americans' way of life, such that they are dependent on government annuities. Jakob's family is caught up in the growing conflict that ends with the Sioux Massacre, or the Dakota Conflict, led by Little Crow and during which thirty-eight warriors were hung in Mankato in 1862 and their bodies mutilated after death.

In descriptive language, Maltman writes about the "beauty and terror" of life on the prairie from the 1840s to 1862 and how the reverberations from that time that still haunt the Senger family and others in 1876.

1. Identify what caused the fragile friendship between the Senger family and their Dakota neighbors to fall apart. How do policies of the federal government affect relations between Native Americans and immigrants?
2. Discuss how slavery and the Missouri Compromise affected Jakob's decisions.
3. Discuss Maltman's narrative strategies. How do they affect the representation of the perspectives of Native Americans and white settlers.

Social and Cultural Life

Dagg, Carole Estby. *The Year We Were Famous.* Clarion, 2011. 245 pp. Grades 6–10.

Inspired by Nelly Bly's round-the-world trip in 1889, Helga Estby signs a contract with Miss Waterson, a publisher in New York City, whereby she will receive ten thousand dollars to walk from Spokane, Washington, to New York City by November 30, 1896. In hopes of securing the money to save the Estby farm, Helga and her elder daughter, Clara, set out on May 6 carrying a letter of introduction that testifies to their respectability and is signed by the mayor. They carry the barest necessities. Exceptions are Clara's father's pistol and writing materials. They plan to work for food and lodging. Clara records their journey in diary format, describing, for example, their encounter with Ute Indians who offer them food and shelter, their narrow escape from jail when Clara shoots a man who attacks them, and Clara's rescue of her mother from rapids. They walk in rain and snow, get lost in lava fields in Idaho, and sleep under the stars. Helga, a Norwegian immigrant, is an advocate of women's suffrage, and Dagg weaves information about women's suffrage in the West throughout. There are references to the 1896 election as the women pay visits to President William McKinley and the wife of William Jennings Bryan. The walk's outcome is different from what they hope, but Clara, who hears for the first time her mother's past history with the man who is her real father, has ambitions to go to college and be a writer. In her notes, Dagg provides known facts about her great-grandmother's and great-aunt's transcontinental walk and pinpoints the fictional characters.

1. Discuss examples of the ways that Clara and Helga represent the "new woman."
2. Related reading: Matthew Goodman, *Eighty Days: Nellie Bly and Elizabeth Bislands' History-Making Race around the World* (Ballantine, 2013).

Holm, Jennifer L. *Our Only May Amelia.* HarperCollins, 1999. 253 pp. Grades 5–7. ALA Notable, 2000; Newbery honor, 2000.

Holm draws on the transcription of her great-aunt's diary and on oral histories in her novel about a twelve-year-girl growing up in a pioneer Finnish settlement in Washington's Naselle River valley in 1899. May Amelia, the only girl in a family of seven boys, is constantly reminded that she is not "a proper young lady," as she defies convention and her father by participating in activities that are viewed as her brothers' domain. She describes a settlement without nearby roads that depends on the river Naselle for transport so that she and her brothers travel by boat to the Island Schoolhouse when released from their farmwork and from helping out at home. Integrated into her accounts of her misadventures and family life are facts about the logging camp and salmon industry. Her descriptions of Astoria (where she goes to escape her grandmother, who blames her for her baby sister's death) and the geographical setting are supplemented by photographs of the area at the time. In her notes, Holm provides information on immigration and Finnish settlers in Washington Territory.

1. Discuss the challenges, opportunities, and contributions that May Amelia and her extended family find in Washington Territory.
2. How would you describe the relationship between the Chinook and immigrant settlers?

Kelly, Jacqueline. *The Evolution of Calpurnia Tate.* Holt, 2009. 340 pp. Grades 5–8. ALA Notable, 2010; Newbery honor, 2010; *Booklist* Top 10 HF, 2010; YALSA BB, 2010.

In Texas in 1899, eleven-year-old Calpurnia, "spliced midway" (2) between three older and three younger brothers, is expected by her mother to conform to a traditional womanhood. But it is apparent from Calpurnia's first-person narrative and from her observations of the natural world that she records in a notebook given to her by her eldest brother, that she resists this model. Her interest in science is encouraged by her grandfather, who introduces her to Charles Darwin and gives her a copy of *Origin of Species.* Quotes from Darwin that emphasize individual differences and adaptation preface each chapter as Calpurnia learns the principles of scientific method as part of her grandfather's science curriculum, which ranges from Copernicus to Newton, Linnaeus, and women scientists, even as her mother institutes a regimen of cooking and knitting lessons. The clash between a traditional education for girls and Calpurnia's wish to be a scientist is highlighted by Calpurnia's Christmas gift from her mother, *The Science of Housewifery*, which is followed by a telegram announcing the news that Calpurnia and her grandfather have been recognized by the Smithsonian for their identification of a new species of a plant. Kelly presents a girl struggling for a new life in a novel that deals with issues of culture and gender at the turn of the nineteenth century.

1. Discuss the extent to which Calpurnia may hope to move beyond the "distaff life of womanly things" (218).
2. Suggested reading: Peter Sis, *The Tree of Life* (Farrar, Straus & Giroux, 2003).

Richards, Jame. *Three Rivers Rising: A Novel of the Johnstown Flood.* Knopf, 2010. 292 pp. Grades 8–10. YALSA BB, 2011.

On May 31, 1889, after heavy rain, South Fork Dam breaks and the water from Lake Conemaugh pours down the river valley, destroying East Conemaugh and Woodvale on its path to Johnstown, Pennsylvania, the meeting place of three rivers. Basing her verse novel on the chronology of events, Richards interweaves geographical setting, explanations for the neglect of the dam, and the graphic description of the flood within the story of the romance between sixteen-year-old Celestia Whitcomb, whose parents are wealthy members of the South Fork Fishing and Hunting Club, and Peter, a hired hand whose father is a coal miner. The minute-by-minute chronology of events immediately before and during the flood is narrated by different characters, including the wife of the train driver who blasts the whistle in warning just ahead of the water. Their voices bring a sense of immediacy to the oncoming danger and destruction as they see houses swept away and people escaping, as well as those who are unable to scramble to safety.

Celestia describes the terror of being swept through the torrent while clinging to a door. There are scenes of fire and rescue, and accounts of the help that comes, including the arrival of Clara Barton and the Red Cross. Richards provides statistics of the death toll, a chronology of the dam's history, and further resources. Her novel also provides a social history of class in the nineteenth century.

1. Discuss how Richards addresses the question of culpability for the dam's collapse.
2. Compare witness accounts in the novel to accounts by Pennsylvania Railroad employees. Related website: "Johnstown Flood National Memorial," National Park Service (www.nps.gov/jofl/index.htm).

Emergence of Modern America and World War I

(1900–1928)

The American West

Ingold, Jeanette. *The Big Burn.* Harcourt, 2002. 295 pp. Grades 7–10. Spur, 2003.

In the summer of 1910, devastating fires consumed 2.5 million acres of public forest land. Ingold's novel centers on the wildfires that, fanned by gale-force winds, result in a blowup in the Coeur D'Alene National Forest, in Idaho. The disaster is experienced from the perspectives of sixteen-year-old Jarrett Logan; sixteen-year-old Lizbeth, who lives on a homestead; Private Seth Brown, enlisted in the Twenty-Fifth Infantry; and Ranger Samuel Logan. Jarrett, fired from the railroad when he makes the wrong decision to put out a wildfire instead of keeping watch on the track, is one of the many volunteers who sign up at the US Forest Service in Wallace. Unlike many, though, Jarrett receives advice and training from his ranger brother, Samuel, who takes him out on patrol before he is sent out with fire crews.

Chapter headings chart the spread of the wildfires by location and date, beginning on July 13 and ending on September 3. As they spread, homesteads such as Lizbeth's are destroyed, and the military is called in. There are vivid images of fast-moving walls of flames threatening the lives of firefighters and the towns of Wallace and Avery. Also, there are accounts of firefighting crews working, often futilely, to contain the fires, and scenes of people being evacuated on crowded trains—a last chance to escape the conflagration. "Field notes" in the text include information on the causes of forest fires, disagreement as to how they should be managed, and an explanation of the weather conditions that caused the blowup. Sam's perspective of his service in Avery and of the army's role in maintaining order is accompanied by a history of the Buffalo Soldiers. In her afterword, Ingold describes the equipment and training used in fighting today's forest fires. She provides information about resources used for her research and includes a bibliography.

1. Discuss how Ingold's story illustrates some of the difficulties encountered in fighting forest fires in 1910.
2. Related reading: Tim Egan, *The Big Burn: Teddy Roosevelt and the Fire That Saved America* (Houghton Mifflin/Harcourt, 2009).
3. Related website: "U.S. Forest Service History," Forest History Society (www.foresthistory.org/ASPNET/USFHSHome.aspx).

Larson, Kirby. *Hattie Big Sky.* 2006; Turtleback, 2008. 289 pp. Grades 7–10. ALA Notable, 2007; *Booklist* Top 10 HF, 2007; Newbery honor, 2007; NSSTB, 2007.

In December 1917, sixteen-year-old orphan Hattie Inez Brooks travels from Arlington, Iowa, to Montana to take over the homesteading claim left to her by her uncle Chester. In order to "prove up" on her claim, she must cultivate forty acres, preferably with flax and wheat, and "set four hundred eighty rods of fence" by November 1918 (25). Hattie describes her uncle's small shack and her challenging life as a "honyocker," which a cowboy tells her is "a hayseed, squatter—it's all the same" (16). In her "Honyocker Homily" columns for the *Arlington News*, Hattie writes about her new life and the skills she is learning, from sowing and harvesting crops to quilting. Larson's novel does not idealize life on the prairie. Despite the backbreaking work and drought, Hattie is determined to be successful in her venture and holds out against Traft Martin, a local rancher, who wants her land. But she is already in debt when a freak storm destroys her harvest, and she is finally forced to give up her claim.

Hattie forms warm relationships in the community, including her friendship with homesteaders Perilee and Karl Mueller. But during World War I, there is fear and prejudice among neighbors. Men like Karl, who were born in Germany, are required to register as alien enemies, attacks are made against Lutheran churches, and German books are burned. There is constant pressure to buy war bonds and show patriotism, but there are those who stand up for their neighbors. Letters from Hattie's friend Charlie convey news from the front in France. Larson bases her story on her great-grandmother's homesteading experience and notes that many of the anti-German incidents are based on actual events.

1. To what extent do people stand up to the bullying of their German-born neighbors?
2. Compare Hattie's accounts of homesteading with *Inside and Outside the Home: Homesteading Life in Montana, 1900–1920*. Use search box on Montana Historical Society's website (http://mhs.mt.gov).

Larson, Kirby. *Hattie Ever After.* Delacorte, 2013. Grades 7–10. 230 pp.

In the sequel to *Hattie Big Sky,* Hattie leaves the boardinghouse in Great Falls, Montana, in 1919, where she has been working to pay off her debts, to seize the opportunity to travel with a vaudeville company to San Francisco as their wardrobe mistress. San Francisco, Hattie reasons, will allow her to solve the mystery of the letter and token sent by a Ruby Danvers from San Francisco to her uncle Chester. But she also sees San Francisco as a city where she can achieve her ambition of becoming a reporter, which has been fueled by writing columns about her homesteading experiences for the *Arlington News* back in Iowa and by reading articles by female reporters Ida Tarbell and Nellie Bly. Upon arriving in San Francisco, Hattie applies for a job at the *Chronicle* but finds that there is no easy path to the coveted title of reporter. Outside the newsroom, eager young men, "stringers," wait for the break that will enable them to get ahead; and in the newsroom, there is just one female reporter who carries her own byline. Cleaning offices is the only job available for Hattie until she uses her initiative to work her way into the newsroom as researcher and then reporter.

Hattie's experiences are set against descriptions of the newspaper world, the vaudeville theater, and the underworld of confidence tricksters. Hattie's interviews and articles address how World War I affected the lives of women in the workforce. Hattie meets some well-known figures of the time, including President Woodrow Wilson, who visits San Francisco to promote the League of Nations. Larson provides extensive notes on her research and identifies where she has fictionalized events.

1. Discuss how the novel addresses women's equality in the workplace.
2. Discuss Hattie's work as a reporter. In what ways can her approach to journalism be compared with the work of pioneer woman journalists such as Nellie Bly?
3. Related website: Bly's news articles are available at the website Nellie Bly: The Pioneer Woman Journalist: A Resource Website (www .nellieblyonline.com/bio#where).
4. Related website: "Ida Tarbell, *The History of Standard Oil* (1904)," Books That Shaped America, Library of Congress (www.loc.gov/ exhibits/books-that-shaped-america/1900-to-1950.html).

Adult Fiction

Doig, Ivan. *The Whistling Season.* Harcourt, 2006. 352 pp. ALA Notable, 2007; Alex, 2007.

In 1957, Paul Milliron, Montana's school superintendent of public instruction, has been charged with closing down one-room schools, a decision spurred by the launching of Sputnik, because the chairman of the Appropriations Committee argues that school consolidation is the answer to meeting this challenge to US science education. Unhappy at the prospect, he thinks back to his education in a one-room schoolhouse. He reminisces back to 1909, when his father, a homesteader and widower with three sons, answered the advertisement "Can't Cook but Doesn't Bite." The arrival of Rose Llewellyn and Morris Morgan, introduced as her brother, herald far-reaching changes for the Millirons and the Marias Coulee community. When the school loses yet another teacher, Morris is persuaded to stand in her stead. He proves a gifted teacher who expands his students' knowledge across all eight grades—demonstrated in their success in the new standardized tests. Students receive lessons on the history of astronomy as Morris prepares them for the return of Halley's comet in 1910. Morris recognizes Paul's ability and teaches him Latin after school.

Doig's story illustrates the centrality of the one-room schoolhouse both to the family and to the scattered surrounding community. But Morris and Rose have a "history" of their own, and Paul must decide whether to keep silent or inform his father. In 1957, Paul draws on Morris's teaching as he works out how he might yet save the one-room schools. Paul's descriptions of family and school life in Marias Coulee include explanations of the "Big Ditch" irrigation project that conflicts with the practice of dry farming.

1. Identify and discuss advantages and disadvantages of the one-room schoolhouse for rural communities.
2. Related website: One-Room Schoolhouse Center (http://oneroom schoolhousecenter.weebly.com).

Erdrich, Louise. *The Plague of Doves.* HarperCollins, 2008. 313 pp. ALA Notable, 2009; Pulitzer finalist, 2009.

Yoked together in a narrative that weaves back and forth in time are the tangled relationships and interlocking stories of the population of Ojibwe and whites living in or near Pluto, North Dakota. Evelina Harp, part Ojibwe, part white, hears from her Ojibwe grandfather, Mooshum, about the murder of a family in early 1911, and the lynching of the innocent Native Americans who found the bodies, including the young boy, Mooshum ("Holy Track"). Erdrich structures her novel to show how the past continues to reverberate in the lives of those living in the 1970s. Evelina, for example, learns from Sister Mary Anita Buckendorfer, granddaughter of one of the lynchers, that Mooshum was strung up but cut down before he died because his grandfather was a member of the lynching party. Dr. Cordelia Lochren, who as a baby was the sole survivor of the murders, discovers that she had saved the life of the man responsible for murdering her family. Central to the novel are the stories of the generations of the Peace family. Evelina's friend Corwin Peace, whose ancestor Cuthbert Peace was one of those lynched, learns to play on the violin that had once belonged to Cuthbert's brothers, Henri and Lafayette Peace, who saved the life of the grandfather of Judge Coutts during an expedition to claim new land. Judge Coutts marries Evelina's aunt Geraldine and narrates his own story, stating his objective is to "maintain the sovereignty of tribal law on tribal land" (115).

The stories of a community's past, intimately tied to the land, circle back to Billy Peace, a religious fanatic who abuses his family and whose story and ending are narrated by his wife, Marn Wolde, who is related to Warren Wolde, who committed murder in 1911. Warren dies in a state hospital after listening to a violin played by a visitor named Peace. Erdrich bases the lynching of Holy Track on the lynching of thirteen-year-old Paul Holy Track in 1897.

1. Choose a character such as Evelina or Corwin Peace and discuss how the past has shaped their lives.
2. Related website: "Thomas Spicer Family Murders, 1897," US Gen-Web Project (www.rootsweb.ancestry.com/~ndemmons/narration spicermurders.htm).

Keesey, Anna. *Little Century.* Farrar, Straus & Giroux, 2012. 322 pp. *SLJ* BAB4T, 2012.

In 1900, after the death of her mother, eighteen-year-old Esther travels from Chicago to Century, Oregon, where her cousin Ferris "Pick" Pickett, owns Two Forks Ranch. She agrees to Pick's plans that she lie about her age and files a claim to be a homesteader on the understanding that Pick will buy her out when he has the money to do so. The homestead includes the lake Half-a-Mind, a valuable water supply for Pick's cattle. In the meantime, Esther learns to ride a horse, sleeps at the small shack on the homestead, and plants alfalfa grass.

Through her rich cast of characters representing Century's small community, Keesey depicts the enmity between cattle ranchers and sheep ranchers over grazing rights on the range, which erupts into violence, including the massacre of sheep by "buckaroos" and the murder of Joe Peaslee, a local storekeeper. Events narrated from the perspective of Esther, and to a lesser extent, of Pick and Ben Cruff, a shepherd with whom Esther falls in love, reveal the morals and motives of a community struggling for a future in a land of scarce resources.

1. Discuss the arguments made by cattle ranchers against using the range to graze sheep.
2. Discuss how Century is affected by the government's control of grazing land. To what extent does Century's future depend on the railroad?

The American West and Immigration

Adult Fiction

Otsuka, Julie. *The Buddha in the Attic.* Knopf, 2011. 129 pp. *Booklist* Top 10 HN, 2012; Langum, 2011.

In the early 1900s, Japanese "picture brides"—some from the city, some from the country, some from the mountains—are on their way to San Francisco to what they believe will be a new life in which they will not have to work in rice paddies and geisha houses. They pack kimonos, fans, silk sashes, and small brass Buddha statues. On the boat they compare photographs of the young men they are to marry, who look young and handsome in their Western clothes standing in front of nice-looking homes, but when they arrive, they find that the photographs had been taken twenty years earlier. Many husbands are migrant workers and their brides' lives are to be spent laboring in fields, laundries, and restaurants or working as maids. Through the plural narrative—"we"— the different experiences of girls and women are described as their husbands make them their wives. They learn that "home" is a bunkhouse, a tent, an attic. Some live on isolated farms, and others in town. They struggle with language and an alien culture, and they are subjected to prejudice even as they are valued over other ethnicities for their hard work. Otsuka's poetic novel covers every aspect of their lives, including their relationships within and without their marriages and those with their employers. They give birth to children who become American while they dream of leaving lives that have caused them to disappear within themselves. Two chapters describe how they deal with their forced evacuation after the outbreak of war. The last chapter describes townspeople's attitudes on the disappearance of neighbors and employees as "almost all traces of the Japanese" disappear and their names fade from collective memory (129).

1. Discuss the reasons young girls and women left Japan and were unable to return.
2. In what ways does Otsuka's novel provide a comprehensive depiction of their lives once in the United States?

Industrialization

Auch, Mary Jane. *Ashes of Roses.* 2002; Perfection Learning, 2004. 250 pp. Grades 7–10. *Booklist* Top 10 HF, 2002; NSSTB, 2003; YALSA BB, 2003.

Auch writes about the immigrant experience in New York and the Triangle Shirtwaist Factory fire through the experiences of sixteen-year-old Rose Nolan, who arrives at Ellis Island from Ireland, on February 18, 1911. Rose's family is split up when her brother, Joseph is diagnosed with trachoma and her father takes him back to Ireland. Rose, her mother, and her sister find their way to their father's brother's home, where Patrick makes his unexpected guests welcome. But tension builds between the two families, and Rose's mother returns to Ireland, leaving Rose and twelve-year-old Maureen alone in New York. Rose experiences the harsh realities that new immigrants face and finds out the hard way about the dangers of the sweatshops that employ young girls.

When Rose obtains a job at the Triangle Shirtwaist Factory, she is told about the strikes for better working conditions and about how her employers evade the law that specifies space requirements for workers on the ninth floor, where she works. Rose's pride in her job is short lived when she barely escapes being burned in the fire on March 25, 1911, in which 146 workers lost their lives. In an author's note, Auch writes about her resources, mentioning that the tragedy led to some of the first worker-safety laws and to a stronger labor movement (250).

1. Discuss the choices that Rose and her family make as immigrants.
2. Discuss the attitudes of Rose and her friends to their employment and to the union.

Friesner, Esther. *Threads and Flames.* Viking, 2010. 390 pp. Grades 7–10. YALSA BF, 2012; NSSTB, 2011.

In 1910, thirteen-year-old Raisa leaves her Polish *shtetl* to join her sister, Henda, in America. During the voyage, Raisa adopts Brina, whose mother dies at sea, and succeeds in getting them both through Ellis Island. But Henda has disappeared, and Raisa is unable to find a place to stay until she meets Gavrel Kamensky, whose family agrees to take her and Brina in as boarders. After sewing machine lessons, Raisa leaves her job in a sweatshop to work at the Triangle Shirtwaist Factory, where Gavrel works as a cutter and where her friends Zusa and Luciana, whom she met on the boat, also work. Raisa tells readers about working conditions in the garment industry's sweatshops and the Triangle factory and describes the cramped layout of the ninth floor and how she escapes the fire. She also describes how she and the Kamenskys search the morgue for Gavrel and attend funeral processions for the nameless dead. They hear the indictment of safety conditions by the fire chief and follow the factory owners' trial.

Raisa's story is illustrative of the immigrant dream to find a better life, as she attends English classes and works to become a teacher. Her marriage to Gavrel and her sister's marriage into a wealthy New York family demonstrate the possibility of upward mobility. Descriptions of the Kamenskys and the families of Raisa's friends provide a snapshot of New York's immigrant life.

1. Compare Raisa's experience to stories of immigrants living in New York's tenements. Related website: Tenement Museum (www .tenement.org).

Haddix, Margaret Peterson. *Uprising.* Simon & Schuster, 2007. 346 pp. Grades 7–10. NSSTB, 2008.

The stories of three young women—Bella, an immigrant from Italy; Yetta, from Russia; and Jane, a rich girl from New York—are told from each girl's perspective as they become friends during the strike of the Triangle Shirtwaist Factory in 1909–10. The difficulties and poverty facing immigrant girls and the unfair labor practices and unsafe working conditions at the Triangle factory where Bella and Yetta are employed are described in detail. Haddix's novel focuses on the strike for union recognition. Included are descriptions of the beating and arrest of strikers, the preferential treatment of scabs, the call for a general strike as shirtwaist workers at other factories strike in sympathy, the names of prominent labor and socialist leaders, and the participation of rich society women who donate funds for a cause they see as related to women's suffrage. All three girls are at the factory on March 25, 1911, when the fire breaks out and two of them lose their lives. Details of the fire and explanations of why so many died are told from each girl's perspective. In an author's note, Haddix provides more information about suffragettes, the trial and acquittal of the factory owners, and the resulting safety laws. A bibliography is provided.

1. Compare accounts of the fire and strike with interviews with survivors at the website "Remembering the 1911 Triangle Factory Fire" (www.ilr.cornell.edu/trianglefire/).
2. Related reading: Albert Marrin, *Flesh and Blood So Cheap: The Story of the Triangle Fire and Its Legacy* (Knopf, 2011).

Paterson, Katherine. *Bread and Roses, Too.* Clarion, 2006. 275 pp. Grades 5–8. *Booklist* Top 10 HF, 2007; NSSTB, 2007.

In January 1912, the mill workers in Lawrence, Massachusetts, walk out, beginning what is known as the Bread and Roses Strike. The mother and older sister of twelve-year-old Rosa become strong supporters of the strike, and twelve-year-old Jake, abused by his unemployed alcoholic father, is recruited to join the strikers by Italian immigrants. Descriptions of strike activity include the picket lines; the joining together of immigrant women in singing "songs of defiance"; the violence resulting from strikers' confrontations with armed Harvard College boys and the militia; and the arrival of Joe Ettor, representing the Industrial Workers of the World (the Wobblies). Other prominent leaders of this labor organization who speak to the strikers include "Big Bill" Heywood and the feminist and activist Elizabeth Gurley Flynn. Rosa's teacher represents the mill owners' side, and she tells her working-class students that Billy Woods, a mill owner, once worked in the mills as a boy and made his way up through education; however, she omits telling them about his fortuitous marriage.

When children are evacuated to New York and other cities, the novel's setting moves to Barre, Vermont, where Rosa and Jake are sent with other children to live with supportive union workers. The strikers return to work when their demands are met after government inquiries into factory conditions and the violence perpetrated against women who have been jailed. In her notes, Paterson expands on immigrant labor in the textile mills, the reasons for the strike, and Barre's stonecutting industry.

1. Discuss examples of the living and working conditions of immigrant laborers in Lawrence's textile mills.
2. Discuss the role of women in the strike and the strike's effect on children.
3. Related website: Bread and Roses Centennial Exhibit (www.exhibit .breadandrosescentennial.org).

Winthrop, Elizabeth. *Counting on Grace.* 2006; Perfection Learning Company, 2007. 232 pp. Grades 5–8. Addams honor, 2007; NSSTB, 2007.

In 1910, Grace Forcier, age twelve, works as a doffer for her mother in the textile mill at North Pownal, Vermont. In need of money, Grace's mother had provided false papers to prove that Grace met the regulation that working children be fourteen years old. But left-handed Grace finds doffing difficult because her mother operates six spinning frames with a total of 1,632 "bobbins to check" (104). The novel addresses the unhealthy and dangerous conditions in the mill and the curtailing of children's education because of economic necessity, which is exacerbated by the mill owners' monopoly on houses, the store, and the school. Miss Lesley, Grace's former schoolteacher, encourages Grace to study for the certification test for Normal School and writes to the Vermont chapter of the National Child Labor Committee to inform them about illegal practices in the mills. The committee hires photographer Lewis Hines and sends him to document children at work; he then photographs Grace and other children at the mill.

Winthrop's story is based on Hines's actual photographs taken at North Pownall mill. Grace is modeled on twelve-year-old Addie Card, whose identity Winthrop found when searching 1910 US Census data. In supplementary material, Winthrop provides information about Hine and includes his photographs of Addie and the child labor force.

1. Related website: "Photographs of Lewis Hine: Documentation of Child Labor," Teaching with Documents (www.archives.gov/edu cation/lessons). Follow "The Development of the Industrial United States (1870–1900)" link for specific topics.
2. Related reading: Russell Freedman, *Kids at Work: Lewis Hine and the Crusade against Child Labor* (Clarion Books, 1994).

Adult Fiction

Belfer, Lauren. *City of Light.* Random House, 1999. 518 pp. *Booklist* Top 10 HN, 2000.

In 1901, Louisa Barrett, the respected headmistress of the Macaulay School (modeled on the Buffalo Seminary for girls) is caught up in the politics and controversy surrounding the development of the Niagara Falls' hydroelectric power project. Belfer's novel provides a comprehensive depiction of Buffalo, New York, a major inland port and cultural center in the 1900s, which was attracting new electrochemical industries as a result of the distribution of electricity with the new alternating current invented by Nikola Tesla. The hydroelectric project, described in detail, is criticized by preservationists and also by investors who are fighting against socialist ideas of public ownership and regulation. Louisa experiences the dirty politics of the elite circle of robber barons that also controls her personal life and the lives of those whom she loves. Belfer includes information about the Pan-American Exposition, President Grover Cleveland (a former Buffalo mayor), and the assassination of President William McKinley.

In this novel, Buffalo serves as a microcosm for political, social, and cultural issues of the early 1900s: union strikes, racism, and the Progressive reform movement. Descriptions of Buffalo's parks and boulevards, designed by Frederick Law Olmsted, are contrasted with conditions in slums and with the "infant asylum." Actual historical figures include the reformer Mary Talbert, who later became president of the NAACP.

1. How do Louisa's life and career illustrate the gender politics of the era? Discuss how Belfer uses other women characters to illustrate women's status.
2. Discuss the private versus public ownership of electricity. Related website: University of Buffalo Libraries website: "Electricity and Technology," Pan-American Exposition (http://library.buffalo.edu/pan-am/exposition/electricity/).

Vreeland, Susan. *Clara and Mr. Tiffany: A Novel.* 2011. Random House, 2012. 405 pp. *Booklist* Top 10 HN, 2011.

Vreeland's novel is based on the recent recognition of Clara Driscoll's designs for the innovative leaded-glass lampshades made by Louis Comfort Tiffany's Glass and Decorating Company. Her designs include the "Dragonfly" lamp, for which she was awarded a bronze medallion at the Paris Exposition in 1900. From Driscoll's letters and archival research, Vreeland has constructed a sweeping novel of Clara's life and work while employed as head of Tiffany's Women's Department. Driscoll's story is intertwined with that of Louis Tiffany and his company from 1892 to 1908. Included are descriptions of Tiffany's innovative work and the glass-making process.

The novel addresses issues regarding the equality of women designers and cutters, who were excluded from the Lead Glaziers and Glass Cutters' Union and subjected to Tiffany's policy of not hiring married women. Driscoll, represented as a "new woman," was connected with the Progressive movement and persuaded the women in her department to confront union bullying. Vreeland depicts a rich portrait of New York in the Gilded Age, with references to authors and artists and to cultural and political events in a variety of New York settings, including Tiffany's extraordinary New York mansion. She provides excerpts from Driscoll's letters and a link to the essay "The New Woman" on the "Clara and Mr. Tiffany" pages on the website www .svreeland.com/tiff.html.

1. Discuss the status of women in the workplace and efforts made to increase their opportunities in the creative arts.
2. Discuss how Vreeland uses Clara Driscoll as a fictional model for the "new woman." In what ways do Clara's life and work reject Victorian ideals of womanhood?
3. Related website: The Neustadt Collection of Tiffany Glass (www .neustadtcollection.org/home).

Racial Prejudice

Hesse, Karen. *Witness.* Scholastic Press, 2001. 161 pp. Grades 6–9. ALA Notable, 2002.

In this five-act free-verse drama, the voices of eleven characters from a small town in Vermont in 1924 bear witness to the infiltration of the Ku Klux Klan into their lives while revealing their own attitudes toward those of different ethnicities or races. Characters include those with some status in the town: a newspaper editor, a doctor, a restaurant owner, and a constable. A photograph of each character prefaces the text. The seeds of prejudice against twelve-year-old African American Leonora Safer and six-year-old Jewish girl Esther Hirsh have already been sown by some in town before certain community members welcome and join the Klan. Leonora, for example, had been subject to the prejudice of white girls when she was chosen to dance in a special program. Hesse shows the insidious way in which the Klan works its way into the community, appearing to serve its best interests, helping white people in need and "upholding" family values. Reynard Alexander, the newspaper editor, comments that the "Klan is in our homes, our schools, our factories, and stores" (103). Other voices express their doubts about the Klan, such as farmer Sara Chickering, who takes the motherless Esther under her wing. The hate and violence instigated by the Klan against the Safer and the Hirsh families result in the near-fatal shooting of Mr. Hirsh. The community and Vermont finally say no to the Klan and its objectives. Hesse also references political and cultural events of the 1920s, such as the murder of fourteen-year-old Bobby Franks, a Jewish boy in Chicago in 1924, and Clarence Darrow's defense of his accused killers, Nathan Leopold and Richard Loeb.

1. Discuss Harvey Pettibone's statement that men in the Klan are "100 percent American men" (24).
2. Choose a character and discuss their attitudes toward others and the Klan.
3. Related reading: Susan Campbell Bartoletti, *They Call Themselves the KKK: The Birth of an American Terrorist Group* (Houghton Mifflin, 2010).

Schmidt, Gary D. *Lizzie Bright and the Buckminster Boy.* Clarion, 2004. 224 pp. Grades 6–9. *Booklist* Top 10 HF, 2005; Newbery honor, 2005; Printz honor, 2005; YALSA BB, 2005.

Schmidt bases his novel on the state of Maine's destruction of the island community of Malaga in 1912. Turner Buckminster, who has just moved from Boston to Phippsburg, where his father was appointed minister of Phippsburg's First Congregational church, encounters the bigotry of town citizens when he meets Lizzie Griffin, a thirteen-year-old African American who lives on Malaga. Phippsburg's citizen aim to remove the "shanties" and everyone from Malaga, ostensibly so that there would be a clear view of the island from a planned resort hotel on the mainland, and persuade Turner's father that they are right in their cause. Turner, forbidden to visit the island, continues to meet with Lizzie on the mainland. Despite all that Turner can do, the townspeople ruthlessly drive everyone off the island, burning their homes and desecrating their cemetery. Turner later finds that Lizzie died shortly after being sent to the Home for the Feebleminded at Pownal.

Reverend Buckminster finally takes a stand against racial bigotry but loses his life in saving Turner from an attack. Turner and his mother are left to stand against intolerance and demonstrate the true meaning of charity in a novel that lays bare racial prejudice and depicts the socioeconomic and cultural milieu of a small town in the early 1900s. In the author's note, Schmidt provides further information about the history of Malaga. The documentary *Malaga Island* points out that the community of white, black, and mixed-race people on Malaga were regarded as "immoral and shiftless," and the "local stigma" that associated "mixed blood with feeble-mindedness" was the reason eight citizens were sent to the Pownal home.

1. Discuss how and why the Reverend Buckminster finally defies his congregation.
2. Discuss the novel in conjunction with the radio and photo documentary *Malaga Island: A Story Best Untold* (www.malagaisland maine.org).

Vernick, Shirley Reva. *The Blood Lie: A Novel.* Cinco Puntos Press, 2011. 141 pp. Grades 7–12. YALSA BF, 2012; Taylor honor, 2012.

When four-year-old Daisy goes missing, temporarily, in Paradise Woods in Massena, New York, on Saturday, September 22, 1928, Gus, owner of the Sit Down Diner, suggests to the new state trooper, Victor Brown, that Jews are responsible for her disappearance. He tells the trooper that they bake the blood of a Christian child in the foods they eat to celebrate important holidays. He gives the trooper the name of sixteen-year-old Jack Pool, who had mentioned Yom Kippur when eating at the diner. The town is quickly caught up in a wave of anti-Semitism as the trooper raids Jewish businesses and the synagogue, accompanied by an ugly mob who, but for Jack's actions, would have lynched Rabbi Abrams.

Vernick notes the letter to the *New York Times* from the president of the American Jewish Committee protesting the "attempt to plant on American soil the barbarous ritual murder accusation against the Jews" (139). She bases her story on the accusation made against an innocent Jewish boy when a small girl disappeared from Massena in 1928. Other examples of anti-Semitism are mentioned in the novel, and Vernick refers in her notes to use of the blood lie by Hitler and others.

1. Discuss the character and conduct of state trooper Victor Brown.
2. Discuss the responses of the Jewish community and Rabbi Abrams to the violence.

Science and Medicine

Chibbaro, Julie. *Deadly.* Atheneum Books for Young Readers, 2011. 293 pp. Grades 7–12.

In her diary, dated from September 1906 to April 24, 1907, sixteen-year-old Prudence Galewski records her involvement with the case of Mary Mallon, or "Typhoid Mary." Unhappy with Mrs. Browning's School for Girls, Prudence is passionately interested in science and, because of the death of her older brother, in how death sickens and kills. She obtains work at New York's Department of Health and Sanitation as an assistant to sanitary engineer George Soper, who trains her in the science of epidemiology as they collect and organize evidence from those who have contracted typhoid fever. Prudence meticulously records her detective work in identifying Mallon as a healthy typhoid carrier after Mallon's arrest, quarantine, and the trial, where the department presents evidence to justify its actions when sued by Mallon.

Scientific research on cell biology, bacteria, typhoid carriers, and the work of Louis Pasteur are incorporated into Prudence's diary. Prudence, a keen observer, evidenced by the labeled sketches in her diary, is encouraged by a woman doctor to apply to the Pennsylvania Medical School for Women. In her author's note, Chibbaro differentiates "real players," such as George Soper, and fictional characters; explains her time line of events; and provides information on Mallon's later life. She also refers to Jacob Riis's work, from which she drew descriptions of life in the tenements.

1. "Is it right for the department to treat a human being like a contagious disease?" (182). Discuss the issues raised by Mallon's arrest and quarantine. Discuss Prudence's responses to Mallon's treatment.

Adult Fiction

Keane, Mary Beth. *Fever.* Scribner, 2013. 306 pp.

This fictional biography of Mary Mallon, whom New York Department of Health sanitary engineer Dr. Soper identified as the first "healthy carrier of Typhoid Fever in America" (14), begins with her employment in the Kirkenbauer home as a cook in 1899, during which time the small boy Tobias and his mother die from typhoid fever. The narrative, written mainly from Mallon's perspective, ranges back and forth as it covers her childhood in Ireland and her arrival in New York in 1883 at the age of fifteen, and as it traces her move from laundress to the sought-after job of cook. Keane's novel reveals an ambitious young woman who proves a skilled and creative cook, a position that pays better than other options open to women of her class and status. Her first warnings to cease cooking, her arrest by Dr. Soper in 1907, and her first three years in quarantine on North Brother Island are presented from Mallon's standpoint, and she makes clear her anger as she is subjected to constant testing and attempts to force her to agree to have her gall bladder removed. On North Brother Island, the location of Riverside Hospital's tuberculosis sanatorium, she lives in a twelve-foot-by-ten-foot bungalow and is refused visitors. The novel covers Mallon's fight for freedom, including her letters that finally result in her securing a lawyer who arranges for a hearing in 1909, based on the grounds that she was arrested and tested without a warrant. The reasons given for her eventual release in 1910 include the discovery of other healthy typhoid carriers. Traced in detail are the steps Mallon takes to find employment once more as a cook, before she is arrested again in 1915. Central to the novel are Mallon's thoughts as she wonders to what extent she has hidden from herself the truth of her culpability for the death and illness of others. The novel concludes in 1938, when she reflects in her diary on Tobias's death and her quarantine on North Brotherton Island. An added dimension to Mallon's story is her relationship with Alfred Briehof and the setting of the tenements and street life of New York's Lower East Side.

1. Discuss the justification, or lack of justification, for Mary Mallon's arrest and quarantine. Related website: David Rosner, "Beyond Typhoid Mary," Living Legacies (www.columbia.edu/cu/alumni/Magazine/Spring2004/publichealth.html).
2. Related website: Mary Keane's web page, which features a time line and primary documents (http://marybethkeane.com/fever/marymallon/).

Science and Religion

Bryant, Jen. *Ringside, 1925: Views from the Scopes Trial.* 2006. Knopf, 2008. 240 pp. Grades 8–12. NSSTB, 2009.

In free verse, Bryant's cast of nine characters from Dayton, Tennessee, bring differing perspectives to bear on the 1925 trial of Johnny Scopes for teaching the chapter on evolution from the school's science textbook. The run-down town hopes to gain financially from an influx of tourists by being first in line to challenge the Butler Act of Tennessee, which makes it illegal to teach theories of evolution. Characters, including high school students, observe and comment on the trial, its impact on the town, and issues of evolution and religion. With the exception of Betty Barker, member of a local study group, it is a time for some people to think more deeply about the relation between religion and science.

For others, listening to the trial and meeting new people expands their horizons. The character, Paul Lebrun reports on the progress of the trial in his dispatches to the *St. Louis Post-Dispatch.*

Quotes preface each chapter from Thomas Stewart, attorney general for Tennessee; defense lawyers Dudley Malone and Clarence Darrow; and prosecutor William Jennings Bryan. Bryant refers to Scopes's observation that he sat "speechless," "a ringside observer," at his own trial. In an epilogue, Bryant adds notes about Dayton, J. T. Scopes, Bryan, Darrow, the Scopes trial appeal, and the antievolution movement.

1. Choose two characters and discuss how they are affected by the trial.
2. Related reading: Deborah Heligman, *Charles and Emma: The Darwin's Leap of Faith* (Holt, 2009).

Kidd, Ronald. *Monkey Town: The Summer of the Scopes Trial.* 2006; Simon Pulse, 2011. 288 pp. Grades 6–9. NSSTB, 2007.

In this novel, the 1925 "Monkey trial" in Dayton, Tennessee, is viewed through the eyes of fifteen-year-old Frances Robinson. Frances's father is one of the Dayton citizens responsible for planning the trial as publicity for the town, after learning that the American Civil Liberties Union would challenge the Butler Act, which prohibited the teaching of evolution in schools and colleges. Johnny Scopes, a sports coach at Rhea Central High School, is chosen as an ideal candidate for the trial, since he admits to covering evolution when teaching biology from a state-approved textbook.

Frances describes the chief protagonists at the trial proceedings, including William Jennings Bryan, Clarence Darrow, H. L. Mencken (whose dispatches to the *Baltimore Sun* are included in Kidd's text) and cartoonist Edmund Duffy. As an eyewitness, Frances describes courtroom scenes; reports on the dialogue between Darrow and Bryan, taken from the trial transcripts; and describes the circuslike atmosphere. The clash between ideas and beliefs is clearly presented.

Kidd notes his interview with Frances Robinson, who was eight years old at the time of the Scopes trial. He explains that although he used the facts in regard to the trial, he fictionalized other elements of the story.

1. How is the Scopes trial relevant to current controversies about the teaching of creationism and intelligent design in schools?
2. Related website: "Famous Trials in American History: Tennessee vs. John Scopes—'The Monkey Trial,' 1925" (http://law2.umkc.edu/faculty/projects/ftrials/scopes/scopes.htm).
3. Related reading: Jerome Lawrence and Robert E. Lee, *Inherit the Wind* (Ballantine Books, 1997).

Social and Cultural History

Donnelly, Jennifer. *A Northern Light.* Harcourt, 2003. 389 pp. Grades 9–12. *Booklist* Top 10 HF, 2004; Printz honor, 2004; YALSA BB, 2004.

Mattie Gokey, living in Maine in 1906, has a passion for words and is a talented writer. She is encouraged by her schoolteacher Miss Wilcox to apply to Barnard College, where she is accepted with a full scholarship, subject to her passing her school diploma. But Mattie had promised her dying mother to care for her four younger sisters, and her father demands her help on their small farm in upstate New York. She accepts what seems inevitable, including the ring offered to her by Royal Loomis, the son of a neighboring farmer. But circumstances change when she is given permission to work at the Glenmore Hotel.

Mattie's narrative weaves back and forth from the farm and her courtship with Royal to her duties at the hotel, which are disrupted by the discovery of Grace Brown's body in Big Moose Lake and the search for her companion, Carl Grahm, alias Chester Gillette. Woven into Mattie's narrative are excerpts from the letters entrusted to her by Grace Brown, which lead Mattie to the truth about her death. Donnelly's novel sets the burgeoning tourist trade of the Adirondacks against the harsh realities of rural life. She also addresses the prejudice that harms Mattie's friend Weaver. Donnelly provides the full story of Brown's murder in her notes, as well as a bibliography.

1. Discuss how the novel raises issues regarding women and writing and Mattie's decision to leave for New York.
2. Related reading: Theodore Dreiser, *An American Tragedy* (1925; Signet Classics, 2010) (based on Gillette's murder trial).

Hale, Marian. *Dark Water Rising.* Holt, 2006. 233 pp. Grades 6–9. *Booklist* Top 10 HF, 2007.

In 1900 Galveston, Texas, was called the "New York of Texas." The father of sixteen-year-old Seth is persuaded by his brother, who owns a lumberyard in Galveston, to relocate, because new business opportunities will allow him to send Seth and his younger brothers to college. Seth, however, wishes to be a carpenter like his father and is glad when a summer carpenter's job becomes available. Soon after he begins work comes a devastating storm that will destroy more than three thousand homes and, by a conservative estimate, cost eight thousand lives. Seth describes the buildup of wind and powerful surf that first draws people in awe to the beach and the initial flooding, to which Galveston residents were long accustomed. He later describes the scenes as he makes his way to find his parents: deep water, broken telephone poles, flying slates, and people swept away and drowning as their houses are destroyed. He shelters with others in a house that barely holds together. There are detailed and graphic descriptions of the aftermath of the storm, including men forced at bayonet point to clear the scenes of devastation in the business district, the harbor, and at the railroad.

Hale includes photographs of Galveston before and after the storm. She explains that some material was from an interview with a survivor, includes statistics of the damage, and addresses the steps taken to prevent another disaster.

1. Compare Hale's novel to eyewitness reports and photographs at the website: The 1900 Storm: Galveston Island, Texas (www.1900storm .com/nightofhorrors/).

Hesse, Karen. *Brooklyn Bridge.* Macmillan, 2008. 229 pp. Grades 6–9. Taylor, 2009.

Fourteen-year-old Joseph Michtom tells about his summer in Brooklyn in 1903, when his father and mother give up their candy shop for the "bear business." Joseph explains how his mother made the first teddy bear one night after seeing Clifford Berryman's cartoon of Theodore Roosevelt refusing to shoot a bear in Mississippi. As Hesse explains in her notes, toy bears had previously been made from wood and metal, and Rose Michtom's cloth bear, with its movable limbs, became enormously popular. Joseph's Jewish family had escaped from Russia, and his uncle explains that these bears were not symbolic of the Russian "bear" but were "Theodore Roosevelt bears" ("Teddy's bears") and "Very American" (2). Joseph and his sister Emily help with the bears, but Joseph is desperate to go to Coney Island's Lunar Park, whose attractions are advertised in modified newspaper clippings inserted into the text. Joseph's warm family life is contrasted to the lives of the homeless orphans and abused children and youth who shelter at night under the Brooklyn Bridge and whose stories parallel the main text. The milieu of Brooklyn is evoked through the social life of the Michtom family and their friends and in descriptions that include the lighted arches of Lunar Park, a street baseball game, and Emily's "home library."

1. Discuss how Joseph is made aware that he is "lucky" compared to others.
2. Analyze the reasons for Joseph's family's success.
3. Related website: "The Story of the Teddy Bear," National Park Service (www.nps.gov/thrb/historyculture/storyofteddybear.htm).

Wolf, Allan. *The Watch That Ends the Night: Voices from the Titanic.* Candlewick, 2011. 466 pp. Grades 7–12. *Booklist* Top 10 Fiction for Youth, 2012; NSSTB, 2011.

In the notes to his verse novel, Wolf writes that he combines "fancy" with well-researched historical facts in "bringing alive representations of those who lived and died" on the *Titanic* (435). The medley of voices (representing those who helped build and launch the *Titanic*, the captain, the crew, and the passengers) begin with John Snow, who describes his first sighting of the bodies floating like seagulls in their white life jackets on April 20, 1912. The prelude chapter, "Preparing to Sail," dated April 9, 1912, is followed by seven chapters corresponding to the liner's seven watches, ending on April 15 and concludes with Snow's final report and the refrain of "The Ship Rat." The voice of American sea post man Oscar Woody joins those of other crew members as they record their responses to the disaster. Wolf's unique novel also includes the perspectives of the "frozen mass" of "the Iceberg" that has its "part to play" (87).

Interspersed among characters' narratives are informational leaflets handed out to passengers, dialogues, letters, poems dedicated to the "promenades" of first- and third-class passengers, actual Morse code transmissions and distress signals, and Snow's undertaker reports. In his notes, Wolf provides extensive notes for passengers, including John Jacob Astor and Margaret Brown ("Unsinkable Molly Brown"). There are statistics pertaining to the *Titanic* and an extensive bibliography.

1. Compare Wolf's novel to any nonfiction account of the sinking of the *Titanic*. In what ways does Wolf's novel add to, change, or bring a different perspective?

Adult Fiction

Preston, Caroline. *The Scrapbook of Frankie Pratt: A Novel in Pictures.* Ecco, 2011. 228 pp. Alex, 2011.

Using the format of a scrapbook, Frankie Pratt uses memorabilia to tell about her family; her graduation from high school; her years at Vassar College; her travels and romances; and her return home to Cornish Flat, New Hampshire, to nurse her mother and marry her first high school date, now a medical doctor. Photographs, postcards, newspaper clippings, menus, theater programs, fabric swatches, and cutouts of furnishings, fashions, and advertisements provide a sociocultural history of the 1920s. Frankie applies for jobs as a writer, and she includes cutouts from magazines and literary journals, including *Women's Home Companion*, *True Story*, *Harper's Bazaar*, *Vanity Fair*, and *New Yorker* (first issued in 1925). Her journal serves to introduce readers to major writers of the time, as she meets Edna St. Vincent Millay and James Joyce. From fashion tips to marriage advice columns, from movies to popular dances and games, from life on a cruise ship to Parisian cafés with news flashes about Babe Ruth and Charles Lindbergh, Frankie's journal, produced on colorful, glossy paper, presents an entertaining and informative introduction to a past era.

1. Analyze the memorabilia in Frankie's scrapbook and discuss how it contributes to creating a history of mass culture in the 1920s.
2. Discuss what can be learned about the lifestyle, writing opportunities, and culture in the 1920s from an analysis of the covers, advertisements, and stories from *True Story* magazine, at the Internet Archive (http://archive.org/details/truestorymagazin00mag).

World War I

Frost, Helen. *Crossing Stones.* Frances Foster Books/Farrar, Straus & Giroux, 2009. 184 pp. Grades 7–12. *Booklist* Top 10 HF, 2010; YALSA BB, 2010.

In this verse novel set in Michigan from April 1917 through to January 1918, Frost focuses on both World War I and women's suffrage. Eighteen-year-old Muriel and her sixteen-year-old brother, Ollie, are best friends with Frank and Emma Norman, who live on the neighboring farm. In alternating voices, Muriel, Ollie, and Emma tell how life changes for them during the year that Frank and then Ollie enlist and are sent to the front. In free verse, Muriel expresses her opposition to the war even before she loses her close friend Frank, killed at the front, and before Ollie returns, traumatized and with only one arm. Issues address censorship and the Espionage Act of 1917. The presence of the war lingers as Muriel's young sister Grace contracts influenza.

Muriel experiences women's fight for suffrage firsthand when she is sent to Washington, DC, to bring home her aunt, a suffragette, and learns about the abuse to which the suffragettes are subjected as they picket outside the White House. She hears her aunt speak of the hunger strike and force-feeding endured by those who are arrested "for obstruction" while their attackers go free. In an epilogue, Frost provides brief information about the passing of the Nineteenth Amendment.

1. Discuss examples of Muriel's questioning of the war.
2. What effect did the "Espionage Act" of 1917 have on civil liberties and free speech? Related website: The Espionage Act and the Limitations of the First Amendment (http://ows.edb.utexas.edu/site/espionage-act-and-limitations-first-amendment).

Adult Fiction

Mullen, Thomas. *The Last Town on Earth.* Random, 2006. 394 pp. Cooper, 2007.

It is 1918 and Commonwealth, a small Washington mill town, enforces a quarantine to keep out the Spanish flu that is ravaging the neighboring town of Timber Falls. The consequences become clear when the guard Graham Stone, accompanied by sixteen-year-old Philip Worthy, adopted son of mill owner Charles Worthy, shoots and buries an armed soldier who demands food and shelter. The situation is exacerbated when Philip is locked away in quarantine for forty-eight hours with a second soldier—a conscientious objector—whom Philip offers shelter. An atmosphere of fear pervades Commonwealth as neighbors isolate themselves and as people succumb, despite the quarantine, to the flu, about which little is known because of government censorship.

Set against World War I, the situation worsens when Timber Rock's American Protective League, charged with enforcing the draft, forcibly removes Commonwealth mill workers who have evaded enlistment, including those that are sick. Other issues include the fear of spies, the treatment of conscientious objectors, and the voices of dissenters. The book also makes reference to the suffrage movement and its links to the Women's Peace Party, the mill workers' associations with the Industrial Workers of the World (Wobblies), and the Everett strike and massacre in 1916. In his notes, Mullen provides additional information about radical communities such as Commonwealth, the Everett massacre, the American Protective League, and the 1918 influenza epidemic. Further reading suggestions are also included.

1. Discuss the policy of isolation and its relevance to World War I.
2. Related site: "Everett Massacre Collection," University Libraries, University of Washington (http://content.lib.washington.edu/pnwlaborweb/).

CHAPTER 7

The Great Depression and World War II
(1929–1945)

The Great Depression and Prohibition

Bryant, Jen. *The Trial.* 2004; Yearling, 2005. 176 pp. Grades 5–9.

On March 1, 1932, Colonel Charles and Anne Lindbergh's baby was kidnapped from their home in Hopewell, New Jersey. In free verse, Katie Flynn reports on the kidnapping and on the trial in 1935 of Richard Hauptmann in Flemington, New Jersey. A highly publicized trial, its outcome is still debated. When Katie's uncle, a reporter for the Hunterdon *Democrat* breaks his arm, Katie is given permission to take six weeks off from school to help her uncle record the trial. She lists the jury members, discusses the attorneys for the prosecution and defense, and presents the evidence (some circumstantial) used to convict Hauptmann. Katie's in-depth reporting includes the effect of the trial on Flemington, New Jersey, as it is invaded by the media and celebrities, including Jack Dempsey, Ginger Rogers, photographer Margaret Bourke-White, and broadcaster Walter Winchell. Bryant includes quotes from different participants in the trial. In an epilogue, she discusses the evidence and Hauptmann's execution.

Katie's personal life and her reporting on the trial are placed in the context of the Great Depression. She describes the effects of the economy on the town and people's lives. She sees, for example, the boxcars that carry "a new kind of cargo" (81). Headlines from the *New York Times* on Katie's bedroom wall document the issues of the time, such as the repeal of Prohibition, dust storms in the Midwest, and Roosevelt's address to the nation. Bryant writes about her research in the "author's note."

1. Discuss the effects of the economic and political climate of the Depression on the trial and on the town of Flemington.
2. Related reading: Greg Roensch, *The Lindbergh Baby Kidnapping Trial: A Primary Source Account* (Rosen, 2005).

Hale, Marian. *The Truth about Sparrows.* 2004; Square Fish, 2007. 288 pp. Grades 5–8.

In 1933, twelve-year-old Sadie and her family join the many people leaving their Missouri homes because of the drought. Sadie's father can no longer find work as a mechanic or carpenter. Set during the Depression, Hale's story bears witness to the hardships of families making their way across the country with the few belongings they can carry. The Wynn family heads for Texas, and they settle on the Gulf of Mexico coast at Aransas Pass on unclaimed vacant land next to the seawall. Here, Sadie comes to face the reality that a black tar-papered one-room shack with a dirt floor and cardboard-covered walls will be their home for the unforeseeable future.

Sadie learns about the extent of the Depression: thirteen million men out of work, men fighting over garbage, and children sleeping under "Hoover blankets." A lone man sleeps nearby in a cardboard box. Sadie struggles with displacement and loss and with being labeled a "bay rat." But Hale's story shows a family working to make a new start as Sadie's disabled father builds a fishing boat and her mother makes their shack a home. A central theme is the forging of new relationships and support networks with families in similar circumstances.

1. Discuss the effects of the Depression on families and children living at Aransas Pass.
2. Discuss the role of Sadie and her friends in helping their families to survive.

Ingold, Jeanette. *Hitch.* 2005. Graphia, 2006. 288 pp. Grades 7–10.

In 1936, seventeen-year-old Moss Trawnley's plans to attend radio school are shelved when he is told that his part-time job at the airport in Muddy Springs, Texas, is to be given to a man with a family to support. He hitches a ride on a train to Montana, where he hopes to find his father, who had left Moss's mother and siblings in Louisiana to work on a Works Progress Administration (WPA) project. But when Moss finds him, he discovers that his father, bitter from the foreclosure of his cotton farm and too proud to accept WPA work, is now a shiftless alcoholic. After Moss and his father spend a night in jail for traveling on a train without tickets, the court justice of the peace gives Moss a newspaper cutting about the Civilian Conservation Corps. Leaving his father, Moss enrolls in the CCC, which is supervised by the US Army, and goes to Fort Missoula for two weeks' training. He is then sent with others to establish a new CCC camp near Monroe, Montana, under the auspices of the Soil Conservation Service.

The story of Moss's first six months in the CCC incorporates the goals of a New Deal program designed to help boys by providing them with work and opportunities to learn new skills. In camps established across the country, boys like Moss worked on conservation projects: planting forests, building parks and wildlife refuges, and restoring depleted farmland. Moss and his new friends settle into the discipline of camp life as they build barracks and other facilities. They build a reservoir as part of the CCC's efforts to restore farming land depleted by the practice of dry farming. Moss soon shows that he possesses the qualities to be a junior leader. Ingold's story shows how the Depression affected people's morale and behavior and depicts its effects on young people and their families. In a note, Ingold explains that although there was no "Civilian Conservation Company 597" in Montana, there were 4,500 camps nationwide. A select reading list is also provided.

1. Give specific examples of skills and learning opportunities provided by CCC to Moss and his friends.
2. Analyze the CCC's relationship with the local community, including its role in changing farming practices.

3. Related website: "CCC Legacy History Center," Civilian Conservation Corps Legacy (www.ccclegacy.org/CCC_History_Center.html).

Lisle, Janet Taylor. *Black Duck.* 2006; Penguin, 2007. 256 pp. Grades 7–10. NSSTB, 2007; YALSA BB, 2007.

David Peterson's ambition to be a journalist leads him to interview Ruben Hart, rumored to be a rumrunner during Prohibition. Hart tells David about smuggling in the vicinity of Newport, Rhode Island, in 1929. Ruben is fourteen years old when he and his best friend, Jeddy McKenzie, son of the local police chief, discover the body of a prominent local smuggler on the beach and learn about the freighters from Canada and other countries that anchor in international waters, waiting for local craft to unload cases of liquor. Ruben describes the activity on beaches as vehicles line up for their share of the lucrative cargo that helps families during hard times.

Lisle's novel makes clear how many participated in the pervasive corruption accompanying Prohibition in payoffs that involved police, customs officials, and judges, as well as Ruben's father, the manager of the local store. Violence increases when mobsters from Boston and New York muscle in on the locals. The episode of the machine-gunning of three members of the *Black Duck* on December 29, 1929, by the Coast Guard is based on a real event. Excerpts from Newport's *Daily Journal* from 1929 and 1930 about the controversial shootings are inserted in the text. In her notes, Lisle discusses the public outcry following the *Black Duck* incident and the repeal of Prohibition in 1933.

1. Discuss the effect of Prohibition on Ruben's community.
2. Discuss issues raised in Lisle's novel that led to the repeal of Prohibition.
3. Related website: Amendments 18 and 21, at "Bill of Rights and Later Amendments," Historic Documents (www.ushistory.org/documents/amendments.htm#amend18).

Meltzer, Milton. *Tough Times.* Clarion Books, 2007. 168 pp. Grades 5–8. NSSTB, 2008.

Set in Worcester, Massachusetts, this compelling and detailed account of what it was like to live through the Depression is told by high school senior Joey Singer. Joey rises twice a week at two o'clock in the morning to deliver milk, and his father's window-cleaning business is shrinking as factories and businesses close. Newspapers describe the towns around Worcester: their empty, broken-down houses and long lines of people hoping for a day's work. Integrated into the story are examples of numbers of the unemployed and prices of food.

Meltzer's story focuses on World War I veterans' demand to be given the bonus payments promised them by Congress in 1924 but not due to be paid until 1945. Desperate veterans march by the thousands to Washington, DC, to demand that the government honor its pledge in 1932. Joey is witnesses to the violence as Hoover orders the police to clear the Bonus Army from federal property. When the police fail, General MacArthur employs tear gas, tanks, soldiers with drawn bayonets, and the cavalry—armed with sabers—to attack men, women, and children. They set fire to the abandoned apartment buildings and Hooverville camps where the Bonus Army was sheltering. Meltzer especially shows the effects of the Depression on children who ride "the rods," camp out, and beg for food. He provides more information about the Depression and the Bonus Army in the "historical note."

1. Discuss the response to and the effects of President Hoover's and General MacArthur's actions against the Bonus Army.
2. Related website: For primary documents and photographs, see "The Bonus Army March," American Treasures of the Library of Congress (www.loc.gov/exhibits/treasures/trm203.html).

Peck, Richard. *A Year Down Yonder.* Dial, 2000. 130 pp. Grades 6–9. *Booklist* Top 10 Fiction for Youth; Newbery, 2001; YALSA BB, 2001.

In 1937, during the "Roosevelt recession," fifteen-year-old Mary Alice is sent from Chicago to stay with her Grandmother Dowdel, who lives in a small town in rural Illinois. Her father has lost his job, and her parents have moved from their apartment to a "light housekeeping room" that is large enough for only two people. Her elder brother, Joey, who had spent summers with her at their grandmother's, is away planting trees out west with the Civilian Conservation Corps, so Mary Alice travels alone on the Wabash Railroad Blue Bird train with only her cat for company. Met by her formidable-looking grandmother, she is immediately hustled to the wood-sided school with its bell tower and enrolled by the principal, who also serves as the school janitor and coach. With a light touch, Peck tells about life in a small town during the Depression. As Mary Alice explains, "Two topics on everyone's mind there at the end of 1937 were something to eat and money" (57). Her grandmother has strategies for making do, including acquiring the ingredients for pecan and pumpkin pies that she shares at Halloween, trapping foxes for pelts, and charging a steep rent of $2.50 from the artist who arrives to paint murals on the local post office as part of the Works Progress Administration. Peck shows how the townspeople share and are part of a history that goes beyond local boundaries, as they remember Armistice Day by raising money to support a woman whose disabled son was gassed in the trenches of World War I. The novel closes with Mary Alice's marriage to a boy who is a soldier in World War II and whom she met during the year she lived with her grandmother.

1. Identify the details that Peck includes to convey a sense of how people lived in a rural town in the 1930s. Discuss the importance and purpose of celebrations and seasonal festivities to the town.
2. Discuss the government's role in the Depression. See, for example, "By the People, for the People: Posters from the WPA, 1936–1943," Library of Congress (www.loc.gov/teachers/classroommaterials/connections/wpa-posters/).

Ryan, Pamela Muñoz. *Esperanza Rising.* Scholastic Press, 2000. 262 pp. Grades 5–8. Belpré, 2002; Addams, 2001; NSSTB, 2001.

Esperanza's story partly parallels the life of Ryan's grandmother, Esperanza Ortega, who was forced to move from a ranch in Aguascalientes, Mexico, to a "company-owned labor camp in Arvin, California"

(256). In 1930, the day before her thirteenth birthday, Esperanza's father, Sixto, is killed by bandits on his ranch. When Sixto's stepbrothers burn down the ranch house to force Esperanza's mother to marry the elder brother, she escapes with Esperanza and their former servants to a labor camp in California, where their former servant's brother has arranged for them to work and live. Written from the perspective of Esperanza, the novel tells of the transformation of a rich, pampered "princess" who has difficulty adjusting to her "peasant" life in the tiny cabin that she shares with her mother and others but who changes as she works in the camp. When her mother is hospitalized with valley fever after a dust storm, Esperanza works in the packing sheds. The sequence of harvested crops used for chapter headings marks the passing of the seasons.

Included in this vivid account of life in a labor camp is information about the workers' strikes for better wages and conditions, even as there is an influx of additional workers from Oklahoma and Texas. In the author's note, Ryan tells about the deportation of strikers to Mexico (including native-born US citizens) as part of the "voluntary repatriation" program between 1929 and 1935.

1. Discuss the transformation of Esperanza and her attitudes toward Mexican workers.
2. Discuss the arguments made by strikers and the opposing position held by Esperanza's family and other migrant workers.

Vanderpool, Clara. *Moon over Manifest.* Delacorte, 2010. 351 pp. Grades 5–8. ALA Notable, 2011; *Booklist* Top 10 HF, 2011; Newbery, 2011; NSSTB, 2011; Spur, 2011.

On May 27, 1936, twelve-year-old Abilene Tucker jumps off the train on the outskirts of Manifest, Kansas, where her father, Gideon Tucker, has sent her to live with "Shady" (Pastor Howard), a former saloon owner and a bootlegger. The past and present come together as Abilene describes the boarded-up and dingy storefronts of Manifest in 1936. She learns about the secrets buried in her father's and in Manifest's past when she finds a tin box filled with mementos, including a homemade map and letters addressed to Jinx from Ned Gillen in 1918. In one letter, dated January 15, 1918, Ned warns about the "Rattler" and German spies, and Abilene and her friends Ruthanne and Lettie know that they have many mysteries to solve. But their sleuthing takes them into a past that the community of Manifest would rather not remember. In solving Jinx's identity, Abilene also learns the truth about her father's past and why he did not return to Manifest. Sadie, a Hungarian "diviner," tells Abilene stories about Gillen, an orphan adopted by the hardware owner in town, and Jinx, a runaway taken in by Shady. Set in 1917 and 1918, these stories tell about Ned and Jinx's encounter with the Ku Klux Klan, Ned's work in the mines before enlisting in the army, and Jinx's plan to outwit mine owners. Interspersed with Ned's letters and Sadie's stories are Hattie Mae Mack's "News Auxiliary"— gossipy newspaper columns written during 1917 and 1918 in which Hattie Mae observes and comments on community events.

Vanderpool provides lists of the townspeople (characters in her novel) who lived in Manifest in 1918 and 1936. In 1918, Hattie Mae Harper was listed as a journalist for the *Manifest Herald*. Vanderpool bases Manifest on the town of Frontenac, Kansas, a mining town in 1918 with a population of immigrants from many countries. She creates an in-depth cultural and social history of Manifest from 1918 to 1936 and shows how past events, such as immigration, Prohibition, working conditions in the local mines, and the influenza epidemic, affected the community. The letters sent from Ned Gillen to his Jinx tell about the conditions in the trenches in France during World War I. In her notes, Vanderpool gives more information about the novel's topics in a glossary, as well as suggestions for further reading.

1. Identify examples of the effects of the Depression on Manifest's community.
2. Discuss Manifest's community in regard to its diverse immigrant population.
3. Identify and analyze the strategies Vanderpool uses to bring together the social history of a community.

Adult Fiction

Byers, Michael. *Percival's Planet: A Novel.* 2010. St. Martin's Press, 2011. 432 pp. *Booklist* Top 10 HN, 2011.

The heart of Byers's novel is the search for Planet X, which resulted in the 1930 discovery of Pluto by Clyde Tombaugh at Lowell Observatory, in Flagstaff, Arizona. The story follows the young Tombaugh from his family's farm in Kansas, where he grinds and polishes telescope mirrors as an amateur astronomer, to his appointment at Lowell in 1929. Byers conveys Tombaugh's unrelenting passion as he meticulously photographs the night sky and scans the plates using the blinking comparator for evidence of the planet whose existence had been hypothesized by Percival Lowell. Byers sets Tombaugh's story in a larger context as Flagstaff becomes a focal point for astronomers and for paleontologists. Fictional characters include Vesto Slipher, the director of the observatory who has contributed to "Hubble's great theory of the expanding universe," and Alan Barber, who is to resume the "photographic hunt for Planet X" twelve years after Lowell's death (27). Byers's story includes details of mathematical formulas used to locate the planet, information about the Lowell telescopes, and the paradox involving calculations of orbit and mass used to fix Pluto's location. Parallel stories about fictional characters are set against the crash of Wall Street and the Depression. In an author's note, Byers explains that he has adapted Clyde Tombaugh's life from historical accounts but has "shaped and altered historical materials" for his novel (415).

1. Compare Alan Barber's discussion with Vesto Slipher, director of Lowell Astronomy, on Pluto (356–59) with Tombaugh's account of the discovery. Related website: Transcripts of Dr. Clyde Tombaugh, Niels Bohr Library and Archives, with the Center for the History of Physics (www.aip.org/history/ohilist/4916.html).
2. How do Barber's doubts relate to the reclassification of Pluto as a dwarf planet? Related website: NASA, "Pluto Classification and Exploration" (www.nasa.gov/exploration/whyweexplore/Why_We_23_prt.htm).

3. How does Byers's novel illustrate the effects of the crash of Wall Street and the Depression?

Gruen, Sara. *Water for Elephants.* Algonquin Books, 2006. 335 pp. Alex, 2007; YALSA OB, 2009.

Gruen presents an illuminating glimpse into the milieu of the circus during the Depression. In 1931, twenty-three-year-old Jacob is in his final year of veterinary studies at Cornell University when his parents are killed in an automobile accident. Jacob's first-person narrative weaves back and forth between the elderly Jacob, who tells of his frustrated life in a nursing home, and the young Jacob, who, unable to write his final exams at Cornell, jumps aboard the Benzini Brothers' circus train and is hired as the circus vet. Jacob's narrative exposes the underside of the glamour of the big top: the divide between performers and working men, and practices in which wages are withheld and unwanted men "redlighted." The illusory magic of the circus is dispelled as animals are held hostage in a business deal with a failed circus, and the ringmaster tortures the elephant Rosie. The effects of the Depression and Prohibition are seen in raids on a speakeasy and on the circus's alcohol cache, and in the paralysis caused by drinking toxic "Jamaica ginger extract." Black-and-white photographs from circus archives and sources for the author's research are included.

1. Discuss the effects of the Depression on the Benzini Brothers' circus.
2. Related website: Julie Zykan, "The Struggling Circus" (www .columbiamissourian.com/media/multimedia/2007/pages/circus/ index.html).

Vance, James, and Dan Burr. *Kings in Disguise.* 1990; W. W. Norton, 2006. 184 pp.

This classic story of one boy's experience of the Depression was first issued as a graphic novel in 1990. Set in 1932, the dialogue and graphics present a compelling representation of life during the Depression: the destitute and out of work who spend their lives riding trains, sleeping wherever they are able, fending off violence, and stealing for survival. When his father leaves to look for work, twelve-year-old Freddie Bloch runs from home. He is rescued from a hobo predator by Sam, the "King of Spain," who takes him under his wing as they hop a train and travel together. Burr's stark illustrations depict hobos gathered together in fields, on street corners, in protest marches, in a shanty-town—their faces mirroring their desperate lives.

When Fred and Sam arrive in Detroit to search for Fred's father, they are caught up in the hunger march on March 7, 1932, against Ford Motor Company, in which police shoot protestors and arrest suspected communists. The story illustrates the role of the Salvation Army in the Depression as they help Sam, who is injured during the shooting. The novel demonstrates that although there are helping hands and comradeship, there are no false hopes. Sam, desperately ill, finds his way home, but Fred is back on the road searching for "another dream" (184).

1. Compare the novel's representation of the march against the Ford Motor Company's Dearborn complex with the article, "The Ford Hunger March of 1932," Workers World (www.workers.org/2009/us/ford_hunger_march_0402/).
2. Discuss the lessons Fred learns as a hobo.

Immigration to the West Coast

Adult Fiction

See, Lisa. *Shanghai Girls: A Novel.* Random House, 2009. 314 pp.

Spanning the years from 1937 to 1957, the novel begins with Pearl's family's comfortable life in Shanghai, where she and her sister, May, work as part-time models and are known as "beautiful girls." But in 1937, their father, deep in debt, arranges for them to be married to the sons of "Old Man Louie" who live in Los Angeles. The girls and their mother are forced to flee when the Japanese approach Shanghai. Pearl and her mother are raped by Japanese soldiers on the way to Hong Kong, and Pearl's mother dies as a result. When Pearl and May arrive at Angel Island, San Francisco, they are interrogated by immigration officials who are suspicious of Louie's family records. As Pearl and May later discover, Louie has sold and bought "paper sons" to circumvent strict immigration laws. See's novel includes details of these laws and their effects on families. She explains in her notes that the sisters' interrogations are taken from transcripts of actual examinations.

See provides a wide-angle view of Chinese immigrants and their culture in Los Angeles. When the sisters arrive at the shabby apartment of Louie's family, they are put to work in their autocratic father-in-law's businesses in China City. Over the years, they see Louie's businesses burn down, and they learn that the Chinese cannot own property, that many people will not rent to them, and that Pearl's daughter is not welcome at a school outside China City. After Pearl Harbor, Pearl describes the effects of World War II on Chinese immigrants. The establishment of Mao Tse-tung's People's Republic of China in 1949 and the Korean War bring new discriminatory laws. Pearl's family falls under suspicion when government agents search for suspected communists under the "Confession Program." The situation of Pearl and her family exemplifies the fear, arrests, and suicides experienced by Chinese immigrants in the 1950s. See provides information on her sources and distinguishes fictional characters and actual people.

1. Discuss the effects of immigration laws in the 1930s and 1940s on Chinese immigrants.
2. Identify the changes that World War II brought to Chinese immigrants.
3. Discuss the implication of Pearl's statement that some may see "girls who are yellow in race" as "red in ideology" (244) in relation to the US government's fears of communism.

World War II

Bruchac, Joseph. *Code Talker: A Novel about the Navajo Marines of World War II.* Dial, 2005. 231 pp. Grades 6–9. *Booklist* Top 10 HF, 2005; NSSTB, 2006; YALSA BB, 2006.

When he was six years old, Kii Yázhi was sent to the Rehoboth Mission School where, he tells his grandchildren, he was there told that his language and culture were useless. Stripped of his Navajo identity, he was renamed Ned Begay. But he studied hard and secretly spoke Navajo with his friends, so he was ready to sign up when the US Marines came looking for recruits fluent in Navajo and English to be trained as code talkers. He signed up in 1943 at the age of sixteen. After training, he is sent with the US Marines to the Pacific and plays a vital role in relaying and receiving coded radio messages as the Americans invade Bougainville, Guam, Iwo Jima, and Okinawa.

In an author's note, Bruchac provides a history of the Navajo, including reference to the government boarding schools where "everything that was Indian was forbidden" (220). He explains how the Navajo code talkers' secret work remained classified until 1969, when their dedication and bravery was finally acknowledged. A select bibliography is included.

1. Discuss Ned's Navajo perspective and attitude toward war and how his culture and traditions enable him to excel as a marine.
2. Discuss the treatment of the Navajo in the US Marines.
3. Related website: Central Intelligence Agency, "Navajo Code Talkers and the Unbreakable Code" (use search box at www.cia.gov).

Davis, Tanita S. *Mare's War.* Knopf, 2009. 341 pp. Grades 7–10. King honor, 2010; NSSTB, 2010; YALSA BB, 2010.

In chapters titled "Now," Octavia tells how she and her older sister, Tali, are driving to a family reunion with their grandmother, Mare, from San Francisco to Bay Slough, Alabama. In the chapters titled "Then," Mare reminisces about her past and tells her granddaughters about her decision to join the Women's Army Corps in 1944 despite being underage. As Mare writes in the note she leaves her mother, "Even colored girls can join the Women's Army" (46). After passing the required written examination, she goes to Des Moines, Iowa, where she studies sanitation, first aid, maps, typing, coding, and signal duties. She tells her grandchildren how she and her companions adjusted to life the GI way. After extensive physical and field training at Camp Oglethorpe, she is shipped out to Birmingham, England, as part of the 888th Central

Postal Battalion, commanded by Major Charity Adams. The battalion was responsible for redirecting mail to US personnel in England and Europe.

Mare describes long shifts in wartime England, with rationing, blackouts, and the ever-present danger from V-1 bombs, before she is sent for duty in Rouen and Paris.

Davis addresses important aspects related to the enlistment of African American women in the Women's Army Corps. Davis points out that women's contributions to World War II have not been sufficiently recognized in textbooks and provides sources that document that history.

1. Discuss ways that Mare and her colleagues experience segregation and attitudes held about members of the Women's Army Corps in the United States and overseas.
2. Related reading: Charity Adams Earley, *One Woman's Army: A Black Officer Remembers the WAC* (Texas A&M University Press, 1989).

Fletcher, Christine. *Ten Cents a Dance.* Bloomsbury, 2008. 394 pp. Grades 9–12. NSSTB, 2009; YALSA BB, 2009.

When her mother loses her job in a Chicago packing factory in 1941, fifteen-year-old Ruby leaves school and packs pickled pigs' feet in brine for $12.25 a week. A talented dancer, she is accepted as a taxi dancer at the Starlight Dance Academy. Ruby finds that it is not an easy life: the pay is only a nickel a dance plus tips. The real money, she discovers, is in catching "fish," those who would buy extras for an attractive girl's company. In her notes, Fletcher writes that her story came from a family member who was a taxi dancer and explains more about the gray area of the taxi-dancing business, popular in the United States from the 1920s until World War II, and in which girls could earn more money than in a factory or other socially acceptable jobs.

Ruby spends time at Chicago's "black and tan clubs," including the best jazz club in town. She experiences the underside of Chicago as she extricates herself from Paulie, a would-be local monster with whom she had become romantically involved, by enlisting the support of the "policy king," head of a gambling syndicate. Her story also illustrates how World War II affects her life as a close friend enlists and her younger sister becomes a victory girl. By the close of the novel, Ruby is working in an aircraft factory in San Diego, and her mother and sister have a new life away from the stench of the stockyards and meatpacking factories.

1. Discuss how Ruby's story exposes racial prejudice.
2. Discuss Ruby's choices and decisions.

Flood, Nancy Bo. *Warriors in the Crossfire.* Front Street, 2010. 142 pp. Grades 6–9. *Booklist* Top 10 HF, 2011; YALSA BF, 2011.

The invasion of Saipan by American forces in 1944 is filtered through thirteen-year-old Joseph, whose family is caught in the cross fire as the Japanese defend the island. Joseph narrates how the native islanders are subject to the orders of the Japanese, who vigorously enforce curfew, close schools and stores, desecrate their church, and readily execute those who show resistance. Joseph has also heard the Japanese warning that American "white-faced soldiers were hungry to eat" island children (39). Flood integrates into her story the actual flight of many islanders to caves in the cliffs, where they faced hunger and thirst and risked being shot. As the signs of battle increase, Joseph's father, broken by beatings, returns home to die. After carrying his body through rain, shells, and gunfire to the river, Joseph leads the family to the well-hidden cave shown to him previously by his father.

Central to Flood's story is the friendship between Joseph and Kento, Joseph's half-Japanese cousin. Their relationship is strained by conflicting loyalties due to the war. When Kento appears at the cave to ask for help, Joseph assists him with the rescue of Kento's mother and sister, who, together with other Japanese civilians, have been rounded up by Japanese soldiers who are forcing them to jump from the island's "Suicide Cliff." American helicopters, meanwhile, circle above, dropping leaflets exhorting people to surrender rather than jump. When Joseph's sister is wounded, an American soldier directs the family to a camp set apart for islanders. Information about the invasion and "Suicide Cliff" is provided in Flood's notes along with a short reading list.

1. Discuss how the setting and traditional culture of Saipan shape Joseph's character. How is Japanese culture important to him?
2. Discuss the strategic importance of Saipan.

Lisle, Janet Taylor. *The Art of Keeping Cool.* 2000; Atheneum, 2002. 256 pp. Grades 5–8. ALA Notable, 2001; *Booklist* Top 10 HF, 2001; O'Dell, 2001.

Set in Rhode Island in 1942, Lisle's story tells how suspicion and prejudice destroy a man in time of war. Thirteen-year-old Robert remembers the year that he, his mother, and younger sister left their farm in Ohio to stay in their grandfather's cottage on Sachem's Head while his father, a bomber pilot, was based in England. Three months after Pearl Harbor, there has been a noticeable buildup of artillery at nearby Fort Brooks. The wartime setting is heightened by the description of blackout regulations, rations, and heightened security, and by Robert's father's letters describing the dangers of bombing missions, before he is reported missing. As sightings of German submarines and the torpedoing of ships off the coast increase, suspicion builds against a German artist, Abel Hoffman, who has been seen observing the fort and its guns with binoculars from a closed area. Robert expresses his doubts about Hoffman, but Robert's cousin Elliot, a promising artist, has spent time with Hoffman, eager to learn from a leading German expressionist painter who is creating a new body of work. Through Abel's story, the boys learn about the persecution of German artists by the Nazis, who despised "degenerate" works of modern art and forbid them to be sold or exhibited. Abel had escaped to the United States, but as Lisle's story shows, fear can overcome tolerance and reason as Hoffman is subjected to mob violence.

1. Discuss Hoffman's persecution in Nazi Germany in relation to his treatment in wartime Rhode Island. Discuss Hoffman's actions and relationship with the Rhode Island community in the context of

war. Related website: "Degenerate Art," A Teacher's Guide to the Holocaust (http://fcit.usf.edu/holocaust/arts/artdegen.htm).

2. Discuss how the war has affected Robert's family. In what ways are the story of Robert's grandfather, his father, and Elliot connected to the story of Hoffman?

Pearsall, Shelley. *Jump into the Sky.* Knopf, 2012. 344 pp. Grades 6–8. ALA Notable, 2012; NSSTB, 2012; *Booklist* Top 10 HF, 2013.

In 1945, thirteen-year-old Levi's aunt Odella decides that Levi's father, who has been in the army for three years, should take responsibility for his son, so she puts Levi on a train to Fayetteville, North Carolina. Uncle Otis comments on the inadvisability of sending to the South "a colored boy" who does not know the rules, but Levi does not understand his uncle's warnings until he experiences the Jim Crow laws in Fayetteville. Levi arrives at Camp Mackall only to find that his father's battalion has been reassigned. Calvin Thomas, a paratrooper with the 555th Parachute Infantry Battalion (known as the "Triple Nickels"), and his wife, Peaches, offer Levi temporary shelter until Cal receives his orders to join the battalion in Pendleton, Oregon. Levi travels with them and finally meets Second Lieutenant Battle whose letters to Levi and Odella about his service as a paratrooper had been received with incredulity. Against the background of news of the war and the surrender of Germany, Levi hears the frustration of highly trained troops who think that their mission to track Japanese hot-air balloons carrying explosives and bombs and fight the resulting fires may be another ploy to avoid sending them to a war where they would jump alongside white paratroopers. With no signs of Japanese balloons, they are soon deployed in the dangerous mission of fighting forest fires in Oregon and other states. When his father opts to continue a promising career in the army, Levi must decide whether to return to Chicago or go with his father back to the South.

In her notes, Pearsall provides additional information about the 555th Parachute Infantry Battalion and notes her interview with Walter Morris, the first African American selected to become a paratrooper. She explains that many of the names and places are real and that several scenes are adapted from written and recorded interviews with men from the 555th Battalion.

1. In what ways does Pearsall's novel make visible the 555th Battalion's subjection to racial discrimination and prejudice before their integration into the regular army in 1947? Discuss Levi's father's responses to the paratroopers' anger over their wartime service.
2. Identify narrative strategies that convey characters' awareness and fears of war.
3. Related reading: Tanya Lee Stone, *Courage Has No Color: The True Story of the Triple Nickels, America's First Black Paratroopers* (Candlewick Press, 2013).

Peck, Richard. *On the Wings of Heroes.* 2007; Puffin, 2008. 160 pp. Grades 5–8. NSSTB, 2008.

Peck seamlessly interweaves historical details into Davy Bowman's first-person account of his everyday life in a small town in Illinois during World War II. Davy evokes a sense of nostalgia as he describes his neighborhood, his boyhood games, and holiday rituals with his older brother Bill and his father, who owns a gas station. But things change with the bombing of Pearl Harbor. The older boys, including Bill, enlist, and Davy and his best friend, Scooter, are soon collecting various materials for the war effort. Peck re-creates the experience of the home front: patriotic songs, war posters, rationing, a neighbor's victory garden, women's changing roles, and the war's effect on families. There are myriad fascinating details presented, such as the government's need for spiderwebs to use as the crosshairs of guns. The war is brought closer when Bill, a bomber pilot, is reported missing. A sense of the past is also conveyed through elderly characters still caught up in memories of the Civil War and World War I. Davy's story thus can be seen as part of the longer historical memory of a community.

1. Related website: "World War II on the Homefront: Civic Responsibility," Smithsonian Education (www.smithsonianeducation.org/ educators/lesson_plans/civic_responsibility/index.html).

2. Discuss the different ways Davy fulfills his civic responsibilities during the war.
3. Examine war posters on the Smithsonian website (www.smith sonianeducation.org/educators/lesson_plans/civic_responsibility/index.html). What are the main themes of these and of posters mentioned in Peck's text?
4. Discuss the challenges Davy's family faces in operating a gas station during the war.

Salisbury, Graham. *Eyes of the Emperor.* 2005; Laurel Leaf, 2007. 256 pp. Grades: 7–10. *Booklist* Top 10 HF, 2006; NSSTB, 2006; YALSA BB, 2006.

Sixteen-year-old Eddy Okubo's father is a first-generation Japanese American who reveres Japanese culture and traditions. After listening to the war news about Japan, Eddy fudges the date on his birth certificate and joins the US Army, because he is determined to prove that he is American—"a nisei, born and raised" in Hawaii (5). After the bombing of Pearl Harbor, Eddy finds that the military treat Japanese Americans with suspicion and prejudice. The army, however, has a special task for Eddy and his fellow soldiers, who are taken to Cat Island, Mississippi, where they become part of a dog-training program approved by President Roosevelt. The premise is that Japanese have a different scent from white people, and therefore, dogs can be trained to track, attack, and kill any invading Japanese. Eddy and his friends, in effect, will be used as dog bait (126).

Eddy's first-person narrative conveys his courage and determination to fulfill his assignment and prove his worth as an American soldier. Salisbury's novel documents the prejudice against Japanese Americans civilians and soldiers. His research included interviews with eight of the twenty-six men who served on Cat Island. The names of the "Boys of Company B" are listed at the beginning of the novel.

1. "You are the enemy," Eddy and his fellow soldiers are told at the beginning of the dog-training program (129). Discuss the assumptions and ethics of the program.

Salisbury, Graham. *House of the Red Fish.* 2006; Laurel Leaf, 2008. 320 pp. Grades 5–8.

In a companion novel to *Under the Blood-Red Sun* (Delacorte, 1994), Salisbury's story here centers on Tomi Nakaji, whose fisherman father was arrested after the Japanese attack on Pearl Harbor along with other innocent fishermen of Japanese ancestry. Tomi's father's sampan was sunk, with ten others, in the Ala Wai Canal. Tomi's grandfather Joji, a Japanese citizen, forced to kill his homing pigeons, was also arrested. It is now 1943, and Tomi, just beginning ninth grade, has decided to raise his father's sampan from the canal. He confronts the prejudice of his former friend Keet Wilson, who resorts to harassment, thievery, and violence to prevent Tomi from rescuing the boat.

Salisbury's story shows how fear and tension in expectations of another Japanese attack or invasion affect Tomi and his family. Reference is made to the Businessmen's Military Training Corps, whose real mission was to "take care of *enemy aliens*" (43). But Salisbury's story also shows the support that Tomi and his grandfather receive, including help in securing the release of Tomi's grandfather. Salisbury also provides a glossary and a "reader's guide."

1. Discuss the role of fear in explaining characters' actions.

Smith, Sherri L. *Flygirl.* Putnam, 2008. 275 pp. Grades 7–10. *Booklist* Top 10 HN, 2009; NSSTB, 2010; YALSA BB, 2010.

Seventeen-year-old Ida Mae Jones loves to fly. Her father, a licensed pilot, had taught her to fly his crop duster, but when she takes the test for her pilot's license, the white instructor tells her that "no woman" is going "to get a license out of" him (8). When the Japanese bomb Pearl Harbor, Ida Mae joins the Women Airforce Service Pilots (WASP). Using her deceased father's pilot's license and relying on her light skin and brown hair, she applies for training at Sweetwater, Texas. Ida leads a double life as she makes friends with white girls, enters "whites-only" facilities, and dances with her white instructor. Although Ida must be constantly on guard and loses one of her best friends in WASP when her plane catches fire, she perseveres and earns her wings.

Smith integrates information about the training and work duties of the WASP into Ida's flying experiences. In one mission, for example, Ida pilots a B-29 bomber. Above all, Smith's novel tells how a young woman is forced to live her life as a lie in order to achieve her dreams and serve her country.

1. Discuss Ida's reasons for flying and serving her country despite discrimination and the dangers of posing as a white woman.
2. Ida wonders whether she is identified first as a woman or as "colored" (48). Discuss some of the ways in which Ida deals with issues of gender and race.
3. Discuss examples in the novel of the military's practice of discrimination against African Americans and women.
4. Related website: Wings across America (www.wingsacrossamerica.us).

Adult Fiction

Belfer, Lauren. *A Fierce Radiance.* 2010; Harper Perennial, 2011. 532 pp.

The development and mass production of penicillin during World War II is at the center of this novel, set in New York City. Claire Shipley, a photographer for *Life* magazine, is sent to the Rockefeller Institute of Medical Research to cover the testing of penicillin. There she observes patients treated by Dr. James Stanton; they recover but then die because of insufficient supplies. Vannevar Bush recruits Stanton to oversee research for the mass production of the latest war weapon. The book covers the history of the discovery of penicillin, the difficulties experienced in its production, the processes that eventually proved successful, and ethical concerns from multiple perspectives. In Belfer's story, the stipulation that the government, not companies, such as Merck and Pfizer, own the patents to penicillin production is used as the trigger in a murder plot that shows companies' eagerness to profit from developing penicillin "cousins" from soil samples. The treatment of Shipley's young son's pneumonia is used to highlight the ethics of the testing and use of newly discovered drugs.

The novel evokes the atmosphere of wartime New York. Characters based on real people include Vannevar Bush; *Life* magazine editor

Henry Luce; Pfizer's John Smith; and Anne Miller, the first American to be cured by penicillin. The journalistic work of fictional Claire Shipley, writes Belfer, was inspired by and sometimes "based on actual stories that ran in *Life* magazine during the war years" (530).

1. Discuss the relationship between World War II and the development of antibiotics. Related website: "Discovery and Development of Penicillin," ACS Chemistry for Life (use search box at www.acs.org).
2. Discuss the ethics of the drug companies.

Benjamin, Melanie. *The Aviator's Wife.* Delacorte, 2013. 402 pp.

When the celebrated aviator Charles Lindbergh asked Anne Morrow, the second daughter of Dwight Morrow, US ambassador to Mexico, to become his wife shortly after her graduation from Smith College in 1927, no one was more surprised than Morrow herself. The couple soon became known as the "Flying Lindberghs," as Anne, whom Charles taught to fly and navigate, becomes his copilot in mapping routes for the new passenger airlines and the first woman to be a licensed glider pilot. She also qualifies as a licensed radio operator. Benjamin stays close to the facts about the Lindberghs' lives and careers while exploring the inner life and emotions of Anne. The achievements of Charles, including his groundbreaking 1927 transatlantic flight and his involvement with the aviation industry, the emotional toll of the kidnapping of Charles Lindbergh Jr., and the constant hounding by the press and the public are viewed from Anne's perspective. Of particular interest are Anne's responses to her husband's fascination with the German Reich and her attitudes toward her husband's speeches on the policy of isolationism and his anti-Semitism. In the novel, she expresses her doubts as she writes the pamphlet "The Wave of the Future" (1940), in defense of her husband's political views. She acknowledges the criticism that hurt her personally and later expressed her regrets over not being true to her own beliefs.

The novel makes visible some of the fissures that Anne experienced in her marriage: the pull between being a mother and meeting her husband's demands that she fly with him; the struggle to bring up their five children in wartime under the direction of an autocratic and often absent father; and the need to fulfill her own ambition as a writer, which she realized with the publication of her best seller *Gift from the Sea* (1955). In her author's note, Benjamin clarifies the distinction she makes between what she has imagined and the historical record.

1. Discuss the ways Benjamin adds to and brings a different perspective and understanding to the lives and careers of Charles Lindbergh and Anne Morrow Lindbergh and the significance of her perspective to the historical record.
2. Related reading: Anne Morrow Lindbergh, *The Gift from the Sea* (1955; Pantheon, 2005).

Jordan, Hillary. *Mudbound.* 2008; Algonquin Books, 2009. 340 pp. Alex, 2009.

Set in the Mississippi Delta in the 1940s, Jordan's multiple-voiced narrative tells of how two families are caught up in the hate and prejudice of the Jim Crow South. After six years of marriage, Henry McAllen moves his wife, Laura, and two young daughters from Memphis to an isolated farm. While Henry enthuses over his land, Laura tells about the endless work in a house without indoor plumbing and electricity, and surrounded by a sea of brown fields and mud. She also tells of how she is constantly goaded by Henry's father, Pappy.

Things change when Ronsel, son of Henry's land tenants Florence and Hap, arrives home. Ronsel, who served as a tank commander under General Patton finds it intolerable to be subjected to derogatory treatment after being hailed as a hero in Europe. His narrative highlights the treatment of black soldiers in the military during World War II. He finds a sympathetic friend in Henry's brother, Jamie, a bomber pilot who has also returned home. Jamie and Ronsel, suffering from post-traumatic stress, share with each other that which they are unable to share with their families. Defying Jim Crow laws, Ronsel accepts Jimmy's invitations to ride up front in the McAllen's truck, but when his affair with a white German woman with whom he has a child comes to light, local Klan members, including Pappy, punish Ronsel. The voices of Laura, Henry, Florence, Hap, Jamie, and Ronsel relate from their different perspectives the buildup to the events that change their lives.

1. Discuss Ronsel's experiences in the war and how he confronted discrimination.
2. Discuss the effects of war on Henry and Jamie.

Roth, Philip. *The Plot Against America.* Houghton Mifflin, 2004. 391 pp. ALA Notable, 2005; Cooper, 2005; *SLJ* BABHS, 2004; YALSA OB, 2009.

In this alternative history, Roth imagines what would have happened if aviation hero and isolationist Charles Lindbergh had defeated Franklin Roosevelt in 1940. The young narrator Philip Roth describes the effects of Lindbergh's election on his family and the Jewish community in Newark as anxiety and fear build about a president who has expressed anti-Semitic views and shows his closeness to Nazi leaders. Newark's Rabbi Bengelsdorf endorses Lindbergh and becomes responsible for the Office of American Absorption. The office runs the Just Folks program, in which Philip's elder brother, Sandy, and other Jewish boys are sent to work on farms far away from home, and the Homesteading 42 program, in which Philip's father, an insurance agent with Metropolitan Life, is to be involuntarily transferred to Danville, Kentucky.

The book makes clear how a majority of Americans, including Jews, are lulled into complacency by their protection from a war as Lindbergh signs nonaggression pacts with the Nazis and the Japanese. Tensions in Philip's family and the nation increase as the Nazi leader von Rippentrop is invited to the White House and as anti-Semitic riots spread across the country, when Walter Winchell, a prominent critic of Lindbergh, is murdered. The novel closes with an unraveling of Lindbergh's administration, followed by the election of Roosevelt for a third term, together with the hypothesis that Lindbergh's disappearance is a Nazi plot. Akin to a "who's who" of the early 1940s, the pages of this book teem with names of politicians and leaders of the time—all of whom are included in Roth's biographical appendix. Philip's rich descriptions of his family's Newark neighborhood and the glimpse into New Jersey's mob world add local color to a complex and interesting novel.

1. Analyze the arguments for isolationism.
2. Discuss the reasons for Philip's father's convictions about the Lindbergh administration.

Shaara, Jeff. *No Less Than Victory: A Novel of World War II.* Ballantine, 2009. 449 pp. *Booklist* Top 10 HN, 2010.

This last volume in Shaara's trilogy (which also includes the 2006 *The Rising Tide* and the 2008 *The Steel Wave*) covers the European theater of war after the invasion of Normandy in 1944 to the surrender of Germany in May 1945. As in the previous books, Shaara constructs his text from the anonymously narrated point of view of various participants, which are based on first-person accounts, memoirs, diaries, and letters. Americans are represented by the bombardier Buckley, the rifleman Eddie Benson, and Generals Dwight Eisenhower and George Patton; the Germans by Commander Karl Gerd von Runstedt and Albert Speer, who visits Hitler's bunker during the Russian assault on Berlin. The surprise assault of the Germans, whose tanks surge over American lines in the snow-covered Ardennes in the Battle of the Bulge, is viewed from both American and German perspectives. Details of military strategies and maneuvers are provided, along with dates and maps. Shaara's graphic descriptions bring alive his participants' experiences of war, from Benson's mud-filled foxhole to Eisenhower's diplomacy, and the responses of each to the horrors of the Ohrdruf concentration camp.

Shaara includes Winston Churchill's warning to Eisenhower about the consequences of the Yalta Conference between Stalin and Roosevelt and the negotiations between the United States and Russia for Germany's surrender. The fall of Berlin and Hitler's final orders and suicide are narrated from Speer's perspective. The afterword provides biographical information for major participants.

1. Discuss the consequences of the agreement at Yalta regarding the deployment of Russian and US forces.
2. Discuss what is justifiable in war, using as an example the firebombing of Dresden.
3. Discuss Shaara's approach to reconstructing history.

Relocation

Bat-Ami, Miriam. *Two Suns in the Sky.* Front Street/Cricket Books, 1999. 223 pp. Grades 8–12. *Booklist* Top 10 HF, 2000; O'Dell, 2000; YALSA BB, 2000.

On August 3, 1944, Adam Borstein arrives with his mother and sister and other Jewish refugees at the Emergency Relief Shelter at Fort Ontario, in Oswego, New York, the only camp opened for refugees in the United States during World War II. His family had fled from Zagreb, Yugoslavia, but had become separated when returning to Yugoslavia to search for Adam's grandmother, at which time Adam's father and older brother joined Josip Broz Tito's Partisans against the Germans. Bat-Ami's story centers on the growing relationship between Adam and fourteen-year-old Chris Cook, as interaction between the camp residents and the people of Oswego increases. In alternating first-person narratives, Adam tells about life in the camp and his schooling at Oswego High School, and Chris tells about her neighbors and family, especially her prejudicial father, who forbids her from seeing Adam.

Excerpts from interviews with refugees and from President Roosevelt's speeches head each chapter. Bat-Ami builds her composite picture of the camp from documentary research and interviews with refugees and others, including Geraldine Rossiter. As a girl, Rossiter befriended the young people in the camp, and she serves as the pattern for Chris. Included in the novel are reproductions of official forms distributed to the refugees and war news. The novel addresses the roles of Presidents Roosevelt and Truman in bringing and freeing the refugees.

1. Discuss what the barbed-wire fence means to Adam and to others in the camp.
2. Discuss Oswego residents' attitudes toward the refugees.
3. Related website: "Emergency Refugee Shelter at Fort Ontario (Safe Haven)" (www.oswego.edu/library/archives/safe_haven.html).

Hesse, Karen. *Aleutian Sparrow.* 2003; Margaret K. McElderry Books, 2005. 160 pp. Grades 7–10. NSSTB, 2004.

In 1942, after the bombing of Pearl Harbor, the Japanese navy invaded Kiska and Attu, the two westernmost Aleutian islands. The Aleuts are removed from the other islands by the US government for safety reasons and taken to detention camps in southwest Alaska. It is 1945 before they are allowed to return to their homes. In her verse novel, in which short stanzas are divided into sections dated from May and June 1942 to April 1945, Hesse gives an account of this exodus through the first-person narration of the young Vera. Vera is visiting her mother on Kashega when they are both ordered, with other Aleuts, to board the *S.S. Columbia*, which takes them first to Wrangell and then to Lake Ward, a thousand miles from their home.

Vera tells about the discriminatory discourse leveled against the Aleuts and describes the primitive conditions in which they have to live. They are American citizens, she points out, contrasting their camp to the superior conditions of the nearby German prisoner-of-war camp. Many fall sick and die from tuberculosis and pneumonia; others, including Vera's mother, get permission to live in nearby Ketchikan. Vera tells how the Aleuts continue to celebrate their traditions and keep faith in their religion while at the camp. On returning to the islands, she finds that her home on Unalaska Island had been looted and almost destroyed. Hesse's novel addresses an episode in American history absent from history books. A short glossary of Aleut words is included.

1. Discuss ways the Aleuts were subjected to prejudice and discrimination during and after World War II.
2. Related website: "Stories of the Aleutians," Aleutian World War II National Historic Area, National Park Service (www.nps.gov/aleu/details.htm).

Kadohata, Cynthia. *Weedflower.* Atheneum, 2006. 260 pp. Grades 5–8. *Booklist* Top 10 HF, 2007; Addams, 2007; NSSTB, 2007.

After the bombing of Pearl Harbor, twelve-year-old Sumiko and her family are forced to leave their flower farm in California, and her grandfather and uncle are deported to a detention camp in North Dakota. Sumiko's family members are taken to a local racetrack, where they are housed in horse stables before being transported to a relocation camp on a Native American reservation in Poston, Arizona. Sumiko describes the unjust treatment of Japanese Americans, including the forced sale of their possessions for a fraction of their worth, the intolerable journey, and living conditions in the camps. Sumiko fights the boredom, intense heat, and ever-present dust by helping her neighbor Mr. Moto create a garden using the seeds of weed flowers that she brought from the family's flower farm. As Sumiko comments, the Japanese made the desert bloom with their gardens and crops.

Kadohata integrates changing government policies toward Japanese Americans into her novel, telling how offers were made to resettle the Japanese Nikkei because of a shortage of workers. The novel also pays tribute to those who were willing to pledge loyalty to and fight for the United States when the government prepared to draft young Nisei. Kadohata also provides information about the 442nd Regimental Combat Team.

1. Discuss the rationale behind relocating people of Japanese descent.
2. Discuss examples of reasons people gave for the incarceration of Japanese Americans.
3. Related website: "Japanese Relocation and Internment during World War II," National Archives (www.archives.gov/research/alic/reference/military/japanese-internment.html).

Adult Fiction

Dallas, Sandra. *Tallgrass.* 2007; St. Martin's Press, 2008. 336 pp. Spur, 2008.

Basing her book on the Camp Amache internment camp for the relocation of people of Japanese ancestry, near Granada, Colorado, Dallas explores the effects of the camp (fictionalized as Tallgrass) on the town and community of Ellis through the perspective of thirteen-year-old Rennie Stroud. Rennie comments many Ellis citizens are discussing not whether it is "right or wrong" to "force" people "born on American soil" into camps, but what Tallgrass "would do to the community" (22). As fear builds, doors are locked and acts of vandalism are blamed on the Japanese. Rennie is aware of the different opinions held by people in town, including those held by members of an influential women's sewing circle, the Jolly Stitchers. Then, Susan Reddick is brutally murdered and raped. Although there is no evidence for Japanese involvement in the crime, the harassment of the Japanese continues, including an attempted assault on the camp by a posse of men from Ellis. Rennie narrates how her family stands up against bigotry as they become friends with the Japanese men who they hire to work on the farm, and with the young Daisy, who helps in the house. Dallas's novel is a detailed portrait of a small farming community whose prejudices and sense of decency are tested by the presence of their Japanese American neighbors.

1. Discuss Rennie's comment to her father, who thinks the "Japanese are bringing the war home to Ellis" (152).
2. Discuss the attitudes of women who belong to the Jolly Stitchers. What do these women contribute to the community of Ellis?
3. Discuss Dallas's suggestion that there is perhaps a "corollary between the Japanese evacuation of World War II and the detainees of Guantanamo" in the Iraq War (viii).

Ford, Jamie. *Hotel on the Corner of Bitter and Sweet.* Ballantine Books, 2009. 285 pp.

The relocation of Japanese Americans in Seattle during World War II is told through Henry Lee's flashbacks. After the death of his wife, Ethel, in 1986 and the discovery of the belongings of Japanese Americans at the old Panama Hotel, Henry revisits his relationship with Keiko Okabe in 1942. Despite the deep-seated prejudice of Henry's father against the Japanese, because of their invasion of China, the young Henry bonds with Keiko, another scholarship student subjected to bullying by white students at Rainier Elementary School, where they work together in the school kitchens. The novel shows the effects of Pearl Harbor on young Asians. Henry, forbidden to speak English before Pearl Harbor, must now abandon Cantonese and wear an "I Am Chinese" button. He is told that his friendship with Keiko is tantamount to aligning himself with the enemy. Keiko refers to herself as an American who does not speak Japanese.

Henry and Keiko witness the increasing arrests and discrimination against those of Japanese ancestry until Seattle's Public Proclamation 1 orders the relocation of Japanese citizens. Keiko and her family are relocated to Puyallup, then to Minidoka, Idaho. Woven into Ford's story is the background to the enmity between Chinese and Japanese immigrants, which dated back to the Chinese Exclusion Act of 1882. An added dimension of the story is the jazz scene in Seattle.

1. Discuss examples of how the arrest and detention of Japanese citizens violated constitutional rights.
2. How did immigration laws affect the relationship between the Chinese and Japanese communities in Seattle?
3. Related website: Sharon Boswell and Lorraine McConaghy, "Abundant Dreams Diverted," *Seattle Times*, June 23, 1966, with photographs of Camp Harmony, Puyallup (http://seattletimes.com/special/centennial/june/internment.htm).

Otsuka, Julie. *When the Emperor Was Divine.* Knopf, 2002. 143 pp. Alex, 2003.

A Japanese American family's experience of being evacuated to camps far away from their home in Berkeley, California, during World War II is told from the different viewpoints of the mother, the girl, the boy, and the father—who, because their names are not specified, represent all Japanese Americans subjected to relocation. In spare, haunting prose, Otsuka writes of prejudicial treatment levied against all Japanese Americans. Their ordeal is first recounted from the mother's perspective, who upon seeing Evacuation Order No. 19, begins preparations to leave, including dealing with the family's pets. Their stay in whitewashed horse stalls at the Tanforan racetrack; the long train journey to the desert in Utah; and their arrival at the hot, dusty camp, without any shade, is narrated from the perspective of the eleven-year-old daughter. Haunted by the vision of his father being taken away by the FBI, the seven-year-old boy imagines his father's return while they live in a barracks without running water, surrounded by barbed wire and watchtowers with armed guards.

Otsuka's novel addresses the lasting psychological effects of the government's policies and treatment on family members. They are ostracized, for example, by former neighbors and friends when they return to their vandalized home. The father eventually arrives home, broken and depressed. In "Confession," the father speaks in first person as he admits to all the spurious accusations made against him: "So go ahead and lock me up. Take my children. Take my wife. Freeze my assets" (142). Otsuka provides a note on her sources.

1. Discuss the father's treatment and arrest and the content and significance of his confession.
2. Discuss the effects of the evacuation on the boy and girl.

Postwar United States
(1945-1979)

The Cold War

Gantos, Jack. *Dead End in Norvelt.* Farrar, Straus & Giroux, 2011. 341 pp. Grades 5–8. Newbery, 2012; O'Dell, 2012; YALSA BF, 2012.

In this novel set in 1962 in Norvelt, Pennsylvania, eleven-year-old Jack tells about the summer during which he is grounded. He is released only to be a scribe to elderly Miss Volker, who writes obituaries for the local newspaper but has arthritic hands. In her obituaries, Miss Volker provides not only the personal histories of the dead and their contributions to the local community; she also links the days of their deaths to historical events that occurred on that same day. Miss Volker's passion for history is evident from her needlepoint map of old Norvelt displayed on her wall and from her "This Day in History" columns she had once written for the local newspaper.

The study of history is central to the novel, as Jack reads his favorite history books and spends time with Miss Volker. The past suffuses the present as Jack reads about the lost world of the Aztecs, events in world history, and local history. War movies feature the Pacific in World War II, and the Cold War era of the 1960s is represented by Jack's father, who voices his fears of attacks by the "Russian Commies" (9). The history of the influenza epidemic of 1918 is integrated into the mysterious deaths of several elderly women in Norvelt. Gantos's story is also laced with humor. In a final scene, Jack and his father provide the town with another piece of Norvelt history as they fly over the town's outdoor movie screen and drop balloons filled with red paint on the screen as "torpedoes" skim "across the water toward the Bismarck" (339).

1. Compare the values held by Jack's mother in regard to surviving hard times to those held by Jack's father.
2. Discuss Eleanor Roosevelt's importance to Norvelt.
3. Related website: Norvelt and Penn-Craft: Pennsylvania's Subsistence-Homestead Communities of the 1930s (www.lib.iup.edu/depts/speccol/exhibits/norvelt.html).

Klages, Ellen. *The Green Glass Sea.* Viking/Penguin, 2006. 318 pp. Grades 5–8. O'Dell, 2007; NSSTB, 2007.

In 1943, Dewey Kerrigan, almost eleven years old, joins her father in Los Alamos, New Mexico, where he is working on the Manhattan Project. The need for secrecy has been impressed on Dewey, and this is reinforced by the physically remote "Hill" surrounded by guards and fences. While on a mission to the White House, her father is run down and killed by drunken soldiers celebrating the end of the war in Europe, and Dewey is invited to stay with the Gordons, who also work on the "gadget" that will help win the war. The experience of living in the atmosphere of secrecy and heightened tension of Los Alamos, where exhausted parents work long into the night, is narrated from the perspectives of Dewey and the Gordons' daughter Suze.

In 1945, as time draws near for the "gadget" to be tested, rumors circulate about its dangerous and destructive nature. Dewey and Suze observe the test from their viewpoint on the mesa, and the Gordons later take them to Trinity, where they walk on the sea of green glass, called Trinitite. The protests against the use of the bomb are set against the euphoria of a successful test. The novel ends with the news announcement about Hiroshima. Klages includes a brief historical note and a reading list.

1. Discuss how the novel adds to your understanding of the Manhattan Project.

2. What does Klages's novel have to say about gender and science?
3. Discuss the various responses of characters in the novel to the atomic bomb.
4. Related websites: Voices of the Manhattan Project (www.manhattanprojectvoices.org); Manhattan Project (www.nuclearfiles.org).
5. Related reading: Steve Sheinkin, *Bomb: The Race to Build and Steal the World's Most Dangerous Weapon* (Flash Point/Roaring Books Press, 2012).

Klages, Ellen. *White Sands, Red Menace.* 2008; Viking/Penguin, 2010. 337 pp. Grades 5–8. NSSTB, 2009.

In this sequel to *The Green Glass Sea*, set in 1946–47, Klages continues the story of Dewey and the Gordon family, who have moved from the Hill in Los Alamos to Alamogordo, New Mexico. The focus of the scientific community is now on the establishment of the V-2 rocket missile program at White Sands. Klages highlights the division between those who, like Suze's father, believes in the V-2 rocket as the means to a future space program, as well as its use for defense, and those who worry about the dangers of the atomic bomb, including Suze's mother, who actively campaigns against its use. Details of the V-2 and its origin in Germany plus a description of one of the launches witnessed by Dewey and Suze appear alongside descriptions of the beauty of the White Sands National Monument. The Atomic Energy Act, the new products and technologies developed in the war, and the marketing of products using the term *atomic* are also integrated into Klages's story. The moral dilemmas of the new atomic age are well laid out in this family story in which there are also choices to be made.

1. Discuss the opposing viewpoints of Suze's parents.
2. Discuss the response of Suze's social studies teacher to the idea that the government is censoring reports about radiation sickness in Japan (150–51).

Levine, Ellen. *Catch a Tiger by the Toe*. Viking, 2005. 200 pp. Grades 6–8. *Booklist* Top 10 HF, 2005; NSSTB, 2006.

Through the first-person narrative of thirteen-year-old Jamie, Levine re-creates the atmosphere of fear and distrust that pervaded neighborhoods, schools, and the workplace during the McCarthy era in the 1950s. Jamie is aware that her grandmother emigrated from Russia, and she has been warned to keep her mouth "zipped" about family affairs. When Jamie's father, a math teacher, is fired from his job and denounced in the newspaper as a communist, Jamie is removed from the school newspaper and shunned by her friend Elaine and others. Her mother is fired from her teaching job and discovers that she is on the FBI list called "The Red Channels."

Woven into Jamie's story is a clear explanation of the objectives of the House Un-American Activities Committee and the threat to democracy during this period. Jamie fights against her unjust removal from the school newspaper and learns about the "Hollywood Ten" and Senator McCarthy. Her father, summoned before Senator McCarthy, refers to his First Amendment rights and to McCarthy's undermining of the Constitution. In an author's note, Levine provides a definition of communism and further describes how McCarthyism affected people's lives and freedom. She gives more information about the execution of Ethel and Julius Rosenberg and appends a bibliography.

1. Jamie's father invokes the First Amendment when questioned by Senator McCarthy. Discuss examples of violations of the First Amendment in Levine's novel in conjunction with the Bill of Rights (www.archives.gov/exhibits/charters/bill_of_rights.html).
2. Discuss Paul Robeson's testimony before the House Committee on Un-American Activities, on June 12, 1956: "'You Are the Un-Americans, and You Ought to Be Ashamed of Yourselves': Paul Robeson Appears before HUAC," History Matters (http://historymatters .gmu.edu/d/6440).

Myers, Walter Dean. *The Journal of Biddy Owens: The Negro Leagues.* Scholastic, 2001. 141 pp. Grades 5–7.

Seventeen-year-old Biddy is employed as an equipment manager and a scorekeeper for the Negro League's Birmingham Black Barons. From May to October 1948, he records in his journal details of the plays and scores for all the games of the season, whether exhibition games, industrial league games, or games against other teams in the Negro League. He documents the long bus tours to cities all over the country, the names of the opposing teams, details about individual players (including Willie Mays), and about the All-Star Players and the Negro League World Series. He worries about the financial survival of the Negro League as more black players are recruited into the major leagues. Biddy also writes about the discrimination the team faces in a segregated society. Socioeconomic and political contexts are integrated into Biddy's accounts of his home life and his decision to go to college, and through, for example, the news of President Truman's decision to desegregate the army.

In his historical note, Myers provides a history of the Negro National League and charts the integration of black players into the major leagues. There are photographs of the Birmingham Black Barons and well-known players, a map, and a list of teams in the Negro League. Myers's novel is a title in the *My Name Is America* series.

1. Discuss how discrimination affected black players.
2. Related reading: Kadir Nelson, *We Are the Ship: The Story of Negro League Baseball* (Jump at the Sun and Hyperion, 2008).

Taylor, Theodore. *The Bomb.* 1995; Harcourt Brace, 2007. 208 pp. 197 pp. Grades 6–10. O'Dell, 1996.

Fourteen-year-old Sorry lives on the unspoiled island of Bikini in the Marshall Islands and tells how the families on Bikini are forced to leave their homes when, in 1946, it is chosen as a test site for nuclear bombs (Operations Crossroads). They are given assurances that they can return home within a short time, which varies from a few months to two years. Sorry's uncle Abram, who speaks English, hears the radio broadcasts about Hiroshima and understands that the island will be poisoned for many years, but most of Bikini's inhabitants refuse to listen. When Chief Juda makes the hasty decision that they should relocate to Rongerik, a smaller island without the resources to sustain them, Abram makes plans to obstruct the dropping of the bomb. When his uncle dies of a heart attack, Sorry carries out his plan by sailing his canoe back to Bikini Atoll.

Taylor describes the transformation of Bikini Island into a nuclear testing site. In a separate narrative, he provides a history of the development of the atomic bomb. In his "factual epilogue," Taylor tells how some members of the original families returned to the devastated island only to be poisoned by radiation that remained in the sand, after President Johnson had mistakenly announced in 1969 that it was safe for habitation.

1. Taylor states that the removal and relocation of the people of Bikini created a "modern Trail of Tears" (197). Discuss the use of rhetoric and propaganda by the Americans in removing the Bikini residents from their island.
2. Discuss Taylor's novel as an indictment of nuclear war.

Wiles, Deborah. *Countdown.* Scholastic, 2010. 377 pp. Grades 5–8. *Booklist* Top 10 HF; NSSTB, 2012.

In this book set in Washington, DC, in 1962, eleven-year-old Franny Chapman knows well the instructions she has been given for when everyone sees the big flash. They are to "duck and cover." Meshing Franny's first-person narrative with rich documentary materials, Wiles brings a vivid sense of how it was to live with the fear of a nuclear attack as the Cuban Missile Crisis came to a head. Wiles's text reproduces President Kennedy's October 22 radio broadcast, as well as photographs of the Cuban missile sites and the subsequent news headlines on the gravity of the situation. Interspersed with Franny's story are documents that bring the 1960s and the Cold War to life: quotes from communications between President Kennedy and Nikita Khrushchev, as well as biographical sketches of Presidents Truman and Kennedy, and others who spoke up for freedom, including Pete Seeger and Fannie Lou Hamer. Photographs document the civil rights movement; song lyrics of the time; and civil defense leaflets, such as one showing families living in home bomb shelters. More information on the Cuban Missile Crisis is provided in a note; there is also a bibliography. The setting of Wiles's novel depicts a middle-class suburb that is based on Wiles's own childhood at Camp Springs, Maryland.

1. What information does the documentary material convey about important ideas and movements in the United States over and above Franny's narrative?
2. Discuss the responses in the novel to the Cuban Missile Crisis and to President Kennedy's radio broadcast. Related websites: "The Cuban Missile Crisis, 1962: The Missiles of October," Edsitement (http://edsitement.neh.gov/lesson-plan/missiles-october-cuban-missile-crisis-1962#sect-objective).

Civil Rights

Bruchac, Joseph. *Hidden Roots.* Scholastic, 2004. 136 pp. Grades 6–9. American Indian Youth Literature Award, 2006.

In this book set in 1954 in Sparta, New York, eleven-year-old Henry Camp hears the truth about his family from Uncle Louis, who tells him about Vermont's Eugenics Project and the 1931 sterilization bill, which allowed the state to sterilize those regarded as "feebleminded" or who had "bad" genes. He explains that Indians, regarded as "gypsies," were particularly singled out for sterilization and that Indian children were frequently taken away from their parents, who were sometimes institutionalized. Louis reveals their family roots as Abenaki and Mohican, as well as French, and tells how the sterilization law and policies affected the lives of his wife and his daughter, Henry's mother. In his notes, Bruchac provides a history of the project, telling how it forced Abenaki people to hide the fact that they were Indian, and he compares the sterilization program to practices in Nazi Germany.

1. Discuss the basic premises of eugenics; the relationship between social reform and eugenics; the relationship between hereditary studies and eugenics; and the main reasons Vermont saw eugenics and the sterilization law as necessary to ensure that the population represented "good old Vermont stock," a concern of those conducting *The Eugenics Survey of Vermont*. Related website: Vermont Eugenics: A Documentary History (www.uvm.edu/~eugenics).

2. Bruchac states that Vermont was the thirty-first state to enact sterilization laws. Research what other states passed laws (with dates) to sterilize various groups of people. Discuss the implications of laws based on the belief in a "perfect" society.

Crowe, Chris. *Mississippi Trial, 1955*. Phyllis Fogelman Books, 2002. 231 pp. Grades 7–10. NSSTB, 2003; YALSA BB, 2003.

Crowe presents intolerance and racism in Greenwood, Mississippi, and the murder of fourteen-year-old Emmett Till in 1955 through the eyes of sixteen-year-old Hiram Hillburn. Hiram spent much of his early childhood living with his grandparents and listening to his grandfather's opinions about slavery. When he was nine years old, his father and mother moved to Arizona and refused his requests to visit his grandfather in the summers. As his father told him, he does not want Hiram to be influenced by his "grampa's Southern nonsense" (41).

In mid-August and back in Mississippi, Hiram begins to see Greenwood in a different light. He hears his grandfather speak against the Supreme Court ruling on school integration and witnesses the mean and cruel behavior of his friend R.C. toward two bachelors known as "queer." He is present when R.C. beats up a visiting African American boy from Chicago, whom Hiram had recently rescued from drowning. This same young man, Emmett Till, goes missing after he allegedly whistled at a white woman, and his tortured body is found floating in the river. Hiram attends the court proceedings and listens with incredulity to a trial in which the verdict that sets free two men who had kidnapped and killed Till is clearly a travesty of justice. Crowe includes a historical note and quotations, plus an editorial from the *Commonwealth* newspaper, which covered Till's murder and the trial.

1. Discuss the trial in the text of Crowe's novel and the supplementary material on the *American Experience* web page "The Murder of Emmett Till" (www.pbs.org/wgbh/amex/till).
2. Related reading: Chris Crowe, *Getting Away with Murder: The True Story of the Emmett Till Case* (Phyllis Fogelman Books, 2003).

Draper, Sharon M. *Fire from the Rock.* Dutton Children's Books, 2007. 231 pp. Grades 7–10. NSSTB, 2008.

In 1957, Little Rock's school board has plans to integrate Central High School, and fifteen-year-old Sylvia Faye Patterson, an honors student, has been chosen to attend. Sylvia is ambitious to get the best education available, but her father, a pastor, is aware of the opposition. Sylvia is torn because, proud as she is to be chosen, she is also aware of how she will be ostracized at Central High. After an interview during which she is made aware of the open hostility to integration and a series of attacks, she makes an important decision.

Draper embeds her story in a sociohistorical context that interweaves the pop culture of the 1950s with comments by Sylvia and her sister on discrimination against women of color in entertainment and media. The novel closes as the remaining nine students attempt to enter Central High, followed by the arrival of the military. In a note, Draper describes the students' treatment at Central High and tells about Arkansas Governor Faubus's decision in 1958 to close all Little Rock schools. A list of web resources is provided. The names of "the Nine" who first entered Central High are listed at the beginning of the novel.

1. Discuss the different attitudes toward integration of the schools by Sylvia's family and friends.
2. What were the political and legal implications of Governor Faubus's actions? Related website: "Documents Related to *Brown v. Board of Education*," Teaching with Documents (www.archives.gov/education/lessons/davis-case).
3. Discuss how the novel treats the issues of civil rights and resistance.

Edwardson, Debby Dahl. *My Name Is Not Easy.* Marshall Cavendish, 2011. 248 pp. Grades 7–12. NSSTB, 2012; YALSA BF.

Edwardson explains in a note to her novel that until 1976, students had to leave "bush" Alaska to obtain a school diploma. In 1960, twelve-year-old Luke, whose Iñupiaq name Aamaugak is "too hard" for teachers, is sent with his two younger brothers, Bunna and Isaac, from their Arctic Alaskan village to attend Sacred Heart Boarding School, many miles away. Through a multiple-voiced narrative, Luke and other students tell of their experiences at Sacred Heart from 1960 to 1964. The school is ruled by Father Mullen, who seeks to eradicate their language and culture in making them into educated Christians. Based on real events, Edwardson's story incorporates other abuses of power: the kidnapping of six-year-old Isaac, who is taken from the school by Father Mullen the day he arrives and placed in a home in Dallas, Texas, and the subjection of students to military tests in which a radioactive tracer is administered. Each student's voice, fresh and honest, reveals his or her feelings, but they speak at the end of the novel in a unified voice against injustice.

Set in the context of the Cold War, students practice nuclear bomb drills and discuss newspaper articles on "Project Chariot" in Alaska, which, Edwardson explains in her note, was designed to demonstrate the peaceful uses of atomic energy. She explains that iodine-131 experiments were actually administered to Iñupiaq villages and to Native American students at a parochial school.

1. Discuss the school's use of *in loco parentis.*
2. In what ways do students resist enculturation? In what ways are they changed?

Johnston, Tony. *Bone by Bone by Bone.* Roaring Brook Press, 2007. 184 pp. Grades 6–9. *Booklist* Top 10 HF, 2008; YALSA BB, 2008.

Set in 1951 in Tennessee, Johnston uses "raw language" to emphasize the racial hatred that governs David Church's father, the local doctor, who tells his son that if his friend Malcolm Deeter so much as sets foot over the threshold, he will shoot him. But David and Malcolm are inseparable until, encouraged by David, Malcolm tries out for the local baseball team and, despite his prowess, is told by the coach that he will not have a "nigger" on his "squad." The two resume their friendship when David rescues Malcolm from a vicious rooster and from a circle of taunting white men that includes his father.

Johnston conveys the ugliness of racial prejudice that is extant in a town where the Ku Klux Klan murder without impunity. His bed-ridden great grandmother exudes hatred and bigotry, while his grand-mother is afraid to speak up against David's father, who represents the destructiveness and irrationality of the racism that tears his family apart. For example, David's uncle Lucas, who lives away from the family and travels, has a different view. The relationship between David and his father deteriorates as David approaches his thirteenth year and rebels against his father's attitudes and plans for him to be a doctor. Their final separation comes when his father attempts to shoot Malcolm as he seeks shelter from the Klan at David's house. In a preface, Johnston explains that she is writing from her personal experience of growing up during segregation with a racist father. The language she uses in the novel is his language. It "reflects a way of thinking that has troubled" her all her life.

1. Discuss the attitudes and behavior of members of David's family, including Uncle Lucas, in the context of racism.
2. How would you explain David's father's attitudes, given his feelings toward Tinney, who raised him when he was boy? Discuss David's experience when he visits Tinney.

Levine, Kristen. *Lions of Little Rock.* Putnam, 2012. 298 pp. Grades 5–8. *Booklist* Top 10 HF, 2012; NSSTB, 2013; YALSA BF, 2013.

In 1958, Governor Faubus closes both black and white high schools in Little Rock, Arkansas, to prevent integration, despite a Supreme Court decision that integration should proceed. Marlee, who is just starting the seventh grade, hears the different sides of the debate, including the opinions of her parents, who are teachers and at first hold opposing views. Marlee refuses, despite threats, to give up her friendship with her new friend Liz, whom she meets in seventh grade and who leaves school when it is discovered she is an African American "passing" as white. In her first-person narrative, Marlee tells about the consequences of the closed schools for students and the action taken against teachers who are suspected of supporting integration.

Levine's story addresses how people begin to speak out against Faubus and begin the political process of replacing and reappointing school board members through organizations such as Stop This Outrageous Purge, aimed to stop the purging of teachers from the schools, and Women's Emerging Committee to Open Our Schools. The novel ends with an acknowledgment of what could and could not be achieved at the time. In her notes, Levine provides some background to her story, explaining why she chose to write about the "lost year" that schools were closed to prevent integration and provides a list of books and films.

1. Discuss the reasons Marlee and Liz know that it is not yet time for them to openly acknowledge their friendship.
2. Related reading: Shelley Tougas, *Little Rock Girl, 1957* (Compass Point Books, 2012) (nonfiction).

Magoon, Kekla. *Fire in the Streets.* Aladdin, 2012. 321 pp. Grades 6–9. YALSA BF, 2013.

Fourteen-year-old Maxie is desperate to become a full member of the Black Panthers like her brother, Raheem, and her ex-boyfriend Sam Childs. In 1968 Chicago, Maxie helps the Black Panthers as they speak up for their cause at an antiwar protest during the Democratic National Convention. They state that they stand behind the antiwar movement but ask that white protestors, in return, stand with the Black Panthers in their fight for civil rights. She describes the protest as it turns into a riot, with fires lighting the streets. As a Young Panther, Maxie attends political education classes and works in the Black Panther office after school. On Saturdays, she helps with the Freedom School, designed for young children. The novel documents the programs of the Black Panthers: the free breakfast program, health clinic services, the Ten-Point

Platform, the *Pocket Lawyer of Legal First Aid*, and rules governing how to respond when arrested.

In this companion novel to *The Rock and the River*, Maxie tells of the pain and anger she and Sam feel over the recent deaths of Martin Luther King Jr. and of Sam's brother, Steve. Maxie lives in an environment of fear and violence in which there is a war of bullets between the Black Panthers and a police force whose aim is to suppress the movement. She tells about poverty at home, her mother's irresponsibility, and her brother's efforts to keep them all afloat. The importance of the Black Panther movement as a means of bringing a sense of power to the people is emphasized as Maxie chooses between loyalty to her brother and to the Black Panthers.

1. Analyze and discuss the objectives of the Black Panther Party, including the Ten-Point Platform. Related website: A Huey P. Newton Story (www.pbs.org/hueypnewton/huey.html).
2. Discuss the Black Panther movement in relation to radical protests of the civil rights movement and the escalation of protests against the Vietnam War. Related website: "Brief History of Chicago's 1968 Democratic Convention" (http://edition.cnn.com/ALLPOLITICS/1996/conventions/chicago/facts/chicago68/index.shtml.

Magoon, Kekla. *The Rock and the River.* Aladdin/Simon & Schuster, 2009. 283 pp. Grades 7–10. ALA Notable, 2010; King/John Steptoe New Talent Award, 2010; YALSA BB, 2010.

Set in Chicago in 1968, thirteen-year-old Sam Childs is with his brother Stick when Stick is injured fighting back against white protestors at a demonstration led by Roland Childs, a civil rights activist and friend of Martin Luther King Jr. After witnessing the severe beating and arrest of their friend Bucky, and after hearing the news of King's assassination, Sam is drawn into the world of Stick and the Black Panthers: he learns more about the Panthers' objectives and listens to their talk of revolution.

The novel explores the tensions between the nonviolent approach to achieving civil rights represented by Sam's father and the approach of the Panthers, who are ready to defend their rights by force if necessary. After police shoot and kill Stick, Sam must decide whether he should follow his brother and be akin to "the river," which flows in "motion, turmoil, rage," or be akin to the solid "rock" that characterizes his father's approach to civil rights (282–83). Information about the civil rights movement and the history and objectives of the Black Panther Party are provided in an author's note.

1. Debate Roland Childs's approach to achieving equality versus that of the Black Panthers.
2. Discuss Stick's statements that the Panthers' "guns just represent an idea" and that the Panthers were "really about" helping "hungry kids" and black people who could not afford to see a doctor (232–32).
3. Related reading: *March: Book One*, by John Lewis and Andrew Aydin, art by Nate Powell (Top Shelf Production, 2013).

McMullan, Margaret. *Sources of Light.* Houghton Mifflin, 2010. 233 pp. NSSTB, 2011; YALSA BF, 2011.

After fourteen-year-old Samantha's father is killed in Vietnam, she and her mother move to Jackson, Mississippi, in 1962 to be near her father's family. Samantha is soon aware of racial attitudes held by the parents of her friend Stone McLemore. Samantha's consciousness is particularly raised when her mother, a college teacher, visits Tougaloo, an all-black college, to deliver a public lecture. After the visit, their door is defaced and they receive threatening phone calls. She also begins to understand how segregation affects their maid, Willa Mae. Her mother's close friend, the civil rights advocate Perry Walker, has given Samantha a camera, so she photographs the vicious scenes at a lunch bar when people defy desegregation laws. She takes more photographs when a mob of white men attack black and white protestors against registration tests when she accompanies her mother and Perry to register black voters. The importance of photography to the historical record is demonstrated when Walker's photos he took of men as they were beating him to death led to their conviction.

McMullan's story is placed in the historical context of violent protests in Mississippi, such as those against black student James Meredith, who attended the University of Mississippi in 1962. These are counterbalanced by an episode featuring Eudora Welty, who insists that black people be allowed to attend her presentation. In her notes, McMullan connects her life with civil rights in Mississippi and notes major milestones of the civil rights movement.

1. Discuss the attitudes and actions of Stone regarding civil rights.
2. Discuss the arguments made for resisting civil rights.

Williams-Garcia, Rita. *One Crazy Summer.* Amistad/HarperCollins, 2010. 218 pp. Grades 5–7. ALA Notable, 2011; *Booklist* Top 10 HF, 2011; NBA (Y) finalist, 2010; King, 2011; Newbery honor, 2011; O'Dell, 2011.

Eleven-year-old Delphine and her younger sisters, Vonetta and Fern, are sent from Brooklyn to Oakland, California, in the summer of 1968 to stay with Cecile, the mother who walked out on them. Cecile, a poet now known as Nzila, is not exactly welcoming. They will not be surfing or visiting Disneyland. Instead, they will attend the Black Panthers' summer camp. In the following transformative days, the girls see posters of Huey Newton and Malcolm X on the walls of the center's classroom and learn about the Black Panthers' ideas for revolution. They are challenged by "Crazy Kelvin" to think about their identity as African Americans. Delphine reads about the murder of Bobby Hutton and sees how the police treat those associated with the Panthers when Nzila is arrested and her kitchen trashed. But the sisters' participation in the rally to honor Bobby Hutton by renaming a park in his name demonstrates a new consciousness and pride in their black heritage, and they recite one of Nzila's poems celebrating their African roots.

Williams-Garcia immerses readers in the context of the 1960s as she seamlessly interweaves popular culture of the day with the sisters' conversations and experiences. In a novel that affirms love, family, and diversity, Williams-Garcia introduces younger readers to a civil rights movement with which they may be less familiar.

1. "What's wrong with this picture?" How do Vonetta and Fern use this statement made by "Crazy Kelvin" (64)? Discuss the significance of Fern's poem.

2. Discuss the representation of the Black Panthers in the novel. Related website: A Huey P. Newton Story (www.pbs.org/hueypnewton/actions/huey.html).

Adult Fiction

Morrison, Toni. *Home: A Novel.* Knopf, 2012. 145 pp.

When veteran Frank Money returns from the Korean War, he is told by army doctors that his "craziness would leave in time" (19). But Frank is haunted by images of his best friends dying, of civilians he killed in revenge, and the face of a young Korean girl who was shot in the head while she scavenged for food. On his way to Georgia to rescue his sister, Cee, from the doctor who has used her for experiments on improving the speculum, Frank is picked up by the police, handcuffed, and taken to a hospital, but he cannot remember why, he tells the minister who helps him after he escapes. He may have been in a desegregated army, the minister reminds him, but the racism he encounters in the North can be just as dangerous as the South.

The stories of Frank and Cee, narrated from their different perspectives, tell of the racism in the past and in the 1950s that continues to hurt them. Frank takes Cee back to their hometown of Lotus, where caring women save Cee's life. Morrison shows how her characters find hope and strength. For Frank, this means facing up to the truth about what happened in the war.

1. Discuss the effects of war on Frank.
2. Discuss how Morrison's novel deals with racism and cruelty.
3. Discuss Frank's earlier and later perceptions of Lotus.

Immigrants: Making a New Life in America

Flores-Galbis, Enrique. *90 Miles to Havana.* Roaring Brook Press, 2010. 292 pp. Grades 5–8. Belpré honor, 2011; NSSTB, 2011.

The novel is based on Flores-Galbis's experience of being sent from Cuba to Miami in the 1961 Operation Pedro Pan. At the beginning of the Cuban Revolution, Julian, his older brothers, and his architect father return from a fishing trip to Havana to the sound of gunshots rather than New Year's festivities. Julian sees what revolution entails as he observes furniture thrown from the president's house, properties confiscated, soldiers and tanks, and the long lines outside the American embassy. He learns that Bebo, who works for his family, can now attend engineering school while he and his brothers may be sent away to cut sugarcane and be "reeducated."

Julian's mother arranges for her sons to be sent to Miami, where they are taken to a camp run by the Catholic Church, which arranges for Cuban children to be placed in foster homes or orphanages around the country. Julian describes conditions in the camp, which is ruled by the bully Caballo. When his brothers are sent to an orphanage in Denver, Julian escapes. But life outside the camp has its own dangers as Julian evades the police and helps a young man, Tomás, rescue more Cubans from Havana—a ninety-mile voyage from Miami. Although Julian is eventually reunited with his mother and brothers, who all hope that Julian's father will be able to join them, the novel makes clear the difficulties and risks implicit for Cuban emigrants. But it also acknowledges those who help Julian, including an informal network of Cubans in Miami.

1. Discuss the implications of the Cuban Revolution for the novel's different characters.
2. Discuss the risks and benefits for the children who were part of the Cuban Children's Exodus. Related website: "Exodus," Operation Pedro Pan Group (www.pedropan.org).

Jiménez, Francisco. *The Circuit: Stories from the Life of a Migrant Child.* 1997; Houghton Mifflin, 1999. 116 pp. Grades 6–9. Américas, 1997; Addams honor, 1998.

Jiménez, Francisco. *Breaking Through.* Houghton Mifflin, 2001. 195 pp. Grades 6–12. ALA Notable, 2002; Américas, 2001; Belpré honor, 2002; NSSTB, 2002; YALSA BB, 2002.

Jiménez, Francisco. *Reaching Out.* Houghton Mifflin, 2008. 196 pp. Grades 9–12. NSSTB, 2009.

In *The Circuit,* Francisco ("Panchito") tells how his family left their small village near Guadalajara in the late 1940s and crossed "La frontera." In the stories that follow, he describes his family's life as they follow the strawberry, grape, and cotton harvests on the migrant's circuit, with hours of backbreaking labor; weeks without work; meager pay; and miserable living conditions in tents, shacks, and dilapidated buildings. A major theme is Francisco's love of school and his determination to keep up with his learning, despite his struggle with English, even as he misses months of school toiling in the fields. When at the end of the novel he is practicing a school assignment to recite the introductory paragraph to the Declaration of Independence, a suspicious peer in the school bus reports him to "la migra."

In *Breaking Through,* Francisco tells about his and Roberto's deportation to Mexico, where they apply for and attain visas to reenter the United States. Although they return to Santa Maria and resume work in the fields, Francisco tells about breaking through the barriers that enable him be the first in his family to attend college. Despite desperate poverty, long hours of work, and a father whose health and black moods make things difficult at home, Francisco finds work outside the fields, attends high school full-time, is awarded a scholarship from the California Scholarship Federation, and is accepted at Santa Clara University in 1962.

In *Reaching Out,* Francisco tells about his experiences and studies at Santa Clara University. In this novel, he also writes about the discrimination faced by Mexicans, continued poverty, and his father's bitter disappointment over his failed dreams. Francisco considers leaving the university when his father returns to Mexico to take care of his family, but he is persuaded to stay, is awarded a Woodrow Wilson Fellowship, and accepts an offer from Columbia University's graduate school. Francisco's story continues to illustrate the plight of migrant workers as he tells about his participation in the National Farm Workers Association's march from Delano to Sacramento, led by César Chávez in March 1966.

1. Discuss examples from *The Circuit* that show how the migrants' circuit affects the health and education of Francisco and other children. Discuss factors that make it difficult for migrant workers and their children to break out from the cycle of poverty.
2. Provide examples of the factors that you think led to Francisco's success in *Breaking Out.*
3. Discuss the law and status of braceros in relation to other migrant workers and the role of union contracts in improving conditions for all migrant laborers. Related website: United Farm Workers (www.ufw.org).
4. Related reading: John Steinbeck, *Grapes of Wrath* (1939; Penguin, 2006).

Manzano, Sonia. *The Revolution of Evelyn Serrano.* Scholastic, 2012. 224 pp. Grades 6–10. ALA Notable, 2013; Américas, 2013; *Booklist* Top 10 HF, 2013; NSSTB, 2013; Belpré, 2012.

Fourteen-year-old Rosa María "Evelyn" del Carmen Serrano is unhappy with her mother's Puerto Rican decor and hates the customary smells of rotting garbage as she walks through "El Barrio," Spanish Harlem, in 1969 to her job at the five-and-dime. But when her grandmother arrives, Rosa, who has requested she be called Evelyn, is introduced to new ways of thinking about her family history and about Puerto Rico. She learns the truth behind the newspaper photographs of police shooting into a crowd of people, which she sees in her grandmother's photo album. Her grandmother tells her that the incident took place in Ponce in 1937 during a protest march of members and supporters of the Nationalist Party who wanted a Puerto Rico independent of the United States.

Evelyn learns that the young people sweeping the streets and collecting the garbage are not worthless "hippies," as her stepfather would have her believe, but members of the Young Lords organization who wish to build pride in the Puerto Rican community and take action to force the city to meet community needs. They provide programs such as free breakfasts, testing for tuberculosis and mercury, and education classes. After fruitless appeals to the Spanish Methodist Church for space and increased police action, the Young Lords occupy the church for eleven days, instituting their programs amid growing publicity. Evelyn becomes increasingly involved in the organization while listening to Pedro Pietri's poetry and attending her grandmother's history classes. In her author's note, Manzano writes about her own path to a raised social consciousness and identifies actual historical events and people in the novel. She provides references to the *New York Times* articles she refers to in the novel.

1. Discuss examples of the actions taken by the Young Lords in conjunction with the Sixties Project's "Young Lords Party 13-Point Program and Platform" (www2.iath.virginia.edu/sixties/HTML_docs/Resources/Primary/Manifestos/Young_Lords_platform.html).
2. Discuss the views and hostility toward the Young Lords represented by Evelyn's father and mother.

Veciana-Suarez, Ana. *Flight to Freedom.* Scholastic, 2002. 240 pp. NSSTB, 2003.

Beginning with her diary entry for April 2, 1967, thirteen-year-old Yara Garcia tells about her family's experiences in Cuba, and this is followed by entries recording the family's emigration to Miami and their adjustment to living in the United States, ending in July 1968. She writes about social and economic changes in Cuba under Fidel Castro: the loss of freedom to practice one's religion, the shortage and rationing of food and commodities, the divisions opening up among friends and neighbors as young people join the Communist Youth Union and the Pioneers and are encouraged to spy on neighbors who may be counter-revolutionaries. She describes the camp where she and her peers work in the fields and tobacco sheds for forty-five days. When her family applies for visas, her father loses his job and is sent to harvest coffee. Yara's brother, taken into the military, is not allowed to leave.

On August 18, 1967, Yara and her family take a "Freedom Flight" to Miami and stay with her father's relatives until they can rent a home of their own. In her diary, she writes about the difficulties of her first days at school, her angry father's activities with a military group that is preparing to liberate Cuba, and her mother's more pragmatic approach by getting a job and learning to drive a car—with the help given to Cubans by the US government. Yara's diary is a record of the cultural, social, and economic challenges faced by a family who has emigrated to another country and of how they adjust while holding on to their cultural values and traditions. The broader context of political events such as the Vietnam War is also woven into Yara's diary entries. In "My Personal Exodus," Veciana-Suarez provides information about various waves of emigrants from Cuba, such as Operation Pedro Pan from 1960 to 1962, the Freedom Flights from 1965 to 1973, and the dangerous exodus on boats and rafts that killed many in 1994.

1. Discuss difficulties that Yara and her elder sister encounter as a result of differences between two cultures.
2. Discuss Yara's question, "Do you stop loving your homeland if you live somewhere else and fly that country's flag?" (185).
3. Related website: "Freedom Tower, Miami, Florida," National Park Service (www.nps.gov/history/nr/travel/american_latino_heritage/ Freedom_Tower.html).

The Vietnam War

Burg, Ann. *All the Broken Pieces: A Novel in Verse.* Scholastic Press, 2009. 217 pp. Grades: 6–9. *Booklist* Top 10 HF, 2009; YALSA BB, 2010.

Matt Pin is haunted by fragmented memories of whirling helicopters, "choking mist and whirling fog," and the screams of mothers and crying children as his own mother pushes him away from his home (2–3). One of the children airlifted out of Saigon, Matt lives with a loving, supportive family, but in seventh grade he continues to have nightmares and is unable to speak about the unspeakable—the leaving behind of his little brother, who was mutilated by a land mine while in Matt's care. In exquisite lines, Matt expresses how he feels about his new family and life. When a teammate tells him that his brother died because of him, a family friend and his father take Matt to Vietnam veterans' meetings, where he listens to the memories and pain of American soldiers. He is told that his mother had sent him away out of love for him, not because she blamed him for what happened to his brother.

In a novel dealing with healing and forgiveness, Burg deals sensitively with the psychological pain, guilt, and loss that so many experienced during and after the Vietnam War and shows how these feelings continue to reverberate through a community.

1. Discuss the different meanings of the phrase "All the broken pieces" for Matt.
2. Discuss the different ways the Vietnam War has affected characters other than Matt.

Lynch, Chris. *I Pledge Allegiance.* Vietnam No. 1. Scholastic, 2011. 183 pp. Grades 7–10.

I Pledge Allegiance, the first title in the Vietnam series, introduces four friends—Morris, Beck, Rudi, and Ivan—who have been inseparable since fourth grade and have all pledged to enlist for Vietnam in the event that one of them gets drafted. When Rudi, who is the oldest by a year, is drafted, the others stand by their pledge. Morris, the central character in this book, signs up for the navy. Through his first-person narration, he tells about his experience on the USS *Boston* in the Gulf of Tonkin before he is reassigned to the Brown Water Navy's Riverine Assault Force as a radio operator on a heavily armed river monitor.

1. Discuss the rationale of the pledge and what it means to each of the friends.
2. Discuss Morris's experience of the "reality of war" compared to what he thinks he knows about war (98–99).

Lynch, Chris. *Sharpshooter.* Vietnam No. 2. Scholastic, 2012. 187 pp. Grades 7–10.

In the second book in Lynch's Vietnam series, Ivan, the narrator of *Sharpshooter*, adds his own perspective to the story of the four friends whose communications are incorporated into each book. As a member of a military family, Ivan's family expects him to sign up for Vietnam. He proves an exceptional "shooter" and is selected for the army's Marksman Program and later trained as a sniper. He, too, is assigned to the Riverine Assault Force but is engaged in flushing the Viet Cong from the riverbanks and jungle. The narratives of Morris and Ivan contribute different angles to the war in the Mekong Delta.

1. Discuss Ivan's realization that there are "no borders" to the war in Vietnam (39).

Lynch, Chris. *Free-Fire Zone.* Vietnam No. 3. Scholastic, 2012. 192 pp. Grades 7–10.

The third book in the Vietnam series follows Rudi from Parris Island, South Carolina, to I Corps Tactical Zone, Chu Lai, during which he realizes that his service in the US Marines offers him the chance to be no longer be regarded as a failure. He likes the structure of life in the marines, including following orders. He overcomes the conviction held by some that he cannot stay the course by demonstrating that he is not afraid to kill the enemy and by showing courage when he volunteers to enter a booby-trapped hut and later a hidden Viet Cong tunnel. The novel emphasizes the Combined Action Program, in which marines units lived full-time with local Vietnamese as well as search-and-destroy missions. Made visible are the burnout soldiers experienced fighting in a war with no clear battle lines, an emphasis on body counts while avoiding American casualties, and the killing of those officers deemed inadequate by those under their command (known as "fragging"). Lynch particularly addresses the ethics of war in this book through the representation of Rudi as a marine who crosses the ethical line between killing and murder.

1. Discuss Rudi as the "prototype of a loyal and dedicated Marine" (110).
2. Discuss the purposes and approaches of the Combined Action Program and "search and destroy" missions. How is each approach represented in Lynch's novel?

Lynch, Chris. *Casualties of War*. Vietnam No. 4. Scholastic, 2013. 192 pp. Grades 7–10.

The last book in the Vietnam series is narrated by Beck, who has deferred his scholarship to University of Wisconsin–Madison to enlist in the Vietnam War with his three friends. At the beginning of the novel, Beck is one of four crew members on a C-123 who are engaged in spraying Agent Orange on the jungle of South Vietnam. Through his introspective narration, Beck speaks of his reservations: he does not like to see the spoilage of a country that looks so beautiful from the air, and although fascinated by the machines of war, he has made a pledge that he will fulfill his duty without deliberately killing another person. He is a loner on base, spending his time in the library and educational center. His captain tells him that his intelligence and sensitivity cause him to be a risk; and after two incidents, he is associated with the superstitious belief of "transference" because he is one of those soldiers who is always close to death but never dies, and so transfers death to others. The most important story Beck tells his family and friends concerns a young Viet Cong soldier wearing a crucifix; on seeing Beck's scapular with the face of Christ, gives Beck a chance to escape after the C-123 has crashed in the jungle.

Beck describes the difficulty of going home on a short leave and his efforts to avoid conveying the truth of his service in Vietnam. Later, after retraining and assessment, Beck describes his service on a gunship when he can no longer avoid shooting at the enemy. Beck's story and his experiences add yet another dimension to young men's experiences of the different faces of war in Vietnam. Finally, it is through Beck's perceptive eyes that readers see how war has changed Morris, Ivan, and especially Rudi, as all four friends meet—for the last time. As in all the novels in this series, Lynch brings a vivid immediacy of how it is to be young man fighting in Vietnam: the fascination with weaponry, the raw emotions in dealing with the reality and carnage of war, and becoming acclimatized to the steamy heat. Questions are raised about the nature of war and about the enemy whom they are fighting.

1. Discuss how Beck perceives Morris, Ivan, and Rudi at their last meeting. How has war changed the four friends?
2. Discuss important themes and views about the Vietnam War incorporated in Lynch's series.

White, Ellen Emerson. *The Road Home.* Scholastic, 1995. 469 pp. Grades 8–12. YALSA BB, 1996.

In part 1 of this book, Lieutenant Rebecca Phillips, a highly skilled nurse, is working a forty-eight-hour shift in triage as "medvac" choppers ferry in large numbers of wounded during the Tet Offensive. Her first-person account describes the long and exhausting hours, the pain and fear of the wounded, awful conditions, mortar attacks, and her relationships with the medical staff. She is especially haunted by an incident in which, alone and lost in the jungle with a broken ankle after being shot down in a medvac chopper, she shoots and kills a Vietnamese boy after he had shot her in the arm.

In part 2 of the book, Rebecca's treatment on the way home is used to illustrate the disdainful reception given to Vietnam Veterans by those disillusioned with the war. White shows the effects of war on Rebecca and on Michael Jennings, a GI who has lost a leg and is living at home in despair until Rebecca visits him. White places the war in context with political events in the United States, including the assassination of Martin Luther King Jr. and Lyndon B. Johnson's decision not to seek reelection.

1. Discuss examples of attitudes toward the war in Rebecca's story.
2. Discuss how White's novel addresses the reception at home of Vietnam veterans.

Adult Fiction

Marlantes, Karl. *Matterhorn: A Novel of the Vietnam War.* Atlantic Monthly Press/El León Literary Arts, 2010. 598 pp. ALA Notable, 2011; Cooper, 2011.

In 1969, First Lieutenant Waino Mellas, fresh out of Basic School, is leader of First Platoon, Bravo Company, positioned on Matterhorn, between Laos and the Demilitarized Zone in Quang Tri Province. Marines are described as exhausted and covered with leeches and jungle rot as they slog through the rain, fog, and mud of monsoon season. When not on patrol and in active combat, they are digging fighting holes and bunkers in the hillside. Mellas's initiation as a leader comes when his company is sent out to the valley to blow up a North Vietnamese Army ammunition dump, which is followed by an order to find their way to the almost inaccessible mountain Sky Cap. Marines trek for days in difficult and dangerous terrain without food to meet deadlines transmitted over the radio.

The book emphasizes the politics that drive the decisions of battalion and regimental leaders, including putting Bravo Company at risk in the attempt to retake the Matterhorn. Marlantes writes about the racial tension that permeates Bravo Company as young black and white men learn to live together in a desegregated army. Above all, the novel celebrates the extraordinary bravery, fortitude, and comradeship of Mellas and his fellow marines. A visual chart of the chain of command, maps, and a glossary are included.

1. Identify key episodes that forge Mellas's attitudes toward the war, the men with whom he fights, and those who give the orders.
2. What does the novel have to say about the qualities of leadership in war?
3. Related reading: Karl Marlantes, *What It Is Like to Go to War* (Atlantic Monthly, 2011).

O'Brien, Tim. *The Things They Carried.* 1990. Houghton Mifflin, 2009. 256 pp. ALA Notable, 1991; Pulitzer, 1991; YALSA OB, 1999.

The first of these interrelated short stories tells about the "things" the soldiers in Alpha Company carried with them. There are items of necessity such as C-rations and ammunition, plus personal items: a Bible, tranquilizers, a rabbit's foot. But soldiers also bore a weight within: memories, emotions, and fears as they learned to carry themselves. These stories present a vivid sense of how it was to be a soldier in Vietnam: the boredom, the fear when marching in the blackness of night, the comradeship, and the jokes used to cover over the reality of death.

O'Brien writes that through his stories he is able to bring back the dead to life including his good friend, Kiowa, whom he was unable to save from drowning in a stinking muddy wasteland and fellow soldiers who committed suicide during and after the war. O'Brien writes of his agonizing over whether he should avoid the draft, the guilt and sadness he feels as he stares at the dead body of a young North Vietnamese boy, the revenge he plans against a young medic who almost lets him die from shock when he is shot. Other stories highlight the "crazy" things that happened, such as a young medic's seventeen-year-old girlfriend who arrives in white culottes and a pink sweater only to attach herself to a Green Beret unit. O'Brien demonstrates how stories take on a power of their own and how they bring an emotional truth to the experience of war in Vietnam that goes far beyond generalizations and facts.

1. Discuss O'Brien's attitude toward war as revealed through his stories.
2. Choose a story and discuss what it conveys about the morality of war.

Soli, Tatjana. *The Lotus Eaters.* St. Martin's Press, 2010. 389 pp. ALA Notable, 2011.

"A woman sees war differently," comments photojournalist Helen Adams. The novel begins with descriptions of Saigon in 1975 as the North Vietnamese approach the city. Helen photographs the refugees barricaded from entering Saigon as looters ransack the deserted stores. Scheduled to leave Saigon with her wounded husband, Linh, she decides to stay and photograph the handing over of power. Switching back to when Adams first arrives in Saigon in 1965, the story tells of the decade during which, mentored by Sam Darrow and Linh, Helen moves from being a freelancer to working as the first woman combat photographer in Vietnam for *Life* magazine. She risks her life by accompanying search-and-clear patrols, by being present in a battle zone, and by photographing the Ho Chi Minh trail across the border. She sees the devastating results when villagers are caught up in war. But she also sees Vietnam from the "inside"—its geography, its culture, and its people. Through Linh's story, Solji shows the shifting loyalties of the Vietnamese as they struggle for independence from colonialism.

Solji raises questions about the role of photographers in war: the effects of repetitive images of violence; the boundary between objectivity and empathy; the temptation of becoming addicted to war so that, analogous to the lotus eaters in Homer's *Odyssey*, photographers cannot return home. But it is the vision of a woman photographer that gives this encompassing novel its uniqueness. A bibliography is included.

1. Discuss Adams's attitude toward her work. Compare her life and work with Dickey Chappelle, whom Solji mentions as an inspiration for Adams. Related website: "Dickey Chapelle," Wisconsin Historical Society (search Dickey Chapelle at www.wisconsinhistory.org).

2. How does Linh's story add to your knowledge about Vietnam and the war?

Contemporary America

(1980–)

The Iraq War

Mazer, Harry, and Peter Lerangis. *Somebody, Please Tell Me Who I Am.* Simon & Schuster, 2012. 148 pp. Grades 8–10. YALSA BF, 2013.

Ben Bright had not informed his girlfriend Ariela and his family that he was going to boot camp after graduation, but his friend Niko guesses the truth. A talented singer and actor, Ben eschews the opportunity to meet with a well-known director who is planning a new musical TV show. Ben's reasons for enlisting are clear: he believes that "kids with privileges and skills and talent" should volunteer (16), and he was influenced by September 11, 2001. There will be time for college when he returns. By September, Ben is in Iraq and on patrol when his squad's Humvee is blown apart by a bomb hidden in a toy that a young boy detonates. Ben is sent back to the United States suffering from traumatic brain injury. The novel includes explanations of TBI and charts Ben's slow progress to recovery. Through an anonymous narration with shifting perspectives, the novel addresses how Ben's condition affects Ariela, Niko, and his family, as well as the important role of Ben's autistic brother in his recovery.

1. Discuss the reasons Niko gives for not enlisting in the army.
2. Discuss Ariela's reaction and responses to Ben's condition.

McCormick, Patricia. *Purple Heart.* Balzar + Bray/HarperCollins, 2009. 198 pp. Grades 7–12. NSSTB, 2010; YALSA BB, 2010.

Eighteen-year-old Matt Duffy is diagnosed with traumatic brain injury after nearly being killed by a rocket-propelled grenade while chasing insurgents down an alley with fellow soldier Justin. Suffering from memory loss, Matt is haunted by the scene in the alley, in which he sees a ten-year-old street kid, Ali, whom he had befriended, blown into the air. As Matt is treated and evaluated, and the incident in the alley is investigated, he struggles with the knowledge that he may have shot Ali. It is not until he is back on patrol again that he learns the full truth of why Ali was killed.

Building her story from talking to families whose sons and brothers served in Iraq, Matt's perspective provides a searing and realistic account of life in the army, including the heat, stench, dust, and noise in the streets; the bravery of soldiers looking out for one another; and the terrifying moments when everything explodes and comrades are killed. Her story makes visible the dangers and ambiguities of fighting insurgents who hide in the midst of a civilian population that the army is trying to protect. It also highlights the fact that so many involved are adolescent soldiers, like Matt, or civilian children caught in the middle of a war.

1. Discuss the attitude of a "civil affairs officer" that it is best not to "make friends with these people" (30).
2. Discuss what McCormick's story says about (1) the army's way of dealing with incidents in which civilians are casualties of war, (2) the relationship between Iraqi citizens and the army, (3) the effect of war on young soldiers, and (4) attitudes toward the female soldier Charlene.

Myers, Walter Dean. *Sunrise over Fallujah.* Scholastic Press, 2008. 290 pp. Grades 7–12. YALSA OB, 2009.

Robin "Birdy" Perry is assigned to the Civil Affairs Unit in Iraq, whose mission is to work with Iraqi civilians as part of the phase of Operation Iraqi Freedom that is concerned with bringing democracy to Iraq.

But Robin and the members of his unit realize that they are in a war that is "sloppier, faster, and more violent" than they had ever thought it would be (96). Myers's novel depicts young soldiers, men and women, serving in Iraq: boredom as they wait for orders while stationed in the Green Zone, tension and fear when they venture outside, efforts to help children caught up in war, dealing with the bloody carnage in the streets, and grief when one of their own is killed. Each of their missions highlights the danger of fighting a war among a civilian population. Robin conveys their frustration with never knowing who the enemy is and the changing rules of engagement as they meet increasing danger from improvised explosive devices and insurgents.

The novel deals with some political realities, such as the absence of weapons of mass destruction and Americans' lack of knowledge about Iraq. Robin writes letters to his Uncle Richie, who served in Vietnam and whose experiences are recounted in Myers's novel *Fallen Angels* (Scholastic, 1988). A glossary is provided.

1. Discuss how the novel addresses questions of the US presence in Iraq.
2. How do various characters—from Iraqi citizens to soldiers and commanders—characterize the war?
3. Discuss the implications of Robin's last mission for establishing stability in Iraq.
4. Related reading: Ryan Smithson, *Ghosts of War: The True Story of a 19-year-old GI* (HarperTeen, 2009).

Adult Novels

Fountain, Ben. *Billy Lynn's Long Halftime Walk.* Ecco/HarperCollins, 2012. 307 pp. ALA Notable, 2013; NBA finalist, 2012; *SLJ* BAB4T, 2012.

Nineteen-year-old Billy Lynn and seven other surviving members of Bravo squad are chosen for a two-week "Victory Tour" across the United States to bolster support for the Iraq War after being filmed by a Fox News crew fighting insurgents in "the battle of Al-Ansaker Canal." Their final stop is the Texas Stadium, where they are guests of the Dallas Cowboys. Billy's impressions of that surreal day are interwoven with flashbacks of Iraq and with his feelings about his family, with whom he had spent the previous two days. Billy experiences the disconnect between the reality of war and the meaningless praise he receives from people in the stands, as well as from the wealthy owner of the Cowboys and his guests in the Stadium Club, for whom "terror" is a talking point. He detects the fakeness in public speeches and must, with his squad, partake in an obscene extravaganza at half time, at the end of which they are beaten up by a stage crew. The unreality is reinforced by a Hollywood producer's efforts to get funding for a movie about Bravo's heroism.

Fountain's satiric novel, with its hyperbolic depiction of the culture and aggression of American football, exposes the greed, hypocrisy, and ignorance of corporate America, the public, and politicians who use young soldiers facing death in the field. In contrast, Billy's decision at the end of the novel is a testament to his loyalty and courage.

1. Discuss examples of the divide between Billy's reality of war and what he experiences at the stadium.
2. Analyze the values embedded in the public's praise of Billy and the Bravo squad.

Powers, Keith. *The Yellow Birds.* Little, Brown, 2012. 230 pp. NBA finalist, 2012; *SLJ* BAB4T, 2012.

In December 2003, Private John Bartle, age twenty-one, meets eighteen-year-old Daniel Murphy at Fort Dix, New Jersey, and promises Murphy's mother that he would bring back her son alive. In October 2004, Bartle and Murphy are stationed at an army outpost in Al Tafar, Ninevah, Iraq. As a poet, Powers brings an immediacy to Bartle's experiences of war in passages that describe Bartle's consciousness of the constant presence of death as he engages in combat, patrols the city, and shelters from mortars in settings that evoke the history and beauty of the old city of Al Tafar. Power's novel offers a deep and thoughtful consideration of the war in Iraq, as Bartle, struggling to hold himself and Murphy together, experiences a sense of futility and witnesses the worst that war can bring. But Bartle notes his feelings of disintegration and his concern for Murphy, who seems to be "coming apart." When Murphy leaves the outpost after a mortar attack in which a young girl who worked in the medic tent dies, he is killed and his body mutilated. Bartle's narrative goes forward and backward in time. In Virginia in 2005, suffering from post-traumatic stress, he tries to find patterns in his "kaleidoscope" of memories when he is eventually brought to account for covering up the nature of his friend's death to hide the truth from Murphy's mother.

1. Discuss Bartle's assessment of Sergeant Sterling in relation to his men and his attitude toward the war. Discuss the decisions made by Bartle and Sergeant Sterling when they find Murphy's body.
2. What are some of the important statements the novel makes about the nature of the Iraq War?

Immigrant and Minority Experience

Alexie, Sherman. *The Absolutely True Diary of a Part-Time Indian.* 2007; Little, Brown, 2009. 230 pp. Grades 7–12. NBA (Y), 2007; YALSA OB, 2009; YALSA BB, 2008.

Fourteen-year-old Arnold Spirit ("Junior") makes the decision to transfer from Wellpinit High School on the Spokane Reservation to the high school in Reardan. He tells about his first year at Reardan among white students who, when he first arrives, hurl insulting names at him and then ignore him. He describes his feelings of being "less than an Indian" when he leaves the "rez" (83). A cartoonist, Arnold expresses in pictures and words his loneliness at school, his family situation, the guilt he feels at leaving his best friend, and the hurt when his former friends turn their backs to him at a basketball match. Alexie writes of pain and guilt but also the rewards of crossing boundaries into another world. Despite being born with hydrocephalus, he plays as a freshman on the Reardan varsity basketball team and receives support from fellow students when his sister dies in a tragic accident. He provides an insider's look at the problems of living on the Spokane Reservation—alcohol and poverty—but makes the point that, in comparison to parents of white students, his family is always there for him. He emphasizes the reservation's strong sense of community.

1. Discuss how Arnold's narrative deconstructs stereotypes of Native Americans and their culture.
2. Discuss the significance of the term *loss* to Arnold.

Alvarez, Julia. *Return to Sender.* Knopf, 2009. Grades 5–7. ALA Notable, 2010; Américas, 2010; Belpré, 2010; NSSTB, 2010.

In the summer of 2005, Tyler's father, injured in a tractor accident, hires three undocumented Mexican workers to work on his Vermont dairy farm. Taylor is shocked when he hears that his father has hired illegal workers. His parents, he argues, have brought him up to obey the laws and respect the United States. But eleven-year-old Mari Cruz and her younger sisters also arrive with their father and their two uncles. Their mother had returned to Mexico to see her dying mother but has been missing for months. Interspersed with the main text are Mari's letters, including letters to her mother, in which she writes her side of story about the reasons their family left Mexico when she was four years old, the journey on foot across the desert to cross the border from Mexico, and how it is to live as an illegal alien. She does not mail her letters for fear of being deported by *la migra*, and she is afraid that her family will be split up because her sisters, born in the United States, are American citizens.

Alvarez's story demonstrates the difficulties that both the Cruzes and Taylors face in securing their future and emphasizes the personal relationships forged between the two families. The dangers facing undocumented immigrants are illustrated by the kidnapping and abuse of Mari's mother by dishonest *coyotes* and the fragility of the lives of the Cruzes, who are eventually deported in 2006. As Alvarez points out, Immigration and Customs Enforcement raided workplaces in 2006 in what was called Operation Return to Sender (321).

1. Discuss the attitudes of characters toward the hiring of undocumented workers and toward Mari and her sisters.

2. Related website: For resources on illegal Mexican workers in Vermont, see Julia Alvarez's site for the book (http://return-to-sender .juliaalvarez.com/research-links.php).

Edwardson, Debby Dahl. *Blessing's Bead.* Melanie Kroupa Books/Farrar, Straus & Giroux, 2009. 178 pp. Grades 5–8. *Booklist* Top 10 HF, 2010; NSSTB, 2010; YALSA BF, 2011.

The story of Blessing's family incorporates the history and culture of the Iñupiaq of north Alaska from 1917 to 1989. Because of family problems, Blessing and her brother, Isaac, are sent from their home in Anchorage in 1989 to live with their grandmother (Aaka) up north. Aaka shows Blessing the photo of Blessing's great-grandparents, Nutaaq and Tupaaq, whose story is told in "Book 1: Nutaaq's Story, 1917." Nutaaq tells about the trade fair in Sheshalik, Alaska, where her sister, Aaluk, meets and marries a Siberian. Before leaving, Aaluk gives her sister two beads from a necklace the Siberian had given to her. Nutaaq also tells about the 1918 influenza epidemic that spreads to her aunt's village, killing her parents and leaving a handful of survivors including herself and Tupaaq. She equates the epidemic with prior disasters such as the "Great Starvation," which almost, but not quite, decimated the Iñupiaq (50).

In "Book 2: Blessing's Story, 1989," Blessing narrates in "village English" how she reconnects with her Iñupiaq culture and traditions and with her family history when she is sent to live with her grandmother, Aaka. She learns that Nutaaq never saw her sister again because of the "ice curtain" that closed borders in the Cold War. In 1989, after borders were reopened, Blessing's family meet their Siberian kin when they are brought to the village via a "Friendship Flight." Blessing's mother arrives to be united with her family, and Aaluk's son brings the cobalt necklace. Blessing gives her mother Nutaaq's blue bead that she had found in Aaka's work basket and that she had been wearing around her neck so that her mother is linked again to the family. Edwardson provides a glossary and further information about geographical setting, Iñupiaq culture, language, and her choice of names, as well as the history of trade fairs and other topics.

1. Discuss the cultural and historical changes experienced by the Iñupiaq between the time of Nutaaq and Blessing.

Adult Fiction

Kwok, Jean. *Girl in Translation.* Riverhead Books/Penguin, 2010. 293 pp. Alex, 2011.

When Kimberly Chang arrives with her mother from Hong Kong before communist China takes over the British colony in 1997, they are met by Aunt Paula and Uncle Bob, who leave them at a condemned apartment in Brooklyn. There is no heat, the kitchen windows are broken, the plaster is crumbling, and there are cockroaches. During the following years, Kimberly's mother works off the debt to her sister by working long hours at her sister and brother-in-law's garment factory—a sweatshop in Chinatown. Kimberly also works at the factory each day after school, hiding her out-of-school life from even her closest friend, Annette.

Kwok's novel draws attention to the sweatshops in New York's Chinatown in the 1980s and 1990s. Kimberly's descriptions of the noise, ever-present dust, and illegal child labor are reminiscent of nineteenth-century textile mills. Immigrants who speak little English are trapped into a life of drudgery and earn less than minimum wage. Paid by piecework, Kimberly assesses everything she spends according to the number of skirts she processes in the "finishing" department: "a hot dog was 50 skirts" (58). Kwok's novel highlights the difficulties experienced by a young immigrant girl. Although recognized as a brilliant student in Hong Kong, she incurs difficulties in sixth grade with an unsympathetic teacher because she speaks little English. Kwok accentuates Kimberly's language barrier by placing in italics English words that Kimberly misunderstands. She also experiences a culture divide as she sees American students behave and speak in ways that are unthinkable to a young girl brought up in Hong Kong by a mother concerned with propriety. Things improve when Kimberly is granted a scholarship to a prestigious private school in New York. Representing the successful Chinese student who excels in math and science, she wins a full scholarship to Yale before going on to Harvard Medical School. But in this coming-of-age story, Kwok shows that academic achievement is only one side of Kimberley's story as she begins to form relationships with boys, including Matt, whom she meets at the factory and with whom she has a child. Kimberly has to make some hard choices but ambition and hard work enable her to "become the best surgeon" that she can be (290).

1. Discuss Kimberly's experience working in a sweatshop and how it affects her education and her social life. How important is this work to maintaining a measure of stability for her mother and herself?
2. Discuss Kwok's novel in relation to "Challenging the Stereotype," by Helen Zia (www.pbs.org/becomingamerican/ce_witness8.html), who talks about the stereotype of Chinese Americans as a "model minority" because they go to college and attain advanced educational degrees. This observation, Zia comments, does not take into account the "complexity of the Chinese American experience." Related website: Becoming American: The Chinese Experience (www.pbs.org/becomingamerican/).
3. Discuss how both her cultural differences and "talent" for school affect Kimberly's relationships with her teachers and fellow students.

Select Bibliography

Baer, Allison L. "Pairing Books for Learning: The Union of Informational and Fiction." *History Teacher* 45, no. 2 (2012): 283–96.

Beck, Cathy, Shari Nelson-Faulkner, and Kathryn Mitchell Pierce. "Historical Fiction: Teaching Tool or Literary Experience." *Language Arts* 77, no. 6 (2000): 447–555.

Boatright, Michael D. "Graphic Journeys: Graphic Novels' Representation of Immigrant Experiences." *Journal of Adolescent and Adult Literacy* 53, no. 6 (2010): 468–76.

Brown, Joanne, and Nancy St. Clair. *The Distant Mirror: Reflections on Young Adult Historical Fiction.* Lanham, MD: Scarecrow Press, 2006.

Bruchac, Joseph. "Interview with Joseph Bruchac." *Journal of Adolescent and Adult Literacy* 52, no. 5 (2009): 445–47. (Bruchac discusses the role of the Abenaki and other Native Americans in American history.)

Cart, Michael. "A Genre without a Readership?" *Booklist* 109, no. 16 (2013): 51.

Clapp-Itnyre, Alisa. "Battle on the Gender Homefront: Depictions of the American Civil War in Contemporary Young Adult Literature." *Children's Literature in Education* 38, no. 2 (2007): 153–61.

Curtis, Susan. "History, Fiction, Imagination, and *A Mercy.*" *Early American Literature* 48, no. 1 (2013): 188–93.

Edgington, William D., Edna Greene Brabham, and Jami Bice Frost. "Assessing Values in Historical Fiction Written for Children: A Content Analysis of the Winners of the Scott O'Dell Historical Fiction Award." *Journal of Children's Literature* 25, no. 2 (1999): 36–49.

Groce, Eric, and Robin Groce. "Authenticating Historical Fiction: Rationale and Process." *Education Research and Perspectives* 32, no. 1 (2005): 99–120.

Harris, Marla. "A History Not Then Taught in History Books: (Re)Writing Reconstruction in Historical Fiction for Children and Young Adults." *Lion and the Unicorn* 30, no. 1 (2006): 94–116.

Hegedus, Bethany, and Kekla Magoon. "Two Books, Two Authors: An Inside Look at a Unique Partnership on the Civil Rights Movement." *Multicultural Review* 19, no. 2 (2010): 20–25.

Hill, Lawrence. "Freedom Bound." *Beaver* 87, no. 1 (2007): 16–23. (Discussion of "The Book of Negroes," the records on which *Somebody Knows My Name* is based.)

Hinton, KaaVonia, Yonghee, Suh, Lourdes Colón-Brown, and Maria O'Hearn, "Historical Fiction in English and Social Studies Classrooms: Is It a Natural Marriage?" *English Journal* 103, no. 3 (2014): 22–27.

Huftalin, Amy, and Louis Ferroli. "Literature That Increases Social Studies Knowledge and Skill in Text Reading." *Illinois Reading Council Journal* 41, no. 1 (2012–13): 10–29.

McElmeel, Sharron L. "Getting It Right: Historical Fiction or Not." *Library Media Connection* 27, no. 4 (2009): 40–41.

McManus, Janie M. "A Novel Idea: Historical Fiction and Social Studies." *Social Education* 72, suppl. (2008): 8–9.

McTigue, Erin, Elaine Thornton, and Patricia Wiese. "Authentication Projects for Historical Fiction: Do You Believe It?" *Reading Teacher* 66, no. 6 (2013): 495–505.

Monnin, Katie. "Aligning Graphic Novels to the Common Core Standards." *Knowledge Quest* 41, no. 3 (2013): 50–56.

Ostenson, Jonathan, and Rachel Wadham. "Young Adult Literature and the Common Core: A Surprisingly Good Fit." *American Secondary Education* 41, no. 1 (2012): 4–13.

Richards, Janet C. "Question, Connect, Transform (QCT): A Strategy to Help Middle School Students Engage Critically with Historical Fiction." *Reading and Writing Quarterly* 22, no. 2 (2006): 193–98.

Rochman, Hazel. "Talking with Ellen Klages." *Book Links* 17, no. 2 (2007): 26–27.

Rycik, Mary Taylor, and Brenda Rosler. "The Return of Historical Fiction." *Reading Teacher* 63, no. 2 (2009): 163–66.

Salisbury, Graham. "Interview with Graham Salisbury." *Journal of Adolescent and Adult Literacy* 49, no. 4 (2005–6): 352–55. (Discussion of *Eyes of the Emperor*.)

Sandmann, Alexa. "Contemporary Immigration: First-Person Fiction from Cuba, Haiti, Korea, and Cambodia." *Social Studies* 95, no. 3 (2004): 115–21.

Seymour, Eric, and Laura Barrett. "Reconstruction: Photography and History in E. L. Doctorow's 'The March.'" *Literature and History* 18, no. 2 (2009): 49–69.

Slotkin, Richard. "Fiction for the Purposes of History." *Rethinking History* 9 (2005): 221–36.

Ware, Thomas C. "Fiction Still Fights the Civil War: 'It Ain't over Though It's Over.'" *War, Literature, and the Arts: An International Journal of the Humanities* 20, nos. 1–2 (2008): 329–38.

Wasta, Stephanie, and Carolyn Lott. "Where Are the Facts? *Jason's Gold* Gives Meaning to the Gold Rush." *Social Studies* 97, no. 1 (2006): 3–7.

Zanowski, Myra. "Historical Novels in Verse: A Fusion Genre." *Journal of Children's Literature* 36, no. 1 (2010): 37–43.

Index

www.ingramcontent.com/pod-product-compliance
Lightning Source LLC
Chambersburg PA
CBHW071110100726
47908CB00008B/2334